Prima Facie

by

E. J. Richards

Jhambutti Books

Published by

Jhambutti Books
Bow Tie Bear Animation
Watercress Cottage
Salisbury Road
Donhead St Mary
Shaftesbury
Dorset

ISBN 978-0-9927613-1-8

Author's Foreword

Prima Facie is set in Roman Britain, in AD 60, when Nero was Emperor. The main character is Tiberius Sextus Valerius, a surgeon with the Roman Army. He is stationed, along with his assistant, and slave, Gallius, in the area now known as Dorset, on the borders of Somerset and Wiltshire.

During his investigations Tiberius visits local settlements, particularly Durnovaria and Lindinis, which would correspond to modern day Dorchester and Ilchester respectively. Other places mentioned by name are Aquae Sulis, Glevum and Iscalis, which are Bath, Gloucester and the lead mines at Charterhouse, in the Mendip Hills.

The Roman Army has been in occupation for less than 20 years and have yet to fully take over parts of South West Britain. The area could be considered to be at the edge of the Empire. Many of the local inhabitants are starting to become Romanised, but some are still clinging to their previous way of life. Not all are happy with being part of the Empire, as evidenced by the Iceni revolt.

In AD 60, medical practices were very different to modern day procedures. Diagnosis was generally based on the theory of humours, such as blood, bile and phlegm, where an imbalance would create a disease. Treatments were then geared towards restoring the balance between these different fluids. A detailed knowledge of anatomy, such as might be gained from dissection of bodies, was not considered necessary or appropriate, and therefore a doctor would have little or no knowledge of the structure of internal organs or of principles such as the circulation of blood. In common with today, there were many different schools of thought about causes of diseases, and Tiberius would have been taught a variety of treatments, with differing rationales. At the time, Athens was considered an important area in the training of doctors, which was conducted along the lines of an apprenticeship. Not all doctors or healers would have had detailed training, and a Greek trained surgeon would be viewed as a top consultant might be today.

Prima Facie

Roman Britain, AD 60. Autumn.

Day One

I stood in the doorway of the infirmary, watching soldiers milling about the courtyard in front of me, some laughing and boasting of their prowess, others silent, possibly wondering how soon they would be skilled with sword, spear or dagger. My slave, and assistant, Gallius, and I had just set and splinted a broken arm, the result of a training accident earlier that afternoon. Most of these sessions for new army recruits produced some injuries, but they were usually minor cuts, grazes and bruises. The air was fresh after the recent deluge of rain and, as I inhaled deeply, I found a faint tang of smoke mixed with roasting meats ready for dinner.

Stretching my arms up to release some of the tension from my shoulders, I contemplated the evening ahead.

I ran my fingers through my short, graying hair, and shivered slightly in the damp autumnal breeze.

Just as I was about to go back into the building I heard shouts from the direction of the main gate. I could just distinguish my name being called, and looking over, saw the surveyors, Memno and Agricola, together with the rest of the surveying party, who were returning two days earlier than expected.

From where I was, I could see that the soldiers carried a load. As they came closer their heads remained bowed, and their shoulders slumped as if the burden they carried was too much for their spirits to endure. As they continued their walk towards me, past the barracks, I wondered who had injured himself badly enough for the survey to be cut short. I mentally prepared myself for more work that evening as I stepped forward to meet them.

'What has happened? Has there been an accident? Who has been injured? Bring him into the infirmary, so that I can see the damage.' Turning to Gallius, who appeared in the doorway behind me, I issued orders. 'Lights. I'll need some more lights, and some dressings, also a needle and thread, I expect. Make sure everything I need is there.'

My questions and orders fell into the shared silence of sorrow and my voice faltered. I stood as the procession passed me, the mud underfoot holding me fast.

Shaking off my hesitation, I hurried after the group and was in time to see them place a bundle on the table of the operating room. At first I thought there was some mistake. This shape in front of me was no person, and why did they not remove the cloak so that I might see.

'Tiberius, we live in sad times indeed.' The soft voice of Memno, the head surveyor, fell upon my ears, but did not register.

I drew closer to the table and lifted up the corner of the cloak. The wet tunic that encased the limbs and torso began to drip on to the floor. The noise insinuated itself into my mind. Drip, drip, drip.

'Memno, what happened?' Drip, drip, drip. 'Where did you find him?' Drip, drip, drip. 'Where is his …?' I could not bring myself to say it. The words fought to stay inside. The horror seemed less if it were not named.

Memno looked at me, his eyes lined with pain. When he spoke, his words were dragged from a throat full of grit.

'The soldiers found him, in a stream. I ordered him to be brought back here. He was in a stream, caught in an overhanging tree. We'll need to bridge the river there; it's too deep for a ford. There, where they found him, just like this.'

Drip, drip, drip. His eyes were drawn once more to the body in front of us, as were mine. We three were the only ones left in the room, two living souls and one dead body.

The long tunic encased the arms and legs of the latter, leaving lifeless hands and feet naked to the air. It clung to the body like a removable skin, outlining the contours of the abdomen and chest, on which there were no discernible wounds or injuries. The unknown man lay as if asleep, but the cause of his death was all too obvious. At the neck, instead of a face, head, features that would have identified him, was a stump of bone, sinews and vessels. This man's head had been severed from his body.

As my eyes slowly registered what lay in front of me, my hand reached out almost of its own accord. The surgeon's training that permeated my very soul asserted itself to protect my other senses.

'Look, Memno, the head has been totally severed by some sharp blade. I need to have the rest of the body cleaned before I can examine it properly.'

As I was speaking, I glanced over at my friend who was, even now, swaying slightly on his feet. 'But that must wait until tomorrow when the light will be better. For now, we will leave this unfortunate soul.' Replacing the cloak, I ushered Memno from the infirmary towards my quarters.

'I'm not hungry,' was Memno's response when we were seated with bread, meat, vegetables and wine before us. However, his shaking hand and glazed eyes did not support this, and I had no hesitation in pressing him to refresh himself with just a little undiluted wine, or a small portion of bread.

'Corolius, from the farm nearby, sought my advice again today. He's been feeling unwell again of late. I bled him and he'll be staying the night in the infirmary. Have some olives,' as I passed the dish over to him. 'The books that I ordered from Alexandria arrived today. I set Hadrian to start the copies. Let me refill your glass.' I picked up the jug to top up his half-empty goblet, and mine. 'How is the road survey? Are you making good progress?'

'We're doing well. We've surveyed most of the stretch between here and Iscalis. Much of the ground is hilly, with lots of marshes and rivers in the valleys.'

'Is that holding things up?'

Memno shook his head, his words becoming slightly slurred, 'No, not much. But this might. I can't see it will be easy to get the soldiers to work on that stretch now. Superstitious lot.'

He waved his cup about, which I hastened to refill when it was put down on the table. As Memno spoke he unconsciously lifted his goblet and sipped, or ate small amounts. I ensured that his cup was never drained nor his plate empty, and in this way I endeavoured to replace the pallor of his face with colour and vitality.

My quarters and the infirmary are sited away from the main barracks to ensure peace and quiet for those who are ill, and tonight, there were even fewer sounds than usual penetrating into the room.

I looked towards the window, and imagined I could see beyond the wooden walls, to where the soldiers would congregate. There would be just the one topic of conversation this evening.

I turned back to Memno, whose head was becoming too heavy for him to easily support. The sound sleep that threatened resulted in him needing assistance to reach his bed. Let him sleep.

It is seldom that men such as my gentle surveyor friend must endure such horrors. We doctors, who are more used to injury and disease, must be stoic. But even I, used as I was to the violence of war, admit that this crime touches something deep within me.

For crime it must have been. This was no accident. And if my soul was troubled, how much worse for that of the victim who lay in the infirmary. How was he ever to find peace, when the resting place of his spirit, his very identity had been cruelly wrested from him? Was he doomed, to forever wander these foreign shores?

Indeed, were these lands alien to him or was he on his native soil? With no knowledge of who he was, how were we going to name him? If he could not be named, how could he be honoured?

I had always, until now, found the people of this Britannicus, my newly adopted land, to be peaceful. It is true that I had heard many tales of unrest and revolt in various parts, and of resistance, both active and passive, to the civilisation that we Romans have brought.

But until now, I had not been touched by violence or insurrection in the eight years I have lived here. Until now.

What type of people would hack a man's head from his body, and why? These questions and many others gyrated round my mind, given energy and spin from the wine that I had consumed in far greater quantities than usual.

Retiring to my room and dropping on the bed, I sought the release that Memno had found, but this was to be denied to me for some time.

Images of headless corpses somersaulted round the room, which in turn twisted and shifted, floors became walls, and ceilings melted and folded.

Day Two

Just as I feared that sleep would never come, I woke to find thin sunlight penetrating my window shutters and nailing my pupils into my brain. How ironic that I, who so often lectured others on the dangers of over indulgence in wine and strong foods late at night, should now suffer like this.

But the way to clear my head and body of the excess humours that would cause fear and paralysis of mind and muscles would be a little water, bread and action. The puzzle that lay in my infirmary would provide the necessary mental stimulation while Gallius had already supplied the sustenance.

After refreshing myself, I left my quarters and headed to the infirmary.

I had given instructions that the body was to be washed and cleaned so that I might examine it more closely in the bright light of the operating room, but before I could begin I needed to check on the few patients who were currently with us.

I continued on, in the direction of the wards, ensuring that sleep had been obtained, pains eased and fevers reduced. The last to be seen was Corolius, a local landowner, who had consulted me yesterday with vague stomach pains, headaches and lethargy. I could find little wrong with him and, after bleeding him, I felt that I had failed my patient as he manifestly refused to accept my prescription of a herbal remedy, exercise and rubbing. But then this was nothing new for Corolius, as he often had his own ideas and interpretation of my treatments. I sometimes wondered why he consulted me, but maybe he would be in a better mood this morning and see the wisdom in my advice.

'Good morning, Corolius, I trust you slept well.' I checked his left arm, which had been the site of the bleeding, finding the wound looked healthy and with a well formed scab.

'Very well.' He stood up with a sinuous grace. 'I feel almost a new man. Thank you for your hospitality and advice.'

'Has Gallius provided you with an infusion this morning?'

His laugh belied the look on his face. 'Why do you doctors always make them taste so dreadful? Yes, Gallius made it up for me and promised to prepare further doses for me to take back.'

'Does this mean you'll follow my prescription?'

'Let's just say I'll consider it. But I understand you have a much more interesting … well, should I say patient or what?'

I tried to hide my irritation at his ghoulish interest. 'We did have a body brought in yesterday evening.'

'From what I hear, part of it's still out there.' As he laughed, I turned to make my way out and down the colonnaded hallway to the operating room. Corolius stopped me with his hand on my shoulder.

'There now, I've offended you. Please accept my apologies.' He appeared to take my slight nod as confirmation. 'And now let us go together to view this unfortunate body. It may well be that two heads are better than one, or none.'

Not trusting my voice, I could only nod again and, lifting up the door curtain allowed him to precede me.

I had one brief moment of hope that last night's events were just a nightmare, a hope which dissipated as the sunlight illuminated the shape on the operating table.

Gallius was already in the room and, on my approach he removed the cloth to reveal the body. I heard a sharp intake of breath, and I confess to being pleased that Corolius appeared shocked as he took up a position opposite me, next to Gallius. A soft footfall behind me indicated the arrival of Memno, whose eyes demonstrated a night as disturbed as mine. When he looked at me, he appeared to wish he were somewhere else, anywhere but standing next to me in that operating room. Glancing around at the bodies, both living and dead, I took a deep breath and began my examination.

'Gallius, when you cleaned the body, were there any other cuts?'

'No, Master. The severing of the neck is the only wound, although there are many bruises to both arms and legs.' As he spoke, Gallius pointed out the purple marks around the upper portion of both arms.

'I see, and on the legs you say?' As I questioned him, I held up one lifeless arm to gain a better impression of the extent of the damage.

'It looks the same, as if it were done at the same time.'

I looked closely at the bruises, reaching my hand round the upper arm, to find my imprint almost matched the discoloration on the skin. Gallius saw my actions, and continued speaking, 'It looks as if someone might have held his arm tightly there.'

I nodded. 'Just what I was thinking. It could be that he sustained these bruises when he was assaulted.'

'He would surely have resisted.' Gallius added. 'He looks to have been young and healthy, with good muscles. He would not have been easy to capture or detain.'

Despite the circumstances, I could not resist a smile of genuine delight.

'Well done, Gallius. My teachings have not been in vain. All your observations would seem to be perfectly correct. As you say, he would certainly have struggled, and if we assume that the contusions were sustained during that struggle, then how long do you think he has been dead?'

'The cut is still fresh, the bruising recent. The body was found in a stream, but the flesh is not overly waterlogged. So that would mean...'

As Gallius appeared to falter in his exposition of the sequence of events, I prompted, 'What was the condition of the limbs, the muscles, when he came in?'

'The limbs were not rigid, but somewhat loose.' His voice increased in confidence with every word. 'Therefore he must have died several hours before being found, probably the previous day. That would mean he was murdered two or three days ago.'

'And what does the body say about how he lay after being killed?'

The voice of Corolius cut in before Gallius had a chance to reply. 'Surely you cannot act as seer, or do you propose that this corpse rise up and tell you what has happened to it? Maybe you could also ask it to tell you who killed him, as well.'

I kept my eyes down, but directed my words to the man standing opposite me. 'The body can give many answers to those who know the signs.' I looked up, and smiled, 'Now, Gallius, what can we assume from the body about its position after death?'

My slave stood back from the table, biting his lower lip and furrowing his brow, before his eyes suddenly opened wide. 'The rubor, Master.'

I nodded encouragingly at him. 'What about it?'

'There is rubor, redness about the legs and back. Lots in the legs on all surfaces.' Gallius' hands moved, describing patterns in the air. His eyelids closed as if he were seeing the corpse through different eyes.

'He must have been on his back, but with his feet and legs lower, as if … the flesh was waterlogged as well … as if he were lying on the bank of a stream.' He opened his eyes and looked for confirmation.

'Assuming that there is nothing else of significance to be identified that would be my conclusion as well. If you could help me turn him on this side. Now, have you thoroughly examined the rest of the body? Are you sure there are no other marks?'

Gallius nodded vehemently, as he pushed and rolled the torso towards me. As he did so, I noticed Corolius, who had fallen silent again, move forwards.

'But what's this? There is something here, look, just below his shoulder.'

I mentally cursed my slave for being too hasty in his examination. How could Gallius let me down like this? How could he allow Corolius to see something before I did? Hurrying round to that side of the table, I berated Gallius.

'You said there were no other marks. What else might you have missed? I expect you to do your duties accurately. How can I trust you or your work?'

'Master, there are just some old scars, one below his left shoulder. That is all. I did not miss anything.' The hurt evident in his voice pricked at my conscience. Maybe I had been too hasty in accusing him, but the presence of Corolius was like a thorn broken off under the skin.

'All marks may be relevant, Gallius, even old scars.' The brief words would have to suffice for now. I could discuss the matter later with him, when other irritations were gone.

'A scar, under his left shoulder? Did you say a scar, just under his left shoulder?' The detail being discussed appeared to have animated Memno, who almost pushed me out of the way. 'Let me see. I must see the scar.'

Once he was at the table, he reached out his hand and traced the shape made by the whiter skin, slightly puckered in places. 'A fall from a tree when he was eight, trying to reach an orange just out of reach. The surgeon said he would always carry the mark. There will be another on his left lower leg.'

As if mesmerised by the words, Corolius twitched aside the cloth that still concealed the lower limbs. On the left shin there was indeed a second, much fainter scar. Memno silently looked at it before quietly walking out of the room. I caught up with him as he stood looking out over the inner courtyard. The early morning promise of sun had been realised, and there were now sharply delineated shadows thrown over his trunk. He must have been aware of my presence as he spoke without turning round.

'Last month at the baths, I noticed the scars and he told me how he got them, trying to get an orange just out of reach. His younger brother couldn't reach, so he climbed the tree to get it and fell. His mother thought he was dead, there was so much blood. She didn't know whether to cry over his body, weep with relief or to scold him.'

'Who? Memno, who is he?'

'Lucius.'

As the name of the dead man hung in the air, I reached out to support myself on the balustrade. Lucius Octavio Gordianus. I remembered his infectious laugh and ready wit on the many evenings we had spent playing ludus latrunculorum. Lucius. We would never face each other across the gaming board again. Memno continued to speak.

'I sent … he went … to deliver some messages in Lindinis. I was going to send Agricola, but he said Lucius would be better. He was a better rider. I last saw him three … no, four days ago.'

'Memno, are you sure?'

'I'm sure, from the scars. He was in his normal clothes when I last saw him, not this long white tunic that he has on now.'

'You must be certain. Could you be mistaken? We have no other way to identify him.' The look in Memno's eyes was enough to convince me. The body lying on the table behind us was indeed that of Lucius, deputy head surveyor. My limbs felt heavy as my feet took me back into the operating room.

'Memno has identified him as Lucius Octavio Gordianus, from the scars.' My throat was dry as I forced the words out.

'Who would have killed him, and why? Why cut off his head? Why?' The words from Gallius mimicked what must have been the unspoken thoughts of us all. Why was Lucius killed in this way, and where was his head?

'It must be reported, and investigated. His death must be avenged. I will not allow this to pass quietly.'

'I agree, but who will investigate?' It was not until the voice of Corolius hit my ears that I realised I had verbalised my proclamation.

'I will speak to Aurelius. He must support us to bring the perpetrators to justice.' Even as I spoke, a half-suppressed laugh from Corolius reinforced the doubt I had that Aurelius would support our cause. As the local law officer, he had the authority to hear and pass judgement on local crimes, but he was wary of disturbing the sometimes fragile peace between the Romans and the indigenous tribes.

'It is a long ride south to Durnovaria, most of one day at least from here. Please, I must insist on a detour, to stay at my farm overnight if you are determined to go. Let me repay your hospitality with mine, and it will reduce your journey tomorrow. You wouldn't reach there tonight now, anyway. But we should leave soon, if we are to arrive before nightfall.'

The offer from Corolius, welcoming and reasonable though it was, did not inspire comfort in me. His manner always irritated me, and I did not relish the thought of spending more time than necessary in his company, but he was right in his calculations. I gave a brief nod in acceptance, and Corolius left the room. I returned to my quarters with Gallius, so that he could prepare a pack, as I would need my toga when I met with Aurelius.

Soon Corolius and I were riding out of the garrison, with Gallius a short distance behind us.

Our journey took us almost due east, across ground that was undulating, cut by streams and rivers, with many woods and thickets. This was good agricultural land, and there were several farms and villas scattered across the landscape. Bird song was flung about by the fitful breeze and mingled with the calls of labourers in the fields.

The rain from yesterday had turned patches of the soil into thick, cloying mud, which at times hampered our progress. At length, turning off the main road, we continued for some distance through partially cultivated fields, many now standing bare as their crops had been safely stored away against the coming winter months. Corolius pointed out the different produce he had been growing, and I was surprised at the extent of the estate. The ground started to rise, and a stream gurgled and chuckled downhill, away from us.

As we rode up the gentle slope, the setting sun highlighted the red tiles of the main house. They gleamed as if made from rubies, matched by the splendour of the autumnal colours of the woods behind the buildings.

The house itself was long and low, forming an 'L' shape with the hint of a formal garden in front. To one side, set back and partially hidden were buildings that I could hear were stables.

The apparent meaningless activity resolved into purpose as I discerned slaves and workers returning to their quarters after a day in the fields, a kitchen girl collecting a handful of herbs, and fresh supplies of wood being taken to a hidden fire. The smell of sage, mint and freshly cut wood perfumed the air.

'Welcome to my house.' The words of Corolius, my travelling companion, and now host, broke into my reveries.

'I could almost think myself back in the hills above Rome,' I said.

'I'm afraid that we lack many of those comforts. Our heating is still rudimentary, but the baths are nearly finished. Come inside and we will eat.'

As we were speaking two slaves had materialised and we relinquished our tired mounts, Gallius going with them to stay in the slaves' quarters. The door through which we passed opened into an atrium and Corolius ushered me into a fine room.

The walls were a deep red, with panels of blue, while underfoot was a mosaic of geometric patterns, the colours serving to complement the walls. In one corner was a brazier, the heat not yet penetrating far into the room, unlike the aroma from the wood and pinecones that blazed there.

'You are welcome in this house.'

The voice came from the woman, obviously the mistress of the villa, who had entered the room behind me. She was short, but slender, her actions calm and unhurried, except for a certain nervousness of her hands, which flickered over surfaces and reached out for walls as if to remind their owner of her location.

'Ah, Julia,' said Corolius, 'I'm glad you've joined us. We have a visitor this evening. Tiberius, you know, the doctor at the garrison. He needs to speak to Aurelius tomorrow.'

Those few words seemed to encompass his opinion of me. In his eyes I was deserving of no more explanation. Julia moved towards me, extending those anxious hands.

'I'm so pleased to meet you. As I said you're very welcome.' Her voice was melodic, with an underlying huskiness that I longed to hear again.

Turning from me, she addressed her husband, 'Corolius, have you arranged for a room to be prepared for our guest?' A bored look was the response she got. 'Come Tiberius, let me show you where you can wash away the dust and grime of your journey.'

I gladly followed to take advantage of the opportunity to freshen up. Her presence in the room had reminded me of the mud spattered across my garments, and limbs. As I rejoined my host, I found him as taciturn as before. We both sat in uneasy silence for a few moments, until Julia reappeared, deep in conversation with a man, and a boy of about ten.

'Tiberius, this is Petronus, my son, and Germanicus, his tutor.'

Petronus' energy lightened the atmosphere. 'Are you a soldier? Mother said you'd come from the garrison. I'm going to be a soldier when I'm older.' With that he produced an imaginary sword, to be matched against mine. 'Germanicus used to be a soldier. I'm going to fight, just like he did.'

After a short spell of mock sparring, his youth won the day and after sinking back into my seat, I declared that, 'No, I'm not a soldier. I'm a surgeon, able to patch up the fighters after they've been wounded.'

'I'm not going to get wounded. Germanicus did. He lost the end of his finger.' The victorious fighter celebrated by running round the room.

'Petronus, I've told you before. You do not run in here. Now stop disturbing our guest, and either sit quietly, or return to your room.' His father's voice produced an immediate effect, and subdued the boisterous child, who sat down at his mother's feet.

'I'm sorry if Petronus annoyed you. He has such energy.' Julia's hand rested on his head, her fingers playing with a lock of his hair.

'I know how they can be.' I said. 'I have grandchildren myself, a boy about the same age, and a girl a few years younger.'

'Do you see them often?'

'Not as much as I'd like. Marcus, my elder son, has a farm some miles from the garrison, and Anthonius, my younger son, lives further north.'

'And your wife?'

'She died some years ago.' The pain of her departure was still there and I was almost grateful for the interruption from Corolius.

'Julia, must you interrogate every guest that comes to this house? Tiberius has no wish to be giving details of his personal life. Is the food ready? Germanicus how are Petronus' studies? Is he being attentive?'

As Julia stood and hurried out, her husband's eyes followed her as he listened to the report from Germanicus. Corolius then lapsed once more into introspection as Julia returned and we prepared to eat.

Throughout the meal we spoke of many mundane things. As her fingers delicately browsed over the various dishes, Julia was keen to know if fashions had changed much now that Nero was emperor. I regretfully informed her that I was not the person to bring her such information.

As I had not remarried after the death of my wife some twelve years previously, I did not take such an interest in hairstyles as I once might have done. Every husband knows that it is better to risk one's life walking on thin ice than to not notice a wife's new hairstyle or tunic.

As we were eating, various slaves moved in and out of the room, bringing in dishes of baked carp, roasted duck and vegetables flavoured with liquadem. One girl in particular caught my eye. She was dark skinned, with brown hair and eyes that had a defiant glint in them.

Although she would have been perfectly at home in some colourful Mediterranean town, here, in this paler land, she had an almost exotic beauty that made her stand out from the rest. The long woollen tunic she wore only hinted at the figure underneath, but the grace with which she moved promised much.

'I see you've noticed Lydia.' Corolius' voice cut into my thoughts.

He reached out his hand to pull her closer as she placed a platter of figs, apples and damsons on the table in front of him. She appeared to respond as any dutiful slave would do, but I noted a tenseness about the shoulders and the way her chin tilted up slightly that indicated otherwise. 'Would you like her tonight?' he continued.

The offer was made carelessly, and as I lifted my wineglass, I considered it in the same vein. She had a certain attraction, and she would ease some of the aches and pains from the day. My hesitation was sufficient for Corolius to presume acceptance.

'She's yours. Lydia, you must look after our guest.' As Lydia nodded and withdrew, I heard a faint gasp or maybe a sigh from Julia at my side. As I turned to look at her, I caught the last remnants of an expression of disgust, or was it disappointment?

The smile of a perfect hostess quickly covered up any possibility of my understanding her previous feelings, but the withdrawing of Germanicus' hand from her arm was not so rapid. I excused myself soon after we had finished the meal, pleading that the journey today had been long and arduous, and I would need to do the same again tomorrow. Corolius smiled as I left the room, but whether that smile was directed at me or Julia, it was impossible to say.

As promised, Lydia was waiting in my room. When I pulled back the curtain to enter, she stood up.

'What would you like me to do for you, sir?' Her voice was hard and brittle, with none of the soft huskiness of her mistress. As I looked at her standing in front of me, I saw, not a slave girl who would pamper and relax me in whatever way I wished, but a young girl, no a young woman, of eighteen or nineteen.

Her face was hardened by toil and grief, and the defiant glint in her eyes was now replaced by dull acceptance. If the degradation of her station in life were taken away, the exotic beauty that was presently a mere faded promise would shine. In this frame of mind I had no wish to use her. Sleep would bring the release from tension I sought.

I waved my hand to dismiss her from my chamber, but she misunderstood the gesture. Slipping her tunic off her shoulders, she let it drop to the floor, before moving towards me, to put her arms round my neck. I pushed her away, with more force than I intended and moved to sit on the bed. For a moment she stayed where she was, before coming to kneel in front of me, gazing up at my face. Her nakedness disturbed me. I was conscious of how enjoyable it would be to use her body tonight, but the way in which her master gave her away so freely was confusing.

'Lydia, I have no need of you tonight. You may go.' Her response was surprising. Most slaves would relish the release from submission that I was offering her, but she was doing the opposite.

'Please sir, don't send me away. My master told me to look after you. He will be angry if I have not pleased you.' She grasped my hand to emphasise her pleading. 'He will ask me in the morning what I did for you. Would you prefer a male slave? Would you prefer to watch me with another? What is your desire? Ahh, I see in your eyes that you would like me.' With that she took my unresisting hand and placed it over her breast, where my fingers couldn't help but feel and caress her soft skin and firm nipple. 'I am very skilled in many aspects. You will not be disappointed.'

She moved closer and guided my hand down where she coaxed the further exploration of my fingers. With her other hand she gently stroked and massaged my shoulders, chest and thighs, moving my clothing aside as she went. I could resist no longer and lying back, I closed my eyes and let her work her magic.

Day Three

It was later than I had hoped when Lydia brought me bread, fruit and wine in my room. I had been desirous of an early start, but it appeared that my host and hostess had not yet risen. As I ate, several times Lydia seemed on the point of saying something. At last, as I had nearly finished, she spoke.

'Take me with you sir. Please, take me with you, away from here. You could buy me from Corolius and Julia, and then I would be free.'

'Even if I wanted to buy you, you would still be a slave. You wouldn't be free.'

'I wouldn't be here and that would be enough.' Her voice was low and had tones of despair and hatred.

'I'm sorry Lydia, but I have no intention of buying any slaves at the moment. I move about so much with my job and when I'm not working, I spend time with my sons. I don't maintain a house of my own at present.'

As I said these words, her eyes glazed over. In her case they were truly the doorway to the soul, as something inside seemed to have died. Any man would have found it difficult to resist the appeal that she had.

'Next time I see them, I'll ask if they need any more house slaves. But I cannot promise anything, and anyway Corolius may not wish to sell you. I suspect that he will want to keep you, in which case I can do nothing.'

She looked at the floor for a few moments, before silently leaving the room.

As Gallius and I rode out of the farm that morning, visions of Lydia kept returning to my mind. Pleasant memories of holding a soft and yielding body, something I had not done for some time, mingled with the question of why she was so desperate to leave the farm. But soon the monotony of the journey took my mind off that particular imponderable and onto the reason for my trip. More circles presented themselves. What if Aurelius decided to take no action? What if Memno was mistaken and it was not Lucius? If it was not Lucius, then who? Was it some other poor Roman soul?

No, Memno was sure it was Lucius, and I was sure of Memno. But why was he killed? Why Lucius? Why in that monstrous way? The footfalls of our horses provided a backdrop to the pounding questions to which I had no answers at present. To keep repeating them in my mind over and over again would surely serve no useful purpose.

At midday we paused to refresh both ourselves and our horses. We were not riding hard, but they were still in need of water. We rested for a short time under a tall oak that grew near the road, with the gentle gurgle of a stream providing a melodic backnote to the drone of bees. The bread and fruit that had been provided sated our hunger. I suspect that Corolius was not, in fact, the provider of this fare but that Lydia, hoping to win my approval for her prospective purchase had acquired it without his knowledge. Corolius was a strange man. If asked, he would almost certainly have given the best of his larder, but he may not have offered or even thought to offer. I was in no doubt that he had some ulterior motive for giving me Lydia the previous night, although what that reason was, only he knew.

As we remounted our horses, preparing to resume our journey, I heard a rumble behind us.

Looking back I could see a heavily laden cart, pulled by two patient mules, trundle into view. I smiled as I recognised the stout man holding the reins, sat in the middle of the seat, almost filling it. Guiding my horse, I rode alongside, so I could talk to Remus. Gallius dropped back, and I could see him chatting to the slave who sat on the back edge of the cart, swinging his legs as he rested against the amphorae of wine.

'Tiberius, I thought I recognised you, and I was right.' The greeting from Remus was in his characteristic throaty voice. 'But you're a long way from home, you and Gallius, aren't you?'

'I have business in Durnovaria.'

He cast a glance in my direction, 'Thought you might, from what I hear. Right again, aren't I?'

'What have you been hearing?' I tried to make my voice sound casual.

'I gets about, I hears things. I've just come from the garrison myself. You were busy, you and Gallius, in the operating room, with Memno. Didn't get to speak to you, but your wine order's all there, well marked. Don't you let them soldiers get their hands on it.' He lifted one hand up to waggle his plump finger at me. 'Yours is the finest wine, not acetum. Don't get it mixed up, or you'll be blaming me when you don't like it.'

'I'm sure Gallius will make sure he gets the right amphorae.' I certainly didn't want to be provided with acetum, which was supplied to the garrison. When mixed with water, the low quality wine did make a refreshing drink, although I knew that many soldiers had taken a liking to the local beers. I preferred my stronger and sweeter wines.

If Remus had been up at the garrison, he would certainly have heard talk of Lucius.

He travelled extensively in the area, supplying not only the army, but also the majority of the farms and taverns, with imported wines. I returned to my original question, 'So what have you been hearing?'

'Lots of gossip about headless bodies, ghosts, and …' He paused, and sucked noisily through his teeth before continuing, 'This is only gossip, mind you. Don't know that I heard right, but I did hear that someone at the garrison was involved.'

I smiled, 'To some extent, they're right. I'm involved, at the moment.'

He shook his head violently, causing the hood of his cloak to fall back from his smooth head. 'No, not you, someone else. Someone on the other side, you might say. Someone who should know better, if you know what I mean.'

'But who?' The words jumped from my mouth, to be greeted with a frown.

'Well, that's the thing, don't know, do I? Didn't get no names, did I? No one wanted to give names, like. Maybe no one knew any names.' He shrugged, as he pulled the reins, and the mules ground to a halt. He indicated a turning off the main road. 'This is where I'm heading.' He nodded at where the main road continued on, 'You're down that way, but … I'd be careful, if I was you.'

I nodded. I intended to be.

The sun was already setting after the short autumn day, as we finally entered Durnovaria. It had been some time since I had visited the town, and the dusk made the narrow streets and wooden buildings appear unfamiliar and sinister. The words of Memno, spoken as we had mounted our horses yesterday, returned unbidden to my ears, 'Take care of yourself.' There was a similar echoing speech from Remus.

My tired nerves started to see shapes that were not there, hear voices that issued from no human throat and feel the cold edge of steel in the cutting wind. We continued down the main street increasingly desperate to find the mansio, where we could claim lodgings and rest.

At last the columns of the portico appeared in front of me. The shadows thrown out by the many lights seemed to exude safety and security. I gladly dismounted, the ground reaching suddenly up to jar my ankles and knees. An attendant caught my arm, or I would have fallen.

'I'm fine. Let me be.' My response was un-necessarily gruff, but the lateness of the hour and the hard ride had taken its toll. 'I'm sorry, but I need a room, and some food.' Almost as an afterthought, I added, 'And lodgings for my horses and slave.'

'Certainly sir, and your name?'

'Tiberius Sextus Valerius. I'm here on official army business.'

'Please follow me.' The attendant inclined his head and indicated the door with his arm.

I abandoned Gallius and the horses as I was shown into the building. The entrance atrium, with the light from the many lamps reflected in the still waters of the central pool, was quiet, and ours were the only footsteps. We moved on through a large communal area until we reached a range of smaller rooms beyond. Lifting the heavy curtain at one entrance, he motioned me inside.

'I will send someone to attend to your needs,' and with that he left me alone. Within a few moments, a young male slave appeared. He brought with him a bowl of water and cloths, with which I could cleanse my skin of some of the dust of the day. As I did so, I gave orders for food and drink to be brought to me, and he soon went about his errands. The quality of the roasted and flavoured beef, which he brought, was average, but the honeyed pastries more than made up for any prior deficiencies.

I slept badly that night, my dreams disturbed and tangled, with images of Lydia, Lucius and nameless shapes cart-wheeling and dancing across my vision. Demons rose up from the very ground, pursuing me, catching at my heels, forcing me to flee from the delights which I longed to sample.

Day Four

When I woke, entangled in the sheets, I felt as tired and weary as if I had indeed been running all night. A session at the baths was required before I could see Aurelius, and accordingly I visited there prior to leaving the mansio.

The attention and the immersion in water, together with sweet smelling oils to cleanse my skin, did much to revive my flagging spirits. After the attendant had assisted me into my gleaming white toga, it was in a greatly improved humour that I emerged out into the sunshine of the new day. Gone were the fears and anxieties of the previous night, to be replaced by a sense of purpose and anticipation.

It had been some time since I last saw Aurelius, having had no reason to consult him, but I have always found him easy to speak to, even after a gap of several months.

I therefore had a lightness of step as I made my way to the forum, where I found a small tavern, just opening. The east facing position meant that the light penetrated deep inside, and it was here that I breakfasted. As I did so, I caught snippets of conversations, some prosaic and mundane, others tantalisingly suggestive of secrets and rumours.

'… he needs to watch himself. Her father won't stand for much more of that …'

'… there's trouble brewing, you mark my words. The omens are very bad. Only yesterday…'

'… and I tell you, it's mine …'

'… I won't have any arguments this early in the morning …'

'… haven't been any druids round here for years. I certainly don't…'

'… do you really think she does?'

'… I don't know why they allow it. They should just crush this, before it's got a hold …'

After finishing my meal, I stood up and made my way over to the basilica, entering the anteroom where I found myself in the presence of a few others, all of whom had business with the law officer.

We milled about in slight distrust of each other, like elegant and stately triremes in our formal togas, weaving in and out of the local tribesmen, in their checked cloaks, and spiked, white hair. I pondered the likely reasons for us all being here. Was this man here to complain about his neighbours? Was that one reporting the theft of a horse? Were these two recent protagonists over the favours of a lady? The petty squabbles and trifles of everyday life were here played out, with Aurelius acting as the referee, controlling fates and dealing out punishments to those deemed unworthy.

'Tiberius Sextus Valerius. Aurelius Satchii Vespasian will see you now.' The soft voice of a subordinate official sounded at my side. Now was the time when minor misdemeanours would give way to major outrage.

'Aurelius, it is good to see you again.' I reached out my hands to the tall, sparse man, who stood up at my entrance.

'Tiberius, I echo your sentiments.' He grasped my hand in greeting, before indicating a chair. 'How are you, and how is your practice getting on? The remedy you gave for my headaches still works.' He lifted his fingers to rub at his temple, before running them through his thinning hair, now liberally streaked with grey. 'I think of you every time I have to deal with too many trivial disputes.'

'You should not use it too often.'

'I'll remember. And how is Memno getting on with his roads? I hope the road to Iscalis will soon be completed to his usual high standard.'

As Aurelius touched, unknowingly on the subject of my visit, he must have seen something in my face.

'Tiberius, you are pale. Sit.' A frown appeared above his jutting nose. Turning, he issued orders, 'Some wine, bring some wine.'

The liquid restored me somewhat and I answered the unspoken question in his eyes. 'The road is progressing well, and he is on schedule, but ...'

For a moment I faltered, reluctant to state the facts out loud, as if by keeping quiet I could deny them, make my friend return to life. But the truth needed to be uttered. Only then could I move on and create some meaning out of his death.

'The road survey is going well, but one of the surveyors is dead. His body was found, beheaded, three days ago.' I paused to lift the goblet to my lips again, the wine flowing into my mouth untasted.

Aurelius sat, marshalling his thoughts. 'You say his head was severed. Did you find it with the body?'

I shook my head, feeling demons waiting at the edge of my consciousness.

'Yet you stated he was one of the surveyors. You must have identified him. How can you be sure?'

'Memno recognised a mark, a scar on his arm, and another on his leg. He knew the man well.' As I spoke I realised that I had already relegated my friend to the status of a body, an object from which the vital force that made him Lucius had departed. 'His name was Lucius, Lucius Octavio Gordianus. I also knew him well.' There. The deed was done. I had pronounced my friend dead.

Aurelius continued, 'Who do you think murdered him?'

'I don't know.' I leant towards my listener, trying by mere proximity, to force him to acknowledge the importance of my words.

'You must investigate his death. He must be avenged. We cannot allow this to go unpunished.'

'I understand your concerns, yet who am I to punish?' Aurelius raised his thin hands in the air, and shrugged his bony shoulders. 'How should I avenge him? I cannot punish an unknown person.'

'Then you must investigate. Send your men to find out the facts and bring the guilty to account for their deeds.'

Aurelius turned away to lean heavily on the table. His voice, previously strong and alert was now soft and almost inaudible. 'I cannot.'

At first his words rebounded round the room as I struggled to find meaning in them. 'You cannot? What do you mean? What can you not do? You can punish the guilty. You are the law officer. Why do you say you cannot?'

'I cannot investigate. I have no men to spare. I am sorry, but I just cannot spare anyone.' He turned back towards me. My anger clouded my eyes and I almost failed to see the distress written across his face.

'Why can't you spare the men?' I cried. 'A Roman has died, has been brutally murdered and you won't investigate. Why?'

'Tiberius, you must understand. I have to maintain the safety and security of the town and surrounding area. I cannot justify sending my men away to investigate a single death, when I have so much unrest here in the town.' As he spoke, his voice still soft and gentle, my ire subsided, and I started to see the man I knew, again.

Ever logical and considered, Aurelius was seeing the greater picture, whereas I had been seduced by my grief into imagining that everything would stop for my private concerns.

Aurelius continued to speak. 'We are reaping a harvest in this region, from the uprising in the east. I dare not deplete my forces here, when I might need to suppress a similar local rebellion. If you had more information, some idea, some hint as to who might be behind this, then I would be able to act.'

I saw what I must do and hastened to reassure him. 'I understand, really I do. If I am able to obtain more information then ...'

My pause was answered unhesitatingly. 'Then I can and will act. But Tiberius, be careful. Whoever did this once, may not hesitate to repeat their actions.'

I was thinking over the conversation with Aurelius as I made my way across the forum, heading back to the mansio.

I passed through a small market that was now busy with buyers and sellers. Shopkeepers displayed their produce, tempting those passing with the quality, or price, of their wares, and calling out to prospective purchasers. The dull thud of a butcher's knife, cleaving through muscle and bone, threw out the smell of blood, to compete and mingle with the other scents. Bread, fresh from the oven was being stacked on one counter, sending out its strong and seductive aromas. I pushed my way through a group of men discussing the relative merits of different sickles and ploughs.

On the other side of the street, a jeweller was enticing the onlookers with his finely worked wares. I paused to observe, my mind temporarily distracted by the dazzle in front of me. Paternal pride also played a part, as I tried to check if the gold and garnet necklace, the sapphire earrings or the silver enamelled brooches were of the same quality as those my son, Anthonius, produced.

To my casual eye, some were better crafted, others not, and I moved on. My progress was slow, and in many ways I was glad of the normality around me. These people were not concerned with death and mutilation, only with getting a good price or securing a bargain.

Outside the shoemaker's, I could hear a disgruntled customer complaining bitterly about the blisters he had gained since wearing his new sandals. The artisan was trying equally hard to persuade the client to step into the shop so that the matter could be resolved. Their interaction attracted a small group muttering in support of one or the other.

Eventually both parties retired to the relative privacy of the interior, one limping ostentatiously for all to see. The crowd moved on in a fluid fashion, slowing, eddying or backtracking, as each individual person progressed.

As I was heading in the general direction of the mansio, I allowed myself to be carried along until stopped by a tap on my shoulder and a breathless voice in my ear saying, 'Tiberius, it is you.'

I turned round to find myself looking at a smiling face, topped with a rim of dark hair. Bright eyes, made smaller by the chubbiness of the cheeks, gazed up at me.

'Victor, I didn't expect to see you here.'

His hands, amply bedecked with rings, grasped mine, as he said, 'Had to run to catch you up.' He produced a cloth from the bag tied to his belt, mopping at his moist face.

'You know me, travel about a lot. Here, there. Where ever there's people, and a sale, you'll find me.'

My smile at the thought of Victor running soon turned to a frown as I was jabbed violently in the back by an elderly woman, carrying several packages.

'It's very busy here. Why don't we sit down, have a drink and a chat?' suggested Victor.

'We do seem to be creating an obstacle,' I agreed, and we moved over to a tavern, sitting down inside the building, opposite each other at a discoloured, wooden table.

After ordering some wine from the attendant, Victor continued speaking, 'I didn't expect to find you here, not in Durnovaria. I didn't think you left that garrison very often. Gallius here with you, is he?'

I nodded, and Victor continued, 'Well, you tell him that I've been able to get some of those boxes that he wanted, the ones with several compartments. Mind you, they weren't easy to find, and won't be cheap, but they are top quality, top quality I tell you. But then you know that everything I get for you is quality. Wouldn't want me selling you inferior goods now would you?'

The words tumbled out of him with barely a pause for breath. Maybe that was why Victor was such a good salesman. His talk had a mesmerising quality about it that meant you almost felt compelled to buy something, if only so he wouldn't be disappointed.

I sipped my wine, waiting for a chance to speak, which came when Victor picked up his cup, to lift it to his mouth, his rings clinking against the pottery vessel. 'I was hoping you'd be coming out to the garrison soon,' I said.

'Of course I will. I do the rounds. Have to satisfy all my customers, otherwise they wouldn't stay customers for very long, would they?'

He sat forward, resting his elbows on the table, ticking off items on his stocky fingers. 'I've got the boxes, some glass jars, some Samian platters, and of course, your pestle and mortar. In fact,' and he leaned over, glancing to left and right, 'I do also have a very nice glass dish, which I'm prepared to let you have. Mind you, it won't be cheap, but the quality ...'

He raised his eyes to the ceiling, before sighing. 'The quality is very high. It's blue, deep blue. What more do I need to say? How about it? Are you interested?'

'I'll see. The thing I need most is the pestle and mortar.'

'I did have a bit of difficulty obtaining one. I knew you wouldn't want anything that would crack after a few months of use, so I hunted around for one that would last. It might be more expensive to buy, but it's going to last so much longer.' He rested back against the chair, only to lean forward again, as he momentarily closed his eyes and pursed his lips.

'What's wrong?' I asked.

'Nothing, nothing.'

He paused, then continued, 'Well, as you're in the profession, so to speak, it's this boil on my back. Really sore it is, when I lean back. I've had it for two or three months now, but I can't seem to shift it. Nothing seems to work, at least nothing that has been tried so far. What do you recommend?'

'I think you should let me have a look at it when you come up to the garrison, if it's still a problem then.'

'Thank you, Tiberius.' He picked up his cup again and drank quickly. 'Mind you, I hope you're not going to charge too much for a consultation are you?'

'I'm sure we can come to some arrangement.' I smiled at him. 'I might even buy your blue glass bowl, if the price is right.'

'I could give you a special deal, knock a bit off the price, providing, of course, that your treatment is up to scratch.'

I looked at him, and raised my eyebrows, and he continued, 'But then your advice is always beneficial. I suppose I could discount your order by a few sestertii.'

'I was thinking more like a few denarii, myself. Medical knowledge is expensive, but you would be getting top quality help.'

Victor threw back his head and gave a hearty laugh, his chins shaking with mirth. Wiping his eyes, he said, 'And I thought you were committed to selfless helping of the injured and sick.' He drained his cup, and got to his feet, saying, 'Let's talk about it when I'm at the garrison. Should be in about a week's time, maybe a few days more.'

The business that had brought me to Durnovaria suddenly slipped back into my consciousness. 'You will be careful on the road, won't you? There's a lot of unrest about.'

'Ohh, I can look after myself and my stock,' he replied. 'Don't forget, that's why I always have my bodyguard around. No-one's going to argue with Lachlan. I work hard, and I don't plan on anyone taking my goods away from me.' He turned and headed for the doorway, calling back as he did so, 'See you next week, Tiberius.'

The late morning sun struggled through a layer of cloud as Gallius and I headed out of town to start our journey back to the garrison. We were returning directly back home, on a different route to the one we had taken yesterday. I was too preoccupied with plans of revenge, retribution and justice to concern myself with conversation, and we made a silent party as we travelled. The road was undulating, sometimes allowing vistas of a fertile land, dotted with buildings, woodland and farms, whilst at other times, we seemed hemmed in by hills, unable to descry what might be ahead.

Clouds partially obscured the sky, allowing only brief glimpses of sunlight, quickly lost. I too, was bright and hopeful one moment, to be thrown into despair the next.

Aurelius said he could not spare the men, and from what I had heard in the tavern, there was plenty of unrest in the town and surrounding villages, which might need to be subdued. I had not realised that the rebellion, so far away in the east of the country, had spread its ripples of dissent to our peaceful area.

But then, all peace is relative. Many of the local inhabitants would probably claim they had lived in harmony with each other prior to us Romans coming.

A wry smile appeared on my lips, as we passed a burnt out village alongside the road. We would feel that by bringing the might and glory of Rome to this dark land, we improved the lives of all. Perhaps those responsible for this murder felt they were avenging the deaths of their own people in some way. Even so, it was not just. Lucius had not harmed anyone, and he should not be made to pay for the imagined crimes of others.

But this unrest, difficult as it made the situation, gave me the glimmerings of an idea. If Aurelius could not investigate, then why shouldn't I do it? Maybe I could find the perpetrators and bring them before him for justice to be done. But how could I imagine that I, a surgeon, could unravel this tangled web? Especially since five or six days had passed since Lucius had died. The more time that went by, the less chance there was of finding those responsible. Solving a murder needed skills I did not have. It took a special type of person to be an investigator.

The road dipped down to ford a small stream, the horses' hooves sending up splashes of water, as high as our feet.

I thought about the elements required. Observation, deduction, an understanding of human nature. The more I cogitated, the more I felt that in many ways this mystery was just a puzzle, a set of clues to be solved correctly, which would lead to a conclusion if followed in the right way. After all, what was the role of a surgeon? Didn't I just determine which particular conundrum needed to be solved? Surely if I could diagnose and treat disease, based on limited information, then there was a chance I could establish the root cause of this evil as well.

As I seesawed back and forth, Gallius acted as navigator and saw to our welfare. At one point, he steered us off the road to allow a marching column of soldiers to pass. Another time he negotiated a way through a herd of goats, poorly controlled by two young boys. I truly believe that left to myself, I would have let my mount take me anywhere.

When we stopped to eat, my actions were automatic. However, a smile illuminated my face as I thought about Lucius. Of course it was entirely possible that his death had as much to do with his eye for the ladies, as anything else.

Lucius, with his blond, curly hair, and fine physique attracted attention wherever he went, and especially from the fairer sex.

Was a jealous husband, brother or father at the root of this? I dismissed the idea even before it was fully formed. If that were the case, then there would have been no need to disguise the body. A murderer would have knifed or poisoned or beaten Lucius, but not beheaded him, or changed his clothing. A flash of pain from a knife in the dark leaving a complete body to be found would serve the purpose. This was too fancy, too ornate, too ritualistic a killing.

And so the journey continued, as my cogitations revolved in my private world, and the sun traversed its set path. As it was, we rode well into the evening and then night, before the garrison lights became visible.

Day Five

I slept late the next morning, and woke, stiff and sore in body but resolved of purpose. I would undertake the investigation into Lucius' death, and thereby give his spirit peace.

The walk from my sleeping chamber to the baths was short, but felt long. The hours spent in the saddle resulted in my gait causing much ribald jocularity amongst the soldiers and slaves. It was with relief that I reached the bath-house entrance, knowing that my aches would soon be eased. As the attendant was scraping the sweat from my body, Memno entered, also claiming temporary release from worldly discomfort.

'Were you successful?' he asked. 'When will Aurelius send his soldiers to investigate?'

'He can't spare any men at present. There is too much unrest in the town. The revolt in the east has caused agitation this far, and the men are needed to maintain order.' The look on Memno's face made me pause.

'So he's not going to investigate.' The words spilled from his lips, as he slumped down on the bench, turning his head away from me.

My certainty of the previous day seemed to have evaporated along with the aches of the journey. Would I be able to investigate a murder? Would I be able to bring the guilty party to justice? There was a world of difference between misdiagnosing a disease and condemning an innocent man. Or was there? The wrong treatment was just as likely to kill as cure. Looking for reassurance, I offered some consolation. 'I will find those responsible, and then Aurelius has to act.'

Memno lifted his head, pulling his shoulders up, and leaned forward as if to absorb my words. 'But how can you do that? You're a surgeon, not an investigator. Are you sure you should be doing this?'

'I will find those who murdered Lucius and avenge his death.' I spoke the words more to confirm my resolve than to convince Memno, who seemed to have more faith in my abilities than I had.

'You'll need to tell me everything about where he was found, and how. How easy will it be to find the exact spot again? Which soldiers were present? Was Lucius floating down the stream, or at the side? Was there a search made for his head?'

As I fired off my questions, Memno initially seemed in awe, but then as he recovered his composure, gave me his first answer.

'I don't remember.'

'Memno, you must remember. How easy will it be to find the spot again? How far away is it?'

'We found the body in the late afternoon, and returned here the following day.'

'And where exactly were you?'

'We'd marked the line for the road, from here. The ground is undulating further north, as you know. There were some huts, a small village possibly, that had been burnt, and then at the top of the hill, you could look down into the valley. The stream where ...' Memno paused, and then stood up to move into the next room. I followed and we both entered the water.

'Could you see the stream from the hill top?' I prompted, not wanting Memno to dwell too long on the gruesome memories of our friend.

'See? Oh, yes, the course was clearly visible, except where there were stands of trees. The route we wanted to take took us directly through a large wooded area. We were marking out the road as we went. I was on one hilltop and Agricola was on the further ridge. The soldiers went down into the wood, and then they found … they … How will you find out why Lucius died?' Memno raised his hands in apparent frustration before letting them drop into the water, sending drops flying in all directions.

I reached out my hand for a towel, which an attendant passed me. Wiping my eyes and face, I asked, 'Was he floating in the water, or was he lying at the side of the stream?'

'I'm not sure. I wasn't there when they found him … Let me think.' He paused, his eyes momentarily vacant. Looking away, he continued, 'The soldiers said they saw something, and they pulled it out. They certainly had wet sandals.'

Hoisting myself out of the bath, I sat on the edge. 'If they needed to go into the water, then Lucius was probably floating rather than lying at the side. Did you notice how many soldiers had waded in?'

'Four, maybe five. I don't really remember for sure.'

'He must have been in the stream, then. It wouldn't have needed four people to get wet otherwise.'

We moved into the hot steam room, where we both lapsed into silence for some moments, letting our bodies and minds purge themselves of stress.

That night the funeral of our friend took place. He had no relatives present, and it would be several weeks before his parents, so far away in southern Italy, would even know of Lucius' demise. The army had been his life for some years, and we were as close as his blood family.

The procession to the cremation area was subdued, with the musicians playing their mournful horns. I walked with the party out beyond the garrison walls, to the chosen site. There had been much discussion about the location, as Lucius' was the first death that had occurred at this garrison. Gallius kept pace with me, as I accompanied Memno.

Ours was not the loud wailing and crying of professional mourners, but it was no less heartfelt. Agricola, especially, was moved to tears many times.

The distance felt long, but far longer would Lucius have to travel to cross the Styx in Charon's boat.

His fare was put in a leather purse, and tied to his wrist, as we could not put it in his mouth for safekeeping. The body lay on its litter, wrapped, not in the traditional toga, but in a long woollen shroud, that covered and partially obscured the mutilated outline.

On reaching the stack of wood that was to take Lucius into the afterlife, the attendant slaves placed him on his funereal bed. I was one of those who declared an oration over him, along with Memno, and Tralen, the camp commander. May the gods have heard and taken note of the words said, for I remember little of my choked and stumbling speech.

As we then stood back and watched the torches thrust into the heart of the logs, my resolve hardened. I would find those responsible and see them brought to justice. The flames caught and started to jump higher into the night sky, sending sparks up into the heavens, and causing shadows to bound and leap as if in some macabre dance. It became impossible to see anything other than the bright glare of the fire, as Lucius was consumed.

Day Six

I, like many others, slept late the next morning. The funereal banquet had been a sombre affair, with more consumption of wine than of food. It is to be expected that such events have little of the jollity of more celebratory occasions, but there is usually a sense of finality. The feast marks an end point, a boundary that has been crossed, a time to talk about the life that has finished, to consider the worth of the accomplishments. However, in this case, we could only muse on how Lucius met his death, why it should happen to him, and what brilliant things he might have achieved, had he been allowed to live. And so we drank to numb our pain, and to fill the gaping silences in the conversations.

I walked over to the surveyors' office on a day that seemed to mock our grief.

The sun gave out its warmth, unstintingly. Soft, wispy clouds broke up the expanse of blue, creating a pleasing effect. The air was still, enhancing the potential enjoyment. There was an aroma of cut wood, sweetly scented smoke, and roasting meat that drifted to tantalise my nose.

'Good morning, Memno.' My greeting was received with a raised arm as Memno put his other hand to his head. 'Gallius could make you up a potion for your headache,' I continued.

My suggestion was greeted with a cautious shake of the head. 'Thanks, but no thanks,' Memno replied. 'The cure is usually worse than the ailment. It will pass.'

I moved into the centre of the room, where there was a large table, which held a detailed map of the area. Memno stood at my side, and we both gazed down at our immediate world, shrunk down to a single glance.

'Here's the garrison, that's Iscalis.' Memno used a stylus to indicate the various points as he named them. 'And that is where Lucius was found.'

His hand was shaking at this last reference position and, at first I could not clearly distinguish the exact location.

'But that's only ...' I checked the scale, and compared the distances, before continuing, 'only a short ride from my son's farm.'

'It's not much further from here.'

'I know, but I need to see Marcus anyway. I was planning to go some time this month, but I could …' I paused. I was going to say, "kill two birds with one stone", but stopped just in time. 'I could do the two things at the same time,' I finished.

'What do you think you'll find? I've told you everything I can remember about what happened.' There was a querulous note in Memno's voice, and I hastened to reassure him.

'I don't expect I'll find much, but seeing the scene through fresh eyes, as it were, may make a difference.' Where else could I start? The site of discovery seemed as good a place as any I might select. I walked up and down the room, engrossed in gladness at the thought of some action. 'I'll leave Gallius in charge of the infirmary. There are hardly any patients at the moment and it'll only be for a day or two.' I glanced at Memno, noting his weary eyes and furrowed brow. 'I do think you should see him. Ask him for something that tastes nice. He'll make it up in the dispensary.'

Memno nodded, sinking down into a chair, as if his limbs could no longer support him. I left to make my arrangements for travel.

Sitting in the reception room, I watched my daughter in law issue orders to the various house slaves. The warm floor dispelled much of the dampness of the air, and was pleasant under my feet, which had become chilled from the ride. Into my comfort came the words of my elder son, grating on my ears.

'Why on earth are you rushing about the countryside, investigating strange deaths at your age? You should be taking it easy. Give up medicine, the army, enjoy life a little.' Marcus had never been loath to say what he meant, but now the sounds were harsh and brutal.

'I'll do what I feel to be right.' I responded. 'Lucius was my friend. He has a claim on my time and I give it freely.'

As Marcus slammed his goblet of wine down on the table and turned away, Aelia, his wife, spoke.

Her voice was measured and deliberate, and only partially dissipated my disgust. 'Tiberius, don't be angry. Marcus only means that we don't see enough of you. He'd like … we'd both like you to make your home here with us. You could see more of your grandchildren. Isn't that right, Marcus?'

'Yes, that's right. We don't see enough of you.'

To my cynical ears the words had a rehearsed sound to them. My eldest son and his wife would love me to stay with them, so that I would develop an even stronger liking for Julius, my grandson, and then announce him as my heir. Well, they would have to wait much longer before I was ready to sit in a chair all day. But in the meantime I preferred to create the impression of accepting their advice, so that life together was more tolerable.

'I'd love to see more of Julius and Carita, but I can't enjoy life with Lucius' death on my mind. Maybe when this mystery is cleared up, then we can talk again about my making my home here.'

As we were talking we sat overlooking the farm, which was cloaked in early evening drizzle. Several slaves came past the window, their voices low and hushed as they headed for their quarters, and a well-earned rest. More slaves flitted in and out of the room, lighting lamps, arranging furniture, bringing food and wine.

My son slowly shook his head, before asking, 'Why are you investigating? Why doesn't Aurelius send his men? He can't expect you to do his work for him.'

'Marcus, Tiberius did tell you that the men couldn't be spared at the moment. You've heard the stories of fighting and ...'

'That's several days' ride away from here. What does Aurelius think will happen? That this Celtic queen will ride down here in her chariot, sweeping all before her?' Marcus waved his arm, appearing to forget about the half full goblet still in his hand, as droplets of wine splashed onto the floor.

Sounds drifted up from the courtyard into a pause in our conversation.

'… here, careful with that lamp. You've spilt oil over my foot …'

'… when's it going to stop raining? I don't think I'll ever get dry …'

I took a sip from my wine, and marshalled my arguments. 'Aurelius thinks that the rumours will create - are creating - unrest in the town and surrounding district. When I went to see him, there was certainly much talk of this Boudicca and her army.'

'Army? What army?' Marcus sneered. 'More of a rabble, if you ask me. They're no match for us.'

'I can see his point though. He may need his men. Even a rabble can cause a riot.'

'That's still no reason for you to be out looking for murderers. The man's dead. You can't bring him back. It could wait a few weeks.'

'It's already been a week since he was killed. I told you, Lucius was my friend. I cannot rest while his death is un-avenged.' I stood up and walked to the window, only half seeing outside. Why could my son not see that I had a sense of duty to my friend? Light flowed out from the many lamps inside the room, making the gentle slope of the courtyard appear slightly less treacherous. As I stood there two slaves slipped on the muddy surface, bringing a third down with them, their voices easily audible from my vantage point.

'What'd you go and do that for?'

'Wasn't my fault. Rufus pulled me down.'

'It's muddy. I only slipped. Give us a hand up.'

'Get up yourself. I'm not having you pull me down again.'

Weaving through the trio came a fourth slave. The graceful movement contrasted with the clumsy antics of those on the ground. The short laugh that rang out was unmistakably female, and she easily evaded their efforts to grab her.

Smiling, I turned back to the room. 'Marcus, I need to do this for my friend. Surely you see that.'

Later that night, as I lay on my bed, an image hovered around my consciousness. Every time I tried to pin it down, it eluded me. Was it something someone had said? But who, and what? Maybe it was something I had seen. I tried to think back to the journey I had made. At the time it had seemed uneventful, if somewhat uncomfortable.

As I had ridden out of the gates of the garrison, the previously sparkling blue sky had turned dull, with an ominous grey to the looming white clouds. Drizzle had been my companion for most of the journey, broken by periods of heavier rain. The road had been quiet, my solitude interrupted only by some carts trundling along, a party out hunting who had cut across the road, and a few other riders, looming larger as they came towards me. So what was it I was trying to remember? It was to do with the death of Lucius, that I was sure. Or was I? I couldn't establish whether it was central or peripheral. Maybe I was getting old or tired - or both.

Day Seven

I awoke surprisingly refreshed. As I opened the window shutters, the morning sun streamed in, as if eager to draw me outside so that it would have a companion. I had not expected to sleep so soundly. That which had danced teasingly through my memory still would not materialise, but I knew from experience that the best thing to do was to try and put it out of my mind, and accordingly I focussed on the task I had set myself for the day. I would visit the site where Lucius' body had been found. Although at least one day of rain and a night of drizzle had passed in this area, there might be something there that would hint at the perpetrators of this crime.

My breakfast was quiet, as Marcus was already discussing the days' routine with his farm overseer, and Aelia was busy supervising the house slaves.

I was in good spirits as I rode away from the farm, past the cultivated fields, where the final crops were being harvested. The enclosures farthest from the house were empty of human life, populated only by deer, hares and the unseen, but vocal birds. The drone of bees collecting their final offerings from the last flowery sacrifices seemed magnified by the patchy silence, filling the empty spaces.

On more than one occasion the sun on my back made me consider removing my cloak, but passage through a bank of trees reinstated its need. The brightly coloured leaves fought to escape the imprisonment of the branches, so that they could fly and swoop, before congregating in a great gathering.

I reminded myself of Memno's directions. Without his help I would have been unable to find the correct spot, for he had not only given me instructions on how to reach the area, but what to look for once in the vicinity. Past the burnt out village, up onto the ridge of the hill. Looking down to the north, the stream can be seen threading its way through the valley bottom to join with a larger river just out of sight. Ride down the hill and follow the water against the flow, to where the survey was temporarily abandoned, in a wood of beech, oak and birch.

Each time I came to a group of houses, I was convinced I was nearly there, only to be mistaken. Either there was still habitation, or there was no ridge behind to climb, or once on the ridge, there was no stream, or too many. But these disappointments made the pleasure more intense once the correct set was found.

As I entered the wood, I could easily see where the soldiers had previously been. The ferns lay broken and dejected, branches had been snapped and the undergrowth showed signs of many feet having trodden the fallen leaves into the mud. The smell of wet bracken assailed my nostrils, as I dismounted to lead my horse through to the edge of the stream, where I tied him loosely to a low branch.

Pushing my way along the bank, I came upon brambles still bearing their sweet fruit, the juice staining my fingers as I removed the berries from the plant. The purple of late foxgloves contrasted with the bright yellow dandelions, their fluffy seed heads dispersing at my passage. The moderated breeze brought evil scents to hint at the presence of hemlock, and stinking iris. Holly and yew stood out in their dark green foliage, against the delicate white branches of the birch and smooth grey trunks of the beech.

I wandered about the area, unsure exactly what I was looking for. At one point I stepped into the stream, but rapidly regretted this action. It was a pleasant site, one to be enjoyed in other circumstances, but for now, I gained nothing more than cold, wet feet and a deeply embedded blackberry thorn in my finger. Intermittently sucking and squeezing the offending spot, I returned to my horse to begin the ride home. I wasn't sure how much benefit my visit had brought me, but at least I had now seen the area for myself. I valued the evidence of my own eyes much more than a verbal report, even though it might come from a trusted friend.

Back at the farm, I wandered round the barns and outbuildings looking for Marcus. A movement at the edge of my sight brought back the elusive phantom from the previous night. I was now certain it was peripheral to the death I was investigating, but not knowing how it related was irksome.

'Father, were you looking for me?'

'Yes.' My irritation had to be satisfied. 'Who was that?' The way that one of the slaves had moved going into the barn, reminded me of something or someone.

'Just one of the slaves. She's new. Is it important?' There was an underlying hint of reluctance in Marcus' voice, which made me pursue the issue.

'It might be. She reminds me of someone. She's new, you say. I thought you said you hadn't been buying any slaves recently. What's her name?'

'Perdita.' As if realising he had given too much away, Marcus stumbled on. 'I think that's it. Yes, Perdita or something like that. I forget their names. No, I haven't been buying, that is, I … I did a swap, yes, I did a swap with another farmer. He wanted to get rid of her, and I thought she'd come in handy, maybe as an extra house slave for Aelia.'

I knew without even looking at him that he was lying. The olive skin and dark hair were not easy to forget, and neither was the grace with which she moved. This was the memory that had been triggered the previous evening, but how and why? What was Lydia doing here, when she should be miles away on Corolius' farm? It was inconceivable that Corolius had swapped her.

'I want to talk to her.' I fired the words at Marcus, regardless of whether he had finished speaking.

'Certainly. Maybe later, when she has finished her work and you have rested and eaten. Come, let us go back to the house and…'

'Now. I want to speak to her now.' Ignoring Marcus' attempts to coax me away, I strode forward intending to catch Perdita by the arm.

She turned, and a look of panic, surprise and fear flashed across her face as Marcus and I advanced. Our quarry backed away like a wounded fox, her gaze flitting between us.

For several long moments, no one spoke. I stepped one pace toward her but the early evening sun slanting through the open barn door shone into my eyes. Was I mistaken? Could this be a different girl? Moving again, I became more certain. The slave was pressing herself into the stacked bales of hay; a few wisps already stuck in her hair. Her mouth formed words with no sounds.

'Do you know her, Father?'

'I … yes, I do. That is, I remember seeing her at another farm.' I turned to look at Marcus, trying to fix him with my gaze. 'You didn't swap her did you, Marcus?'

'I … well … that is. How else would I have got her? Of course I did a swap. Well, maybe not quite a straight slave for slave transaction, but it was definitely a swap.' His defiant eyes looked straight into mine.

'But Marcus, I happen to know she belongs to Corolius.'

'She belongs to me now.'

Behind me I could hear Lydia gasp. She seemed to stop breathing as she waited for my answer.

'I wonder … I expect she got lost. From what I remember she was brought over from Spain only recently.'

'You appear to know a lot about her.' Marcus kept his attention on me, with narrowed eyes, as he spoke.

'Not really.' I said, carelessly. 'I'll take her back tomorrow or in the next few days. I need to see Corolius again anyway.'

'Why? Why do you need to see him?'

'He's my patient. It's getting dark. Hadn't we better go inside?' Taking Marcus by the arm, we walked away. He seemed reluctant to leave Lydia in the barn, with so much mystery surrounding her. I, too, had many things I wanted to establish, but I wanted to do so without drawing attention to Lydia.

'I understand Julius is doing well with his writing and reading. When are you going to introduce him to Greek? If he wants to be a surgeon like me, he must learn Greek.'

'His tutor thought maybe in a few months' time. But who is that slave, and why are you so interested in her?'

'What slave? Oh, the one in the barn. No, I'm not bothered about her. I just don't want my son getting embroiled in legal arguments, when I can help. After all, don't forget I still own this property.'

As soon as I said the words, I regretted it. Marcus was sensitive about not being able to own the farm, but the law was clear that, as paterfamilias, I had ultimate ownership of all my family's property. I sought to distract him. 'Have you got all the crops in now? Did I understand that you're planning on planting vines next year?'

'Vines? Oh, yes. In the upper pasture. The soil seems suitable there, and the aspect's right. What do you know about her? Is there something going on between you and Corolius?'

'Me and Corolius? No, he's one of my patients as I said.' I turned to my daughter-in-law, who had come out to find us. 'Aelia, how delightful you look this evening. That yellow colour really suits you. Is it a new tunic? I hope we haven't delayed dinner too much.'

Taking Aelia's arm, I headed back into the villa, with Marcus following behind, as I continued, 'I was talking with Marcus about the plans he has for the farm. I think you should extend the house as well, maybe put on another wing.' With such light-hearted chatter, the time passed until we had eaten, and I could retire to my room.

Day Eight

The next morning I rose early and came out of my room to find a contrast from the weather of the previous day. I initially stood in the corridor, and then perched on the stone balustrade. The overhanging roof gave me protection, and I could spend a few moments in quiet contemplation. I watched large raindrops chase each other across the courtyard, before losing themselves in the newly formed stream that hastened down the slope.

The travel plans I had made for today would have to be postponed. I could instead amuse myself for part of the day in the company of Julius and Carita. The inclement weather looked set to last for some hours and would allow me plenty of time to also arrange my thoughts and findings.

I was about to turn away when the sight of someone braving the rain caught my attention.

It was impossible at this distance to see who had emerged from the outbuildings; a heavy blanket provided only meagre shelter to the person. As the figure drew closer, I recognised Lydia. She stopped a few feet in front of me, wrapping her arms around her. As she looked up at me, the heavy, wet folds fell away from her face, leaving it open to the elements. The single word she spoke held many accusations.

'Why?'

'Why what, Lydia?'

'Why?'

'I don't know how you came to be here, or why, but I have to do what's right. You belong to Corolius. I must return you, or arrange for your return.' As I spoke the gusty wind eased, leaving the rain to fall unhampered. It smoothed her hair, and unheeded rivulets ran down her face. Her stance and silence forced justification from me.

'Even if I had not said anything, the truth would have been revealed at some point. It's better this way. You would have to return to Corolius. He is your master. You belong to him. I'll try and think of some story to tell him, so maybe he won't punish you too much for running away.'

I could not tell if rain or tears were wetting her cheeks. My hand was beginning to reach out to wipe her face, when, her head and shoulders slumped with the weight of my words, she turned to trudge back across the mud of the courtyard. I watched the retreating figure until she was obscured by the rain, or was it tears in my own eyes that blurred my vision?

'Who is she?'

I jumped at the voice coming from behind me. 'What's that? Marcus. I didn't realise you were there.'

'You know who she is? You know her, don't you?'

'As I said yesterday, she belongs to Corolius. What I don't understand is what she's doing here. Maybe you could enlighten me.

'I swapped one of the other slaves for her.'

I leant back against a pillar, feeling the damp stone, cold at my back. 'Marcus, we both know that isn't true. Why can't you tell me the truth? You didn't swap Perdita with anyone. How did she come to be here?'

I could see differing emotions fighting for prominence on Marcus' face. As he folded his arms, frowned and dropped his head, I no longer saw a grown man, but my five-year-old son, caught in one of his many misdemeanours.

'Marcus, you know that Corolius could sue you, and me, for stealing her. Tell me what happened so that when I take Lydia back, I can smooth things over with him.'

'I found her. She was in the woods. She said she was lost. I didn't know where she came from. She wouldn't say. So I kept her.'

The short truculent sentences were uttered to the floor. 'I found her. I was out hunting and I found her. I want to keep her.'

I looked out over the courtyard, which now resembled a quagmire. 'I'll take her back as soon as the roads are passable after all this rain.'

'Why should Corolius ever know that she's here?' Marcus squared up to me. 'I want to keep her here. I like her. I want to keep Perdita.'

'She goes back. She doesn't belong to you.' I turned and walked away from him, but my efforts to end the exchange were not successful. I had gone no more than a few paces before Marcus caught up with me.

'You called her Lydia. You didn't call her Perdita, you called her Lydia. How do you know that's her name? You talk as if you know her.'

'Marcus, I told you, I stayed at Corolius' farm on my way to Durnovaria. I noticed her there. That's all.'

'There's something going on. She said she worked on the farm, but her hands aren't used to field work. I'm sure she's a house slave, or something like that.'

'Yes, she was in the house, serving at dinner.'

I continued to walk away, only to hear Marcus say, 'You slept with her, didn't you? Is that why you're so anxious to return her to Corolius, so you can do the same again?'

'I merely want to return Corolius' property to him, and help you avoid the law courts.' I kept my back to my son as I spoke. I did not want him to see the sudden heat that flushed my face at the remembrance of that night.

Day Nine

I lay for a few moments in silence, hearing the air fill with the chorus that heralds the dawn. The previous day, I had indeed spent playing with my grandchildren, although the time when I could bounce Julius on my knee was long gone. I could just about do the same with Carita, who soon tired of the attention, seeking out the ministrations of her nurse, and my games with Julius became more adult. In praise of his skill at writing a passage about Bellerophon killing the Chimaera, I showed him the rudiments of ludus latrunculorum, letting him beat me on some of his first tries.

As the rain had then ceased, Julius conscripted some of the younger slaves, and they used up considerable amounts of excess energy in various ball games. I declined to join them, pleading an unfair advantage in height, instead sitting and whiling away an enjoyable hour or two watching their youthful exuberance.

But now it was time to leave this domesticity behind. As I stepped out of the main door to the cart that was waiting for me, I thought how pleasant it would be to have this lifestyle. A comfortable house, a productive farm, but then the image shattered into a broken mosaic. For the thing to complete the picture would be a peaceful family, and I knew that Marcus and I would not be able to live for very long under the same roof without our fragile relationship suffering.

If I lived anywhere, it would be with my younger son, Anthonius, or in my own house. I smiled as I imagined Marcus' irritation if I did so.

But that day was far off. At present I had other things to think about, such as who killed Lucius and how to return Lydia to Corolius.

As I climbed up onto the cart, Lydia was already sitting there. Sitting down, I brushed against her arm, feeling the tautness of her body, which matched the blankness of her face.

'Goodbye, Grandpa.' Julius came running up to say farewell, with Carita toddling along behind him. 'Thank you for showing me how to play that game,' he said. 'I'll remember to keep practising, so I'll beat you next time.'

'I'm sure you will,' I replied, 'but mind you pay as much attention to your other studies as well. Here you are,' as I slipped two copper coins into his hand.

'Bye bye, Grampa.' Carita waved her doll at me.

'You make sure you're a good girl, and do as your mother tells you,' I said.

She nodded enthusiastically as I slipped a coin into her hand as well. She looked down at it, then ran back to her mother, holding out her hand for examination.

'You spoil them,' came the soft murmur from Aelia. 'Have a safe journey, and come back soon.'

After giving some last minute instructions to the slave who was going with us, to ride my horse and then to return the cart, Marcus came up to me.

'Goodbye, Father. As Aelia said, do come and see us again soon. It's good for Julius and Carita to get to know their grandfather.'

I wanted to ask Marcus if he also wanted me to return. Maybe it would be good for father and son to get to know each other a little better. Maybe I had abandoned my sons to their fates during those long months and years when the life of my dearest Eusibia had been ebbing away. What use is a doctor if he can't even cure those he loves? What use is a father if he can't protect his family?

Marcus continued speaking, 'You'd better get going, before the weather changes again.'

He then turned and went back up the steps to where Aelia was holding Carita, with Julius at her side. All four waved, with varying degrees of enthusiasm, as I urged the horse on and down the track, away from the house.

We had travelled some distance with the only sounds coming from nature's orchestra, before Lydia's words interrupted the birds and insects.

'You could just stop the cart here, and no-one would ever know.'

'But I'd know, and so would he,' I indicated to where my horse was being ridden lazily behind us. 'I have to do what's right, what is required by law.'

Lydia did not speak, but the set of her mouth, which matched the furrow above her eyes, said much.

'I'm sorry that I have to do this,' I continued, trying to ignore her, as I stared straight ahead, concentrating on the road, 'but you are a runaway slave. If I return you, there is less chance of severe punishment.' I could not resist a glance sideways at the girl sat next to me. 'Maybe if you told me why you ran away, it would help.'

Her mouth softened, and she bit her lip as she brought her hand up to scrub roughly at her eyes. 'I'm scared.' were the words she finally uttered.

'Scared? Scared of what?' My response came out quicker than I had intended, and I took a deep breath, as I re-phrased my questions. 'What are you scared of? Is Corolius a hard master? Does he punish you too severely?'

She shook her head to all my enquiries, causing me a degree of exasperation. 'Well, what are you afraid of then?'

Lydia's initial reply of 'Her.' made little sense, until she expanded. 'She hates me, does Julia. She's cruel, and enjoys hurting people.'

'Lydia! You should not say such things of your mistress.' I found it difficult to reconcile this view of Julia with my own recollections, even allowing for the differences in our experiences. We continued on, in silence, for a few moments, before returning to the subject.

'She likes to hurt us, to see us cry with pain.' The tremble in Lydia's voice was matched by a shake in her body, which was transmitted to me through the wooden platform we sat on. 'None of the house slaves like her. She asks for things, then changes her mind, and complains when it is not right.'

'But she is your mistress. She has a right to have things done in the way she wishes.'

'But what gives her the right? Why should she be able to order me about, give me meaningless tasks, that can't be done, and then have me whipped for not doing it right?' Lydia was beating her fists against her thighs, in time to the tears running down her face.

I felt I had no answer to give. I was not accustomed to dealing with or pondering such issues. What did give one person the right to issue orders to another? Why should one human have the right to dictate the environs of another's world? I didn't know. I had been brought up with the idea that we are all born on this earth for a purpose. For some, that is to rule, others to obey. In many ways we are all slaves, bound by the decisions of others, more superior. Our destiny is out of our hands, and we cannot change our fate, we can only accept it. But such philosophical arguments were unlikely to be understood by this simple woman, railing against the natural order of things.

'You must try to do her bidding.' My feeble attempt at consolation was poorly received, as Lydia turned her head, directing her gaze away from me. 'If you try hard to please her, then maybe she will get to like you. Try to anticipate her needs, and meet them without her having to ask.'

This was a new experience for me. I was not used to counselling slaves on how to conduct their relationship with their owners. My success in this may be gauged by the way Lydia wrapped her arms around herself, moving slightly away from me on the bench. There were no more words exchanged during the journey.

The trees behind Corolius' house had shed their ruby leaves and now stood barren against the cloudless sky. The roof tiles no longer shone as we approached the building. Our arrival did not go unannounced, but to my surprise it was not Corolius or Julia who came to greet us.

'Tiberius. I'm so glad you were able to get here so quickly.'

In my confusion I could not understand the meaning of the words Gallius used. 'What are you doing here? Why aren't you at the garrison? Where is Corolius?'

'I sent messengers. To ask you to come. Isn't that why you're here?'

'No, I got no summons. I came because ...' I looked round to my side, where the wooden seat was empty.

It was entirely understandable that Lydia had taken the opportunity to slip down from the cart and disappear into the house. I somehow doubted that she would be able to cover up her absence but everything was so obviously in disarray, that it might go unpunished. At any rate, I would wait and see if any explanations were called for. 'No, I came to see Corolius.'

'I know. That's why I asked you to come.'

Gallius and I gazed at each other as we mentally dissected the conversation and rearranged it. Before we were done, Julia burst out of the door, her nervous energy expressing itself as mild hysteria.

'Tiberius, I'm so glad you could come. Gallius is unsure of the treatment required. Please help him.' Without hesitation she then turned and ran back inside.

'Gallius, what is going on here.' I got down from the cart, as the slave who had accompanied us from Marcus' led the horses away.

'Master, I had a message to come and tend to Corolius, who had been taken ill. The hospital at the garrison was virtually empty, so I felt I could come.' Gallius put his hand to his head, rubbing his forehead. 'I got here yesterday, and found Corolius in bed, very lethargic, and with shaking hands. I realised I needed your expertise, so I sent for you.'

'The rider must have passed us on the way. No matter. Marcus will tell him that I was on my way here anyway.'

As we entered the house, Gallius indicated that we should turn to the left, and then we paused in front of Corolius' bedchamber.

'Now what are the symptoms?' I asked.

'Lethargy, weak but rapid pulse, and loss of appetite. He seems to salivate a lot, and his hands and legs appear stiff.'

'The same complaints as before, but more pronounced. And what treatment have you given so far?'

'Bleeding, an infusion of herbs, same as before.'

'And the response?'

'He did seem to improve overnight, but I am still not comfortable with his progress. I cannot find a cause for this illness.'

'Let's see if our combined thoughts can shed some light on this,' and I lifted the curtain at the entrance to the room. Corolius was lying on his bed, his closed eyes appeared sunken in his pale face.

'Tiberius, we have need of your skills. Gallius seems unable to effect a cure. I fear it is beyond his capability.'

I could feel Gallius' anger emanate along the restraining hand I placed on his arm, as I addressed myself to the man sitting by the head of the bed.

'Germanicus, I didn't expect you to be here. Acting nursemaid doesn't seem to sit easily on your shoulders.'

He stood up, stretching his arms up towards the ceiling, and yawning. 'I felt it my duty to give Julia a break. She's very concerned. And Petronus could not study for worry about his father.'

'I would have thought that exercising the mind and body would have restored both his humours, and yours. But now, if you could leave us, so that I can examine Corolius. Gallius, bring that lamp closer.'

Our evening meal was conducted in near silence; each of us seemed lost in our own thoughts. As Gallius had indicated, Corolius was improving, and much as I would have liked to claim the credit, I felt it was despite, rather than due to my administrations. Within a short time of my arrival, he was able to sit up and take a little broth. I was at a loss to explain this affliction that started and ceased so abruptly.

I retired to my room as soon as I was able, only to be stopped at the doorway by Julia. Her anxiety and concern for her husband were almost palpable, and gave her voice that husky breathlessness that could reach down inside a man and come near to making him forget his duty.

'Will he …? Is he …? Can you …?' Her movements filled in the gaps, as she lifted her gaze to mine.

'I don't know, Julia. At the moment he is recovering, and that is the important thing.'

She caught hold of my arm, the nails of her long, slender fingers impressing themselves in my skin, through the fabric of my tunic. 'Why? Why is he so ill? You must help him.' She lifted her other hand to her brow, as she closed her eyes. 'Please make him better. I couldn't stand to lose him.'

I caught hold of her as she swayed slightly. A hint of lavender and sandalwood wafted into my nostrils. 'Julia, you're tired. You must rest. Let me call your slaves.'

'I'm tired, Tiberius, you're right. Maybe you could help me to my bedchamber. But I'm so worried about Corolius. He's been acting so strangely recently, and there have been so many visitors.'

'Julia, I must insist that you rest.' A movement at the end of the corridor resolved itself into a house slave, who ran forwards to take her mistress. 'Help her to bed, and make sure she is not disturbed.'

The slave nodded, and Julia relinquished her grip on my arm. Looking at me, she again asserted, 'I could not bear to lose him.'

A sudden trick of the light made her eyes appear hard and dry, curiously at odds with her words.

Day Ten

Another night of unsettled sleep passed before I was woken by Gallius bringing some refreshments, and for a moment I fancied myself back at the garrison, with only the puzzles of disease, the dilemmas of treatment and intrigues of the gaming board to tax me. But my slave soon dispelled all lingering dreams.

'Corolius is much recovered. He slept well and is now able to walk a short distance with minimal support. His appetite has also returned and he took some fruit, vegetables and olives this morning.'

Still drowsy, I waved my hand to indicate approval so far of the regime that Gallius was describing. 'Make sure Corolius, and the rest of the household, know he is not to take anything stronger for the rest of today. Tomorrow, if he continues to improve, he can take a little meat as well.'

Gallius nodded, as he replied, 'I've already told Germanicus, who was there when I gave Corolius some massage to aid the return of power in his legs. Will we need to stay longer, or…?'

Sitting on the edge of the bed, I looked up at Gallius. His eyes looked sore, and his shoulders were drooped. 'You look tired. Did you sleep badly?'

'I … um … I was caring for Corolius.'

'Gallius, why couldn't one of the house slaves have sat with him? You didn't need to, surely.'

'Germanicus said I needed to, that you had asked for me to stay with him.'

'I see. Maybe you should have checked with me, as I hadn't given any such orders. You said earlier that Germanicus came in when you were giving Corolius some massage. He seems very concerned about this illness.' I indicated the space on the bed beside me. 'Why don't you sit down? Have you eaten yet? As usual, you've brought me plenty.'

Gallius placed the tray on a low table and sank down onto the bed, next to me. He braced himself with his arms, and let his head drop forward, before raising his weary eyes to mine.

'Germanicus was most insistent that he see what I was doing. He kept saying how strange this illness was, and why couldn't the cause be found.'

'Julia was saying very much the same yesterday.' I said. 'I wonder if there is something in his food or drink making him ill.'

'You think it might be poison? No slave would dare,' protested Gallius.

I picked up some bread, dipped it in the wine and ate. Passing the plate to Gallius, I contemplated the options. As he had said, few slaves would consider poisoning their masters. The law condemning all slaves, should one murder his or her owner, resulted in effective self-policing. No-one wants to die for another's crimes. And even so, I was unsure if it was poison. The paralysis that had brought Corolius down could be due to a physical ailment, but if so, it was something I had not seen before. There were elements of the case that seemed familiar, but at present I could not establish why.

'I don't know what is going on here, but this is not our main concern. We must return to the garrison. Corolius' illness can wait. We need to find out what happened to Lucius. As soon as you're ready we'll leave. I'll find Julia and give her instructions to maintain the improvement, while you prepare the horses.'

It was not Julia, but Germanicus that I found once again with Corolius, who was now reclining in the main room. He was indeed much better, with the previous weakness now almost resolved. His breathing and pulse were also normal.

I gave my prescription and assured them both that I would call again in a week's time unless there were any changes before then. Germanicus followed me to the main door, where Gallius was already waiting outside with our horses.

'Germanicus, please bid Julia farewell from me. I take it she is still resting?'

'Yes. Her husband's mystery illness has quite worn her out, especially with the worry of Corolius' recent behaviour.'

'His behaviour? In what way?'

'Did she not say last night? Corolius has had several unknown visitors recently, that neither Julia nor I were permitted to meet.'

'But Corolius has a large farm. Surely he is allowed to keep his business separate from his family, and his servants.' The worried look that had been on Germanicus' face was replaced with a hard stare, through narrowed eyes, before he, as rapidly, relaxed his features again.

'Of course. Maybe you're right. Maybe the frequent trips he's been making are also business. Perhaps that's why he never reveals where he has been.' Germanicus slowly shook his head, as he continued, 'He's away for several hours, even days at a time. We, or rather Julia, never know where he is or when he will return. The last time you visited, Corolius had already been absent for three or four days, saying nothing of where he had been.'

It was my turn to frown. 'I thought he'd come straight from here to the garrison.'

'No.' Germanicus raised his eyebrows, opening his eyes, and lifted his hands with the palms uppermost. 'He'd been somewhere else first. But don't worry. I'll look after him, and protect his interests while he's unwell. Safe travelling.'

With that he turned abruptly and strode along the corridor leading to the bedchambers. I walked slowly down to where Gallius was already sitting on one of the horses.

The journey back to the garrison was slow. Rain from the previous night had made the track boggy in places, and the horses worked hard to reach the road. In many places it was necessary to ride in single file, until we were on the firmer surface.

By mutual consent neither of us spoke until we were well away from the farm. Gallius then rapidly resumed our conversation of that morning.

'Do you really think that Corolius was poisoned? If so, who could it have been? And why?'

'I don't know. Julia and Germanicus certainly think that his illness has caused him to act strangely. It could easily be a poison of some description.' My brow was furrowed as I fought to drag a memory from the depths of my mind. 'His symptoms certainly remind me of something.'

'But what? I don't think I've seen this before.'

'I have a vague recollection that I've been trying to pinpoint. I saw someone with the same weakness, lethargy and shaking, while I was still an apprentice to Paul.'

'That was more than a few years ago now.'

'I know, Gallius. Even before you and I met. Let me think. Paul was called to a house in Athens where the patient displayed very similar symptoms, before dying. It was a child of five or six, a boy, no a girl, I seem to remember, and there was the same stiffness in the legs and weakness in the hands...'

'But who would murder an infant? Surely it can't have been the same as this. They could not have been poisoned.'

I turned to look at the man riding next to me. Gallius had an expression of abhorrence on his face as he spoke of the death of a child. The scroll of my internal memory unrolled, back to the first time I had seen him. I had bought him in the market in Athens, when he was just a boy of ten or eleven, and he had been with me ever since. He had seen my sons grow up, my wife die and now my grandchildren born. In many ways, my family had been his. He had never really known his parents, according to the trader who was selling him. Maybe he was longing for a family, a child of his own. Had he met the woman who he hoped would bear those children for him? He was still young, tall and healthy, and he could easily make a living as a doctor, once I retired and gave him his freedom.

'You seem very moved by that death. Are you thinking of your own future children? Is there a household that I need to send you to more frequently?'

'Master, I would not presume … No, no, you know I … how cold that wind is.'

I could not resist a smile and further probing at his discomfort. 'You didn't tell me, did Corolius sleep well last night?'

'At times. He was restless for a while, but then slept soundly.'

'But you did not. I wonder, was there someone else, assisting you at this time?' I put up my hand to prevent an interruption. 'Let's see, there was that little dark haired girl, who seemed quite taken with you, or maybe the well built girl with fair hair. Yes, I think she would be a good choice. Wide hips and large breasts. She would bear you many children. I could talk to Corolius and Julia next week, when I visit. I take it you'd like to come with me then?'

The bitter wind did nothing to cool the heat in Gallius' face as he looked away. His muttered words were rapidly whirled out of earshot.

Smiling, I released him from the examination table of feelings. 'As I was saying, the child that died was indeed poisoned, but don't forget, a poison can also be taken inadvertently.'

The smile dropped from my face as I recalled the details. 'It wasn't murder in that case, but a tragic accident. The girl had been watching her mother prepare an ointment and, when her mother's back was turned, she had tasted it. By the time it was realised what she had done, it was too late. She died the same day.'

The road passed through a stand of trees, bending and tossing under the onslaught of the air, which robbed them of their last remaining leaves, sending chill currents to swirl around us. It had been a cold day in Athens, all those years ago. Despite the thick cloak I was wearing, I shivered at the memory.

'But what was the ointment? That would give us a clue. Could it be the same situation? Corolius could have tasted something by mistake. But if that were so, why did he not say so?' Keen to prevent a return to the previous topic, questions now tumbled out of Gallius.

'If I could remember the substance, it might be possible to prepare an antidote. But even if we can identify the cause, if we fail to find the reason, Corolius may still die.' I looked at Gallius as I continued, 'I cannot believe that he knowingly took a noxious substance, which leads us to assume that he unwittingly swallowed the poison.'

'There have been some strange things happening at the farm recently. I was told that Corolius has been going away for several days at a time, yet tells no one where he has been.'

'Yes, Julia and Germanicus were both very keen to give me that information. They were hinting at something, which, at present, I must admit, I quite fail to see.'

'But what if they are poisoning Corolius?' Gallius threw his arm up and out in the air, 'They may wish him to be out of the way.'

I could not stifle a smile at the image thus presented. 'Gallius, what on earth makes you think that? Why would Julia be trying to murder her husband? Why would Germanicus want to kill his employer? They have no reason.'

I paused as we passed a wagon, the inexpertly loaded casks on the back threatening ruin to the driver. Once out of range of his hearing, I continued, 'I am sure that if they did indeed want to, which I doubt, they would have succeeded. They would have had ample opportunity to contaminate his food with a sufficient quantity to kill. Even if they got the dose wrong the first time, they could have given more.' I shook my head. 'No, I am sure it was not Julia or Germanicus. But what made you consider them?'

There was a sullen undertone in Gallius' answer. 'Everyone in the house knows they spend most nights together, especially when Corolius is away.'

'You should not put so much store by kitchen gossip, even if it was imparted from lips that would later give you so much pleasure.'

A quick glance sideways showed the accuracy of my barb. 'But let us not forget, that interesting as the case might be, Corolius is not the focus of our energies at this time. We are still no further forward in discovering the murderer of Lucius.' I then spent some time relating the events that had occurred whilst I was at Marcus' farm, and the visit I had made to the site where the body was found.

The last few miles seemed endless, and I had already planned and mentally enjoyed the soothing properties of the baths when we rode in the gates.

I headed straight there, leaving Gallius to deal with the horses. The image I had in my mind was of the dying child and the grieving mother I had seen in Athens, and it did not go until I was relaxing in the warm water. There, as I let the aches and pains seep out of my joints, confusion also ebbed away, to be replaced by clarity.

Hemlock. That was the substance in the ointment that the child had tasted. Not enough to kill a man, but plenty to rob a smaller body of life. We doctors truly have a two edged sword. That which we can use for good, can also be used to kill.

Hemlock. Able to reduce swellings as an external application, but with the ability to cause death if ingested. I only kept very small quantities, mainly to ease the passage of a soul, when the fight for it has already been lost.

As I emerged from the water, I felt the benefits in both mind and body. My limbs felt less aged and my mind much sharper and clearer. Rubbing myself dry with a towel that the attendant handed me, I contemplated the evening ahead. While in some ways I was as far from ascertaining the reason for Lucius' death, or indeed identifying the murderers themselves, I made the decision to relax and concentrate on other matters. As I exited the bathhouse in lighter spirits, I met the very person I needed.

'Agricola, dine with me tonight. I wish to avenge myself.'

'Tiberius, what do you mean? I have done nothing that warrants vengeance.'

'Ah, but we both know that to be incorrect, don't we? You are guilty of a most heinous crime.'

Backing away from me, Agricola looked round as if to find an escape.

On finding himself cornered by the buildings, a look of confusion flashed over his face, as I continued speaking, 'Yes, that most awful of crimes. Not allowing me to regain my losses. You beat me soundly last time we played, and I claim the right for revenge.' I lifted my hand in the air, as if lodging my stake with the gods themselves. 'After a good meal, which I believe Gallius is even now preparing, we shall face each other across the board. Is it to be ludus latrunculorum or ludus duodecin scriptorum? You may choose, for I feel alert enough tonight to beat you at either.'

As I spoke, I guided Agricola towards my quarters. He seemed edgy, which I put down to the general low mood in the garrison. Everyone had been affected by the death of a colleague. The doctor in me decided that what Agricola needed was an evening of good food, pleasant wine, and a closely fought game. At the entrance to my rooms, I called out, 'Gallius, Agricola will eat with me tonight.' Without waiting for an answer, we moved into my living space, and reclined on the couches. I now had the opportunity to study my friend's face more closely.

'You've been working too hard.' I held up my hand as Agricola started to voice a denial. 'No, I can see it in your somewhat red and puffy eyes. But no matter. I am the person to cure you and restore your humour.'

I rose from my seat and was heading towards the door, when Agricola stopped me.

'I'm fine. I don't need anything. I got some grit in my eyes earlier, and perhaps they're still sore from that.' A smile began at the corners of his mouth. 'Besides, I need all my faculties if I'm to beat you tonight. Who knows what you might add to a potion to aid your chances.'

'Ahh, that's true. I can't beat you, and then risk you denouncing my victory. But you must see me if your eyes are still sore and swollen tomorrow. Then I can safely treat you.' The aroma of baked pike announced the arrival of our meal. 'Gallius, as usual you've surpassed yourself. I don't think I'm going to let some girl with big hips and bigger breasts lure you away.'

'My cooking could soon deteriorate, master, and you're the one who thinks I like her. I haven't said so.' Gallius rearranged the tables so that we could eat from our reclined position. I took hold of his tunic to prevent an immediate escape.

'So it was the dark-haired one. No, Gallius, she's not a good choice. Her hips are far too narrow.'

'But maybe she is beautiful to look at, lithe and supple to hold.' As he was speaking, Gallius traced the outline of a slender woman in the air, half closing his eyes as he did so.

'Agricola, we need your opinion. Should Gallius have a girl who has child bearing hips and ample breasts, with, admittedly a plain face, or go for attractiveness to look at, which may fade with the passing years?'

'He should go for beauty. Who knows what tomorrow may bring, but the memory of that fairness of face will stay with you forever.' There was a wistful undertone to Agricola's voice. 'Gallius, you should go for the woman that stirs your heart and soul.'

'Thank you, and well spoken. Now, master, I must attend to the rest of your dinner, unless you want it spoilt.'

'No, no, away with you.'

As Gallius left the room, his healthy laugh hung in the air like an invocation to the gods, which was answered by the lightness and gaiety with which we ate. Our talk ranged far from these wet and windswept shores, back to the sun-kissed land of our birth.

Agricola spoke of the tumbled mountains of northern Italy, touched with snow in winter, by bees and butterflies in summer. The smell of thyme crushed underfoot would hang in the air and mingle with the pine when he walked the hills as a boy. Plump and juicy olives bedecked the trees, their smooth, dark skins crying out to be handled.

The pigeon rissoles that Gallius brought in, arranged on a platter, evoked memories for both of us, of hunting deer and ducks, their bodies strangely heavy once dead, the spark in their eyes suddenly extinguished as their lives ebbed away.

I, too, recalled long, summer days that were full of light. Crops in the fields that were always ready for harvest and sweet fruit on the trees, just within reach. The honey from our hives was always fragrant and packed with sunshine. The cakes that we were now eating had a dull taste compared to those of our youth. Or maybe we just felt it so. Age brings many things, not least the responsibilities of a man, and is it any wonder that he looks back with fondness on the carefree days when still a child? It is not surprising that we choose to remember the good, and draw a veil over that which is less pleasant.

We lingered long over our meal, and the light outside had gone by the time we were drinking our wine. Lamps spilled their pools of illumination around us, serving to highlight the darkness, and we seemed cut off from all other influences. Gallius had already brought in the two gaming boards, which were now set out on the table in front of us.

'So, Agricola, which is it to be? I believe I gave you the option.'

'Ludus latrunculorum, I think. Your good food and company have made me too relaxed to bet much on the dice.' Agricola lay back holding his goblet on his chest.

'Then we are both in the same position, for we have eaten and drunk the same. I'll set the board up. The usual one sesterce a game?'

'Yes, I'm happy with that. Although maybe I'll change my mind if you win too much.'

I laughed as I set up the red and white counters. Over the many months that we had been playing regularly, the balance was fairly even, and possibly tipped to his favour. The smile on my face faded, as I remembered another player who used to sit there, someone to whom I owed more than one type of debt. Lucius, too, had been a frequent opponent. Agricola had fallen silent, gazing into his goblet, as if for inspiration.

'Red or white?' I asked.

My companion was truly in another world. 'Red or white what?'

'Soldiers, counters. Would you like to be red or white?'

'White, I'd like to be white.'

We played the first few moves in silence, indicating their completion by leaning back against the couches.

'Has Gallius really found a girl?' It was Agricola who spoke first.

'I'm not sure. He certainly spent the night with someone, other than the patient he was watching.' I moved my counter back, to complete the encirclement of a white piece, and removed it.

'Surely you weren't serious about not giving him his freedom. You've always said that when you retire, he would become a freedman.' Agricola took the opportunity to set up a trap of his own.

'Oh, I guess I'll still free him, but I must admit, I will miss his company.'

'Have you ever thought of re-marrying?'

After careful consideration, I decided to sacrifice one soldier, to enable a counter-attack. 'Who would marry me? No, I can't see that I'll meet anyone now, not at my age.'

'You might. You never know when, or where, you'll meet that special person.' Agricola suddenly seemed in a world of his own, as he moved directly into the snare I had laid. Accordingly, I removed four more of his pieces. By now there were many more red than white left on the board, and he conceded the battle.

'Do I take it you've met someone? You certainly don't seem to have your mind on the game tonight.' I got up to fetch the jug of wine from the table where it had been left and replenished both our goblets. Leaving the board, I shifted my position to face him. 'Who is she? Are we ever going to meet her? Or is she to be your mystery woman? It would be nice to have some good news, after Lucius' death.'

Agricola took a long draft, then reached forward to start setting the board up again. 'Oh, it's no-one. No, I've not really met anyone. I was just curious about Gallius and his woman, that was all.'

I leant over to rest my hand on his arm. 'My friend, I know you too well for these games. There is something that troubles you. Is the girl not returning your favours? Is her father disapproving? Is it that she is promised to another? These things may all be overcome, with the right influence and approach. Let me help ...' My words faltered as he turned his head to face me. Despite the flickering lamplight, distress was plainly written in his eyes. I could not bear to see such pain, and I had to look away.

Agricola lifted his goblet again and drained the remainder, before suddenly standing to walk out of the room, out into the night. Should I have gone after him? I don't know. Would my pursuit have changed things? Who can say? We must each choose our path, and then accept the consequences. It is not for me to decide on the actions of another. I made my choice, as did Agricola. Picking up my goblet, I drank deeply, before refilling it.

Day Eleven

'So, Gallius, what do you think of the boxes? Good quality, aren't they? Nothing but the best for the army, that's what I always say, nothing but the best. Mind you, the supplier did try to give me some that would have just fallen apart, at the first hint of damp, but I wasn't having any of it. They may have been all right for where it's sunny and dry, but not here. No, here you need stuff that's going to last.'

I heard Victor well before he bounded into the infirmary office, closely followed by a tall, well built man carrying several packages.

'Tiberius, you're looking well. Just put those down over there, on the table, will you Lachlan?' As he turned back to me, he continued speaking, 'One pestle and mortar, just as you ordered. And one beautiful blue bowl. I'm sure you'll appreciate the fine workmanship. It's well wrapped up, don't worry.'

He turned back to Lachlan, 'Well don't just stand there, open the package. Let the customer see the merchandise, which he can't do if it's all wrapped up.'

Lachlan silently did as he was ordered. His large hands struggled to undo the knots in the fine string that secured the parcel. In the five years that I had known Victor, I had never heard Lachlan speak. But then Victor did enough talking for the both of them. I remembered the day that they had first come to the garrison, with their ramshackle cart, pulled by a tired and stubborn mule. Since then, Victor had done his best to make himself indispensable, and it must be admitted that he had succeeded. Whatever goods or services you wanted, Victor could obtain, given enough notice and the right money. Everybody knew that his prices were higher, and that Victor took his cut, enough to replace the original cart, with a version that was much improved. His new, covered wagon was pulled by two horses, and it was rumoured that he also maintained a farm, complete with several young, female, and male, slaves - a rumour he never denied or confirmed. But buying through Victor was easy, often quicker, very reliable and, to tell the truth, I, in common with so many others, liked the man.

'So, what do you think? I said it was good quality, and you can't say I'm mistaken now, can you?'

As Lachlan removed the straw that had been protecting the bowl and held it up to the light, I could see that it was indeed well made. There was an intensity to the glass that made it almost glow in the midday sun.

'Umm, not bad,' I said, trying to sound non-committal.

'Not bad, not bad. That's the finest workmanship in the whole of the Empire that is, and he says it's not bad.' Victor put the back of one hand to his forehead, and gave an exaggerated sigh, before staging a collapse into a chair. 'I do my best, I get quality goods, even offer special prices for my favoured customers, and what thanks do I get in return? No appreciation of the effort I put in, no appreciation at all. I'll be destitute before long, if this continues, destitute. Ahh, Lachlan, what shall we do?'

I found that I could not prevent a smile coming to my face, as I watched the antics of the two men. Lachlan had replaced the bowl carefully on the table, and was now stood behind Victor, patting him on the shoulders. Victor still had one hand pressed to his temple, and his eyes closed, which he opened as Gallius entered the room, carrying a tray.

'Gallius, your master is ruining me, ruining me, I say. I offer him the finest bowl in Britannicus, no, the finest bowl in the Empire, and he says it is not good enough for him. How can I possible please him? What must I do to gain his approval? Tell me, that I might succeed before I am ruined,' Victor cried out, as he spread his arms wide, allowing the many gems in his rings to sparkle in the light.

'Maybe some refreshments will restore you,' said Gallius as he poured some wine into a cup, and handed it to Victor.

'Thank you, kind sir, it will enable me to survive another day.' Victor drank from his cup, and reached out for some of the olives and bread that Gallius had also brought.

'I really have no need for the bowl, despite its quality.' I picked up my cup, savouring the contents. Replacing it on the table, I slowly shook my head, 'I'd like to, but, no. I can't justify it.'

'Ahh, Lachlan, what a world we live in, that men must justify buying things of beauty. Why not have it just because it is beautiful? Does it have to be useful as well? Think how it would look on your table, greeting you when you returned to your room, with its elegance and grace and colour.' By now, the smile that was Victor's usual expression had fully returned to his face.

'Enough,' I cried, lifting my hands in mock surrender. 'I've made my decision.'

'Put it away again, but be careful. Maybe soon we can find someone who will appreciate the quality, and will want it for the pure pleasure of ownership.' Victor took a handful of dried figs, slipping them into his mouth, with barely a pause in his speech. 'I take it you found the pestle and mortar to your liking, or do I need to take them away with me?'

I shook my head, as he continued, 'Now, what are you going to need for the coming winter? New cloaks, perhaps? I can get some from Gaul, very good at keeping out this wind and rain. A set of scales, to measure out your potions and draughts? I'm sure you need a few more cupping vessels. Can't have too many, I'm sure. What about some new cooking pots and pans?'

'Victor, I think we're fine at the moment.'

'You have a think on it, and if you do remember anything, then let me know. Mind you, I'm not likely to be back here for a couple of months, so if there is anything you might need, you'd better tell me now.'

'I think the only thing I need right now ...' I paused, and Victor leaned forward in anticipation, '... is to have a look at that boil on your back, if it's still a problem, that is?'

He laughed, and slapped the table with his hand. 'You nearly had me then, you really did. Would you mind having a look? It doesn't seem to be getting any better.'

I sucked my breath in through my partially closed lips. 'Sounds as if it's going to need operating on. Could be nasty.'

Victor's laugh was a little more nervous this time. 'What do you mean, nasty? Not painful I hope.' He looked to Gallius, who was standing with Lachlan, sorting out the goods to be bought, and those that Victor would keep. 'Gallius, it isn't going to hurt, is it? I'm not very good with things that hurt.'

Gallius repeated my actions, with a sharp intake of breath. 'Could be, could be. Difficult to say.' He paused and slowly shook his head, before continuing. 'Depends on what price you give him, I'd say.'

This time, Victor's laugh rang out clearly, as he got to his feet. 'Let's get this over with, then we can decide on how much discount I should give.'

I stood up, and indicated the door, before rubbing my hands together and smiling at him. We both went into the operating room, where I selected the instruments I was most likely to need. Victor shrugged his way out of his tunic, remarking as he did so, 'I don't know what the laundry girls do, but they always seem to shrink my clothes.'

119

'I'm not so sure it's the tunic shrinking. Maybe it's you growing.' I said.

He put both hands on his tummy, and wobbled the excess flesh, 'Well, maybe you're right. But then, the more the merrier.'

I grinned, and pointed to the operating table, 'Have a lie down, on your front.' I came and stood looking down at his back, around his right shoulder blade. There was a large red area, not just around the swelling.

I looked up as Gallius came in, the bowl of water he was carrying sending faint, short-lived trails of steam up into the air. He put it down, glanced over at Victor, and selected three or four instruments, placing them in the water. Lifting them out, Gallius dried them on a cloth, and brought them over to me. I took the scalpel in my right hand, and a cloth in the other, as I considered where to cut. Having chosen the spot, I placed the cloth on the skin, and incised the boil with my scalpel.

Victor flinched, as the knife cut in, and I could hear him mutter, 'I thought you were joking when you said it would hurt.'

'Nearly done,' I said, as I made a small slit, through which I could squeeze the collection of pus.

Wiping the creamy-yellow liquid away with the cloth, I continued until red became the dominant colour. Picking up a second cloth, I applied pressure over the site, until a clot had formed.

'There. All finished. Wasn't so bad, was it?' I handed the scalpel back to Gallius who started to clean it, before packing all the instruments back into the case.

Victor climbed off the table, before answering, 'Not too bad, I suppose, not too bad. Any special instructions?' he asked, as he carefully pulled on his tunic, wincing as the material slid over the operated area.

'Not really. Try to keep it clean, and come back if it causes any more problems, sooner rather than later.' I paused, before adding, 'Be careful. There's some dangerous people about at the moment. I wouldn't want to see you hurt.'

The almost inevitable laugh issued from Victor's body. 'Don't you worry. Not only do I have Lachlan, and no-one is going to argue with him, now, are they, but I also have more spiritual protection.' He pulled out the leather thong I had earlier seen round his neck, to show a small, bronze amulet, in the shape of a phallus. 'I was promised total assurance of safety against all robbers, thieves and pirates.' He fingered the pendant, continuing, 'He didn't say anything about doctors inflicting pain though.'

'So, how much discount do I get?' I asked.

He paused, his head on one side, as he rubbed his chin. 'How about ten?'

'I was thinking more like twenty,' I countered.

His laugh rang out again, 'Fifteen, and it's a deal.'

I nodded and we shook hands to seal the bargain. 'You heard that, Gallius, fifteen percent discount. Remember that when you're settling up with him.'

Victor put his arm round Gallius' shoulders. As they left the room I could hear Victor saying, 'Any chance of another cup of wine, to enable me to recover after my painful ordeal, while we settle the accounts?'

That evening, I was sat in my room, reading one of the medical books, on loan from the hospital library at Alexandria, when Memno walked in.

'Tiberius, may I talk with you?'

I looked up from the document I had in front of me. I seemed destined never to get to complete it, but at least I would have the copies, when the originals were returned. 'Of course,' I said. 'How can I help?'

Memno sat down heavily. For some moments he was silent, his breath rasping slightly through parted lips.

'What's the problem?' As I spoke, Memno's respiration rate gradually slowed, but as it did so, small beads of sweat appeared on his brow. The colour drained from his face, leaving blue tinged lips standing out. I was already on my feet and moving towards Memno when he clutched at his chest and keeled over to lie prostrate on the floor.

'Gallius, come quick.' My shout rang out into the corridor, as I also dropped to the ground to support my friend's head in my arms. Gallius ran into the room, almost stumbling over the chair that had fallen back into the doorway. On seeing the situation, he spun round and left as quickly as he had arrived. I stayed kneeling on the cold floor holding Memno as he slowly opened his eyes. The sound of his laboured breathing filled the room, and my inspirations matched his, as if I was trying to do the work for him.

'Master, what would you have me do first?' The incisive tone cut into the air. 'If you hold his arm, I could bleed him.'

Taking my prompts from Gallius, I merely nodded and shifted my position to grip Memno's arm just below the elbow. Gallius expertly opened a small vein and the dark red fluid flowed into the collecting vessel.

'I brought some wine as well.'

'That's good. Mix it with a little water.' I felt helpless as I watched my slave encourage my friend to first take a little to drink and then to swallow it. Memno revived somewhat, as our ministrations took effect, and the blood flow faltered and ceased. His sudden efforts to speak were unexpected.

'Tiberius … I must … speak … must say.'

'Hush, there's no need to say anything now. Rest, and we can talk later.'

'I … must … confess … now, please.' His eyes locked with mine, and I was stunned by the clarity and pleading evident there. I looked away to break the emotional bond, filled with a sense of foreboding.

'Of course we must talk, but not yet. We must get you to a bed, so you can rest properly, and recover your strength.' Turning to Gallius, I bade him get some help to carry Memno. As his footsteps faded, so did Memno's efforts to talk. He lapsed into a quiet sleep, his breathing becoming deeper and softer. Wiping a strand of hair from his forehead, I could feel his skin had lost the clamminess that had been present.

'Master, where shall we put him?'

'What's that? Oh, my bedchamber, I think. The infirmary is too far. Yes, carry him into my room.'

As Gallius and three other slaves lifted Memno and bore him out of the room, I stayed on the floor. The position I had been in had caused a cramp and numbness in my legs, and I was totally unable to stand. A pretty sight I must have made, dragging myself along to lean back against the wall. I could not bear that someone see me in this disabled position, and I made efforts to reach the chair quickly. Soon the numbness was replaced with stabs of pain and the return of feeling, and I could start to pull myself up on my chair. I expected my legs to give way with every movement, but I reached the safety of the seat with no further insult to my dignity. By the time Gallius returned, I felt a reasonable degree of certainty in being able to walk.

Entering my bedchamber, I saw Memno lying, propped up by several pillows. His complexion was returning to normal, although he was still pale. Perching on the bedside, I checked his pulse, which appeared satisfactory. The small wound where Gallius had bled him had a good clot, which had not been displaced with the move.

'My friend, how are you now? No, stay there. Don't try to get up.' I gently placed one hand on Memno's chest to restrain him from sitting up.

'But I … must speak … with you.'

'Later. We will talk later. You must rest now. You are in no state to speak at the moment. When you have recovered some of your strength and had a good night's sleep, we can talk in the morning.'

'The morning may be too late. I … I must tell you. Please don't let me die without confessing.'

I was torn. Should I let my friend speak now, when he so obviously needed rest? Or should I deny him that rest, in order to gain further insights into the mystery that my thoughts had been focussed on? Doctor and investigator strove to gain the upper hand. That which had been instilled in me so many years ago, won the battle, and I pulled the covers up around his torso.

'You must rest now, or you may not see the night out. Sleep now and I promise we shall speak in the morning.' Rising, I turned my back on him to leave the room. At the curtain, one of the slaves was waiting. 'Stay with him overnight and mind you stay awake,' I ordered. 'If his condition changes, you must summon me immediately. Do you understand?'

'Yes, Master,' came the dutiful reply, and with that assurance I returned to my study.

Here there was much activity, which Gallius was directing. The chaos of the furniture that I had just left, was being replaced with ordered disarray.

'Gallius, what …?'

'Master, I have arranged for a bed to be made up in here for you tonight. Memno is not the only one who needs some rest.'

I smiled at Gallius' concern. My own sleeping arrangements had totally escaped me. Of course, if Memno were in my bed, I would have to go elsewhere.

'Thank you.' As we were speaking, the movements in the room resolved into order as the other slaves left. 'No, don't go yet Gallius.' I thought hard about the words to use. 'You did well this evening. Memno might not be as well as he is, if it were not for your quick thinking.'

'I merely did as you have taught me,' he replied.

'I know, but not everyone would have been as calm and organised as you. I … thank you.'

With a nod of acknowledgement, Gallius also left the room, leaving me standing alone. In truth, the thoughts running through my head were painful to admit.

Gallius had acted with a detached professionalism that I had lacked. I, Tiberius, was the trained and experienced surgeon. Yet I was the one who had been unable to think logically and quickly. I had felt flustered and confused. Maybe the time had come for the apprentice to oust the master? Was this not the natural order of things? The old wither and fade as the new shoots take their place. With these thoughts as my bed companions, I lay down for sleep to take me.

Day Twelve

I was still racked with doubt after my night's sleep. Which ranked higher – my promise to the dead, or my responsibilities for the living? Was it right that finding the truth about one, should endanger the other? And to add to my confusion, was I correct in my prescription of rest for Memno?

Would allowing him to talk, and unburden himself, have eased his suffering, or would it have increased it to the point where his weakened spirit could take no more? In the many years since Paul pronounced that I had passed beyond the role of apprentice, I have generally been confident and secure in my knowledge and skills, but now I was unsure, as if I were fumbling in the dark, searching for something which was always half sensed.

As I tried to sit up, I found my limbs entangled in the bedclothes, pinning my legs to the bed, as if I were wrapped for the funeral pyre. Extracting myself, I reached for the bread to break my fast of the night, just as Gallius entered the room.

In his hands he carried one of the boxes from the dispensary, which contained the drugs and potions used in the fight against disease.

'Good morning, Master. Did you not sleep well?'

'Morning. Am I to assume that I look that old and haggard?'

He laughed. 'You are lacking a little of your usual brightness. Also, if you say you slept well, then I would wonder how that happened.' His look was directed at the covers on the bed, now knotted and heaped, like a failed sculpture. 'But I digress. Master, I have been in to see Memno this morning, and he, too, had a somewhat restless night. I thought to give him a sleeping draught.'

'What would you suggest?' My head was in too much turmoil to create things from new. How much easier it would be to agree, or not, with a presented suggestion.

'Balm, coltsfoot, prickly lettuce, thyme and feverfew, mixed with a little wine.' Gallius held the box in his left hand, and counted the ingredients off on his right fingers. 'His breathing is still not easy, which the balm and coltsfoot will help. He needs to sleep, and ensure that his dreams are not too violent, hence the prickly lettuce and thyme. And of course, feverfew, to lift his melancholy.'

I struggled to think coherently. That which Gallius had proposed was almost exactly what I would have given, but I felt the need to change the formula. After all, I was in charge. 'Why not some root of peony? That would act on his melancholy and induce sleep? Or poppy?'

'I felt they were both too vigorous in his present weakened state. We do not want to drive the life out of him along with the melancholy.'

'Maybe you're right, but I would like you to use flax dodder rather than feverfew. Yes, I think that would probably be best. Make it up, but don't give it to him yet. I would like to see him first and maybe talk to him. I can't do that if he's too soporific.'

Gallius carefully placed the box he had been carrying on a table, before coming to stand in front of me. His eyes were fixed on the wall over my left shoulder.

'But Master, I thought I said. I have already given him the draught. I know that is what you have done in previous cases. Memno displayed the same symptoms as Antonus did last month, and Calpernia some weeks before that. Was there something different this time that I missed?'

'No, I believe they were the same, although I cannot at the moment recall the precise details of Calpurnia's ailment. But you should have asked me first.'

Gallius' gaze shifted from the wall to the floor, which he appeared to be studying in minute detail. 'Master, I was under the impression that you instructed me … after Calpernia … that you instructed me to make up the potion for Antonus, by myself. I have only done as I thought you wanted me to. I am sorry if I did not understand you correctly.'

I stood up and dressed, giving myself time to formulate my reply. All that Gallius had said was true, but in my present frame of mind, I couldn't accept that I had been proved wrong yet again. I made a conscious effort to avoid looking at Gallius, if only so that I wouldn't see the pain that part of me knew would be plainly displayed in his eyes.

Striding to the door, I paused before leaving the room, 'I'm going to see the rest of the patients in the infirmary, if that's all right with you.' I did not care how harsh the words sounded. 'Unless you want to take over their care as well.'

'Yes, Master. I mean, no, Master.'

'And get this room cleared up.'

'Yes, Master.'

As I left the room, I heard Gallius breathe out heavily. I could almost hear his shoulders sag as he released the tension. Later, I would apologise, but not now. It would have to be later.

The walk to the infirmary started to reduce my frustrations, but it was too short a distance to fully restore my equanimity. For a few wild moments, I considered continuing to put one foot in front of the other. To go out past the buildings, out of the garrison, onto the road that led through the huddle of shops and dwellings, and into the belt of trees that circumscribed my horizon.

There the ground would be soft underfoot, with a deceptive layer of wet leaves overlying the muddy tracks. Stately trunks would open up the way before me, closing behind, as if to entice me further in.

The air would be full of the chirrup of squirrels, collecting the last few nuts for their winter stores, their movements disturbing the surface covering, releasing the aroma of decaying matter into the atmosphere. The trees would be sending their branches up, holding each other, high above my head. A flash of red might indicate a squirrel or fox; soft brown may mean the rapid exit of hares; grey shapes would hint at the presence of deer.

But duty called. Those pleasures would have to wait for another day. I pulled my gaze away from the dream and back to reality. I went into the infirmary.

The few patients that were currently in residence were not demanding, and even with my present lack of confidence, I could manage them adequately. I paused at the doorway of the occupied room, composing myself and ensuring my countenance was appropriately masked. Lifting up the curtain, I entered the four-bedded area.

'How are we all today?' I endeavoured to give my voice the correct amount of assurance and knowledge, in order to reveal nothing of my inward turmoil.

The soldiers assumed varying degrees of attention, depending on their injuries and ability to move. I moved into the room, turning to my left.

'Now, Justinius, how's the arm feeling?' I sat down on the edge of the bed and looked at the occupant, who had his left arm heavily swathed in bandages.

'Feels much better now, sir. When can I return to duty, sir?'

'Don't be too keen.' The reply came from Carinius, in the next bed, before I could answer. 'Don't want to get back until you're ready. Army'll manage fine without us. Ain't that right, Vetus?'

'Yep.' Vetus, in the far corner, shook his head and grinned, revealing two rows of yellow stained teeth. 'They won't lose much sleep over us, not while we've got the doctor to look after us. You bide your time, young Justinius.'

'They're right.' I smiled down at the young soldier. From his age, this must be his first posting and naturally he would be missing his family. I wondered what part of the Empire this blond haired lad, with his fair skin, came from. It would be a few more weeks before he was back to enjoy the more local camaraderie of his contuburnium. 'That arm needs a little more time to heal, otherwise it'll be no use for fighting.' As his face dropped, and tears threatened to appear at the corner of his green eyes, I hastily continued, 'However, if we give it another two or three weeks, it'll be as good as new. You won't even notice it.'

'Until there's a duty you don't like,' Carinius, chipped in, raising a half-smile on Justinius' face, as he continued, 'Could come in very handy then, for you to say how much your arm hurts like. Get you out of heavy work, that could.'

I smiled as I bent over the bed. The banter within the room was as good a medicine for the raw recruit as anything I could offer. 'Can you move your fingers for me like this?' I held Justinius' well-padded arm as I demonstrated the actions, which he repeated. 'Good, and your thumb? That's great. The fracture is healing well. Don't forget to take regular poppy and the comfrey poultices should continue.'

'Yes sir. Thank you sir.'

Moving on, I came to the next bed, that of the veteran Carinius, now nearly at the end of his twenty-five years of service. I knew that he had plans to settle in the local area, on his retirement. Lifting his leg, I examined the sole of his foot, where he had sustained a deep cut, requiring stitches. However, the wound had virtually healed now, leaving just a thick, red line to indicate its presence.

'And how are you this morning, Carinius?' I asked.

'Not so bad, sir, you know how it is.' He raised himself up on one elbow. 'But my foot's awful painful. I don't think I could walk on it yet, not properly like.'

'I think we'd better see you try then, don't you?'

Carinius groaned a little as he swung his legs out of bed, giving a theatrical wince as his feet touched the floor. He stood up, clutching at the window frame to give himself some support.

'I'm really not sure I should be walking on this foot yet, sir.'

'Get on with it,' was my unsympathetic response.

He launched himself out into the middle of the room, raising chuckles from the rest of the quartet. Carinius' exaggerated and abnormal gait had such a pronounced limp that it threatened to bring a smile even to my lips, but I controlled my mirth.

'I think I've seen enough,' I announced as he reached the doorway.

'You can see I'm not walking well, am I?' he said, as he made a great show of holding onto the doorframe.

'Definitely not.' I answered. Just as he was starting to hobble back, I continued, 'However, the best treatment is to get out marching on it. That'll soon get it back to normal. A few extra long marches, that's what it needs.'

Carinius shrugged his shoulders, and walked back with an even step length, raising his hands and eyebrows at the other three soldiers as he did so.

The chorus of laughs almost drowned out my words as I declared, 'Back to normal training this afternoon.'

As he reached the bed, he looked at me thoughtfully, asking in a more serious manner than I was used to from him, 'Sir, what happened with the surveyor, Lucius? Was he really found with his head chopped off?'

I nodded, not really trusting my voice to work. Luckily Vetus took up the conversation.

'I reckon it was some jealous husband. I certainly felt like punching him one, when he took my girl away from me.'

'I heard she was so glad to be away from you,' came the dry and wheezy voice of the occupant of the fourth bed, 'that anyone would have done. At least that's what she said last night, just after, you know.'

Again there were laughs, this time at Vetus' discomfort, before Justinius spoke.

'Could it be to do with that Boudicca, over in the east? I hear her druids sacrifice prisoners.' The others and I looked at him in amazement, and he faltered a little under our combined gaze. 'My cousin, he's over at Durobrivae. He said, in a letter, about it, about how they sacrifice people, but they do it in secret, like.'

'Well, it's just as well she's over there and we're over here, then, ain't it.' The ever-optimistic voice of Carinius cut in.

'Mind you, I can't see why we're still here, and not over there, helping to show her who's the boss around here. What do you think, sir?' Vetus asked, as I sat down on the edge of his bed to examine his knee.

'I'm not sure. I do know there are a lot of rumours around.' I carefully palpated his kneecap, which had been dislocated. 'Does that hurt much?' as I bent the joint.

He didn't answer, merely balling his hands into fists, and pushing them into the bed as he threw his head back, closing his eyes tightly. As I straightened his leg again, he bent over, rubbing it vigorously.

'What rumours?' he muttered, through clenched teeth, more I suspect to divert my attention from his knee, than any desire to hear second hand gossip.

I thought back to the time I had spent sitting in a tavern in Durnovaria, waiting to see Aurelius. 'Ohh, about druids, lots of local unrest and unease. You need to keep trying to bend this knee, Vetus. It might stiffen up otherwise.'

'Of course, sir. You were saying about druids. Didn't think there were any of them left.'

I moved on to the last bed, saying as I went, 'No, I didn't think so either. It's probably just rumour. But I think you'll find that's why you're all still here. No point in having all the army in one place, if there's a risk of revolt elsewhere.'

'It could be those Christians,' Justinius proclaimed. 'I've heard they chop people up and eat them, as part of their rituals, and then they won't ever die.'

'Got another cousin, have you then?' asked Vetus. 'Where's this one based?'

'Judea, he was in Judea,' came the response.

'Well, young Justinius,' said Carinius, 'you won't need to worry about them. Judea's a long way away. There definitely aren't any Christians around here. I'd soon give them what for, if there were.'

'And how are you today, Suetonius? No, don't sit up.' I placed a gentle restraining hand on the chest of the occupant of the final bed. 'I've told you, your collar bone and ribs will heal better if you lie down.'

He sank gratefully back into the pillows, whispering, 'It still hurts when I cough, or take a deep breath, sir.'

'So don't cough then,' was the almost inevitable repost from Carinius.

'It'll get better,' I said, in what I hoped was a reassuring manner, 'but in the meantime, make sure you take some poppy, for the pain, and the poultices need to continue for you as well.'

As I left the room, letting the curtain fall back behind me, I heard Vetus ribbing Carinius about his return to duty, and I am sure there was at least one pillow thrown, maybe more.

I was later than was usual in returning to my room after the morning's work. The sun was well past its zenith as I sat down to eat from the tray that had been left. The orderliness of my quarters had been restored, and despite my critical eye, I could find no fault. I shifted my attention to the food and started to partake of the nourishment. Biting into the apple created a trail of juice down my chin, but the flesh turned woody in my mouth. The bread was dry, but then tasted heavy and cloying when dipped in wine. Mechanically I moved hand to tray then up to mouth, until the absence of noise inserted itself into my consciousness.

There should have been others about, not least to look after Memno, or was there no further need for observation?

I stood and walked towards my bedroom, my footsteps falling into the silence. Pausing at the door, I surveyed the scene. Gallius stood in the centre of the room, with another slave, who scuttled past me with an armful of covers.

'Master, the rooms are tidied, as you requested.' He stretched over to smooth an unseen crease on the bedclothes.

The lump in my throat prevented me from speaking, and I held onto the smooth wood of the doorframe.

'Master, I arranged for Memno to be moved to ...' His voice faltered as he re-arranged a small dish on a table, setting it down again with a barely perceptible difference in position. The aroma of rose petals and lavender drifted through the still air. My need to know my friend's fate was greater than my fear of the truth.

'Where?' The sound was cracked, and I almost did not recognise the voice as mine. I forced myself to swallow and tried again. 'Where is he? Where did you put Memno?'

'We ... that is I ... he is in his room. Did Belbo not tell you?'

I found that I was sitting on the bed. 'I must go to him. I have my duty to do, as his friend. Why didn't you call me when it happened?'

'I sent Belbo to tell you. Did he not find you? He should be punished for not delivering the message.'

'I should go and see him now.' Somehow my body did not seem to accept the instructions of my brain. My limbs stayed where they were. 'What did you say about Belbo? No, I didn't see him today.'

'Master, you should have him flogged for not doing as he was told.' Indignation was evident in every syllable that Gallius spoke.

'He's just a boy.' Despite my worries and concerns, I smiled. Belbo was about the same age as Gallius had been when I bought him, and in just the same way, Gallius had sometimes failed to fully complete errands. 'No, I won't have him beaten, but I shall speak to him.'

I lifted my head to make eye contact. 'But Gallius, why did you send a boy, when the news related to such a man as Memno? Do you intentionally seek to discredit him or reduce his status?'

'But it was only a simple message. There was almost no need to interrupt you, but ...'

'Gallius. How could you say that this news of Memno is simple? I will not have you insult his memory in this way. If anyone should be flogged, maybe it is you.' As I paused for breath, Gallius' words penetrated my hearing.

'Master, the message was that Memno had woken up after a long rest, felt better and asked that he be moved back to his room, so that you would not be further inconvenienced. That was the message.'

'He is feeling better?'

'Yes, Master.'

'He has just moved to his own room?'

'Yes, Master.'

'He is not … dead?'

'No, Master.'

'I should go and see him.'

'No, Master. You should stay here and rest. You're tired. You slept badly last night, and you need to rest now.' As he spoke, Gallius bent down to remove my sandals, and swung my legs up onto the bed. 'Memno is almost certainly sleeping again now, and you should do likewise.' Almost without my knowledge I was lying down. 'Why don't I get you a sleeping draught to help you into the arms of Morpheus?' he continued.

'No.' My rebuttal came out stronger than I had intended. For some reason I was very loathe to take any medication. Was it that I would not be able to think with a befuddled brain?

In any case, I was tired enough to sleep without any aid. Or was I so muddled already, I did not trust anyone?

The sky had darkened when I woke, and my eyes took some moments to adjust to the reduced light. I could distinguish a figure in the doorway, and I wondered why Gallius was just sitting there.

'Gallius, bring some light, and come over here.'

The figure slowly turned his gaze from the reddened sky.

'I've already sent for a lamp, so I can obey half of your request. But I'm afraid that I can't pretend to be the right person, so maybe I'd better go.'

The voice was familiar yet I could not place it. The identity of the speaker eluded me. 'No, don't go.' I pulled myself upright, to sit on the edge of the bed as I stalled for time to think. Belbo came in, carefully carrying a lamp, which he placed on the table, before running out again, eager to be elsewhere. The darkness moved away and so did my uncertainty.

'Valerian. When did you get back?' I cried. 'It's good to see you again. I'm sorry, but I was still half asleep.'

My nephew's laugh scattered the rest of the shadows, and his embrace grounded me back into reality.

'This afternoon. I would say it's good to see you as well, but, in truth, Tiberius, you look dreadful. I wouldn't want to see my doctor looking like you.'

The presence of my nephew lightened the gloom, which had threatened to settle round me. 'Do I look that bad?'

'Most of your patients look more alive and healthy than you do. I prescribe a shave, a meal and a session in the baths. Which order would you like?'

I gave a few moments thought to the suggestion, before declaring, 'The shave and baths first. Then there will be time for a meal to be prepared.'

'Ah, now you see how fortuitous my arrival was. You requested light, and I supplied it almost immediately. You ask for food after a massage and it will be done.' Valerian adopted an exaggerated pose before producing an elaborate bow. 'I anticipated your every need, oh great and noble master. Now come, your bath awaits you. The water is hot, the oils are sweet, and the masseur has strong, firm hands.'

I smiled at his antics. Valerian had always had a gift with words, and could have made as successful a career in oratory as he had as a centurion in the army.

'I'm coming, but don't forget my old bones won't be able to cope with hands that are too hard.' I stood up, half-pretending to find it difficult to straighten fully. With one hand on my back, I used a chair to support my mock stagger to the door. 'You youngsters, you don't know what it's like to grow old and infirm. I hope your young masseur with the firm hands is also able to be gentle.'

'But master, did I not say? Whatever you wish for, I can provide. Now come, your temple of relaxation awaits you.'

With this, we both moved across the courtyard, to where light spilled out of the bathhouse door, illuminating the occasional gusts of steam that escaped.

An attendant hurried to our side as we entered, and for several long, unwinding moments, we both gave ourselves up into the skilled hands of the barber, masseur and oilers. It was not until we emerged from the final cold plunge that our talk turned from the inconsequential to the present and specific.

'So, tell me, Valerian, if you only came back today, how did you manage to arrange all this?

'The bathhouse, you mean. I do believe it's been here for a while.'

I threw my wet towel at him. 'No, I mean this.' My extended arm swept round the room to include the clean clothes that a slave was holding, ready for when I had dried my body.

Valerian laughed as he extricated himself from the damp material.

'That was easy. I met Gallius just outside your quarters this afternoon. He said you were sleeping, as your night had been very disturbed. Don't forget I know what you're like when you don't get enough sleep. Grouchy, unkempt, like a bear with a sore head.' He ducked to avoid a flying sandal. 'So the obvious thing to do was provide the essentials to get you fit to face the world again.' Reaching down to retrieve the shoe, he seemed to study it intently for a few moments, before asking, 'Was there a reason why you slept badly? Gallius seemed very concerned about you.'

I sat down heavily on the bench, and watched the rivulets of water soak away between the tiles of the floor. 'Memno had some sort of attack last night.' Glancing out of the window, I realised that just one day and one night had passed. 'He nearly died,' I continued, my words coming from a throat as dry as a funeral pyre.

'Oh no. Is he all right now? You must have been worried.' Valerian sat down next to me.

'I have been told he's recovering well.' I braced my arms on my knees, and swallowed a few times. 'I … I found that I could not … when he needed my help, I …'

'I don't understand. You said he is recovering well. You must have been able to assist him.'

'I wasn't the one to aid him.' A laugh totally devoid of mirth escaped my lips. 'No, Gallius was the one who was able to think and act clearly. I just sat there like the muddled old fool I am.'

'You certainly are.' Valerian's peal of laughter was genuine. 'A very muddled and decrepit fool, I would say. I'm not at all surprised that you found it difficult to think quickly.' He reached for his tunic, pulling it over his head, temporarily muffling his voice, as he continued, 'Number one, Memno is your friend. Number two, you weren't expecting anything so severe to happen to him. Number three, you've been trying to do far too many things at one time.' He paused, straightening his tunic before standing and facing me, his gaze making contact with my eyes. 'This news of Lucius' death. Is it true, that he had no head when he was found?'

I nodded in confirmation, not trusting my voice, and Valerian continued, 'And I take it there is still no real clue as to who the barbarians are that did this to him.'

My answer was merely a shake of my head, as I looked down at my sandal, lying on the floor, the laces tangled and knotted.

'With all that lot going on, I'm not surprised that you found it difficult to think straight.' I was about to interrupt when my nephew continued, 'But what you have done is train a good assistant in Gallius, so you could say it was still your skill that saved Memno.' I must have looked puzzled, as Valerian sat down to expand his point. 'You said Gallius acted quickly and efficiently when Memno was ill. He would only have been able to do that if he'd been trained well, and the person who trained him was you.' He finished by pointing the end of his belt at me, before buckling it round his waist.

'But that's just it.' I shrugged my shoulders, and lifted my hands in despair. 'How can I hope to avenge Lucius' death, if I can't even think straight when my skills as a doctor are needed? I can't do everything.'

'I quite agree.'

I looked at my nephew. Did he also doubt my ability to heal the sick? Did he feel that I would never find the murderer of Lucius? Was this indicative of how others felt?

Valerian continued, 'You can't do everything. So don't.' He bent down to lace and tie his sandals, saying, as he straightened up again,

'You have more than half your mind on Lucius, so why not concentrate just on that? Then you are more likely to uncover the mystery surrounding his death. At the moment you'll be far more use doing that, than moping about here.'

'But I can't leave the infirmary.' I picked up my own garments, dropping my tunic into place. 'Who will care for the sick and injured? I cannot abandon my duty there.'

'From what you've said so far, you won't be much good to them in this state. Leave Gallius in charge. He can …'

'No.' My interruption came almost unnoticed by myself. I stalled for time, as I leant down to don my footwear. 'Um, no. I don't think that would be a good idea.'

'Rubbish. It's a great idea, and you know it. You've always said that he would take over your practice when you felt too old to continue. He knows what he's doing. When you are thinking more rationally, you'll realise I'm right.'

'I'm thinking rationally now,' I protested.

'No, you're not.' He shook his head. 'Let Gallius look after the infirmary for a few days. You devote all your time to finding those who killed Lucius. And then maybe you could spend a few days with Anthonius. I know he'd love to see you.'

'You've seen him? How is he?' My younger son had only recently moved to Britannicus, and lived some distance to the north. His letter writing skills were not as good or as regular as I would have liked.

Valerian nodded, saying, 'He's fine. Very busy, setting up the jewellery workshop, but there were lots of customers so I didn't spend much time there. It was only a quick visit, as I happened to be in the vicinity.'

I finished tying my sandals as I contemplated when I would be able to fit in a visit to Glevum, to see Anthonius.

When I stood up, Valerian continued, 'Things here will be fine, with Gallius in charge. Now that that's settled, let's eat. You may have been asleep all day, but some of us have been travelling.'

He got up and moved towards the door. As I followed him outside, a few large drops of water splashed down into the courtyard, causing us to quicken our steps.

We were soon back in my quarters, where a meal was ready waiting for us, and as we seated ourselves, the occasional tap of raindrops became a steady drumming, forming the backdrop to our repast.

Day Thirteen

Despite my unusual sleeping pattern of the previous hours, I had a restful night. The rain continued its melodic sound, lulling me into a slumber. Even the violent cracks of thunder did nothing more than wake me briefly, before I drifted off again. When I did open my eyes and keep them open, it was to a morning just after dawn. Outside, the heavy rain continued, joined now by a fitful wind that intermittently rattled the wooden window shutters. There was barely enough light to make out the familiar shapes of the furniture, although I could distinguish the curtain flapping in the doorway. Could it be the spirit of Lucius, come to spur me into action on his behalf?

I smiled to myself as I lay, luxuriating in the comfort of decisions made and objectives set. Ghostly interventions were not needed, now that Valerian had pointed out what I knew to be the right path. How much better it would be to do one thing well, rather than several tasks badly.

As the light strengthened, so did my resolve. I would concentrate on unravelling a mystery, while Gallius managed the infirmary. After all, the day when I would fully relinquish the practice was drawing closer, to be measured in months or years, rather than decades. When Gallius brought my breakfast, I would tell him.

As if on cue, the curtain flapped wildly before being tamed and pinned to one side. A figure silently moved about the room, placing a tray on the table by my bed and laying out clothes for the coming day.

'Good morning, Gallius.' My simple words caused him to start and drop the tunic he was holding. 'I'm glad that wasn't my breakfast.'

'Good morning, Master. Your breakfast is on the table, as usual. I was sorting your clothes.' He paused, and carefully positioned the garment on a chair. 'I trust you slept well last night, and that the storm didn't wake you.'

I stretched out my arms and legs, before sitting up. 'I feel fully rested, and could almost say that I did not notice any interruptions. My sleep was so sound, I could almost believe you did indeed add something to my wine. Come now, confess.'

'No, no. Of course I didn't. No, Master, no. How could you think such a thing?' As he spoke, Gallius backed away from me. Surprise was written in every muscle and sinew. I looked at him. He had taken my joke more seriously than I had expected. The events of the past days had affected us both.

'Gallius, you shouldn't take my words to heart so much. I was only joking.' I motioned him over, and was relieved to see a wry smile partially ease his tension. 'Come and sit down. We will eat together.' As I leant back against the wall, Gallius brought the tray and placed it next to me. He seated himself on the edge of the bed and I continued, 'I have decided that Memno should remain under your care. You were perfectly right in your treatment yesterday, and you should carry on.'

I broke off some bread and ate it, relishing the flavour. Gallius then reached out his hand, took some apple and slowly lifted it to his mouth.

'But Master, yesterday you said ...'

'Yesterday has gone. I ... I need a break. I have been trying to do too many things, and not been able to concentrate on any one of them. I have decided that you should run the infirmary for a few days, while I clear up the matter of Lucius' death.'

'Are you sure?' Gallius spoke quietly, and slowly. 'Are you sure you wish to leave the care of your patients in my hands?'

'Of course I'm sure. Would I have said it otherwise?' I got up, almost upsetting the tray. Gallius saved it and moved to place it back on the table. As we stood there, face to face, I put my hands on his shoulders. His eyes had a bereft and lost look about them, instead of the usual sparkle. Maybe I had been overly harsh and critical. But now was the time to move forward, not reflect on the past.

'Gallius, I'm sure you can do this. You are a good doctor. In some areas, particularly the use of native herbs, your skills surpass mine. We've talked about this before, that you would one day take over my practice.'

'But surely that day is not yet here. There are still many things I don't know.'

'It will only be for a few days at this point. You must see that I have made a vow to Lucius to find his murderer, and that I must do.'

'But you can't just abandon me,' said Gallius.

'I won't. But you will take over the daily care of the patients, while I unravel the mystery. I will still be here, so that we can discuss any cases you are unsure of.'

'But what if someone asks to be seen by you?'

'If anyone specifically requests my help, then tell them you are in full consultation with me. I wouldn't suggest it unless I was certain that you were able to do this. I know you won't let me down.'

Confidence started to ooze back into his posture as he contemplated the prospect. 'I might need to delegate some of my other duties, so that I can devote enough time.'

'Of course. And you might find it useful to have an assistant, someone to fetch and carry for you. I'm not too sure who might be best. I'll need to have a think about it.'

Even as I contemplated the options, Gallius made his choice, 'I would like to have Belbo.'

I looked at him in surprise. Belbo was only a boy of ten or eleven. He always seemed to be in trouble, in people's way, or nowhere to be found when you wanted him.

'Are you sure?' I asked. 'Belbo doesn't seem the most likely choice.'

Gallius nodded his head vigorously. 'I'm sure. He's a bright lad, and always asking questions. And, well, he reminds me a bit of what I was like at his age. You gave me a chance. I'd like to give him an opportunity.'

'Belbo it is then.'

I felt I needed to clarify my thoughts and start making some sense of the various comments I'd heard. I therefore sat down at my desk, and took out a stylus and wax tablet, in order to write down some of my ideas.

Lucius – found dead, but why? Beheaded, but by whom?

The Boudicca uprising. Is it related to this murder? Celts have been known to sacrifice their victims, but no obvious local revolt happening.

Corolius – is he involved? Was he being poisoned? If so, by whom? Was he involved with a local cult? Seems difficult to believe.

What could Memno's guilt be? Why did he need to confess? What was he hiding?

Were there druids in the area? Who at the garrison could be involved with such an outlawed group? Were there Christians in the area? Did either of these groups have human sacrifices? Were either of these cults involved? If so, in what way?

At this point I put down my stylus, and gazed out of the window. The rain that had been falling steadily since the previous evening now appeared to be easing.

At least I would be able to answer one of the questions I had set myself. I would talk to Memno, but first I needed some exercise to stretch my limbs that were cramped from sitting.

There was a chill in the wet air that demanded a cloak, and once I had procured this, I set out. The mud that now covered most of the ground was treacherous, and I bent my steps towards the road, putting my trust in its solid surface. It seemed to be the only thing with any substance in this quagmire of questions that revolved around in my mind. Part of me knew that I did not really need this walk, that I was only putting off the time when I needed to speak to Memno. What could he have felt the need to confess? Was he, in some way, to blame for Lucius' death? Even as I thought the words, a chill ran down my spine. Was Memno a murderer? No, I could not accept that ... or was I blinding myself to the truth? Had my friend killed another, either by his direct actions or indirectly by non-intervention? I had to know, but whilst there was still some uncertainty, I could believe in his innocence. Once he had pronounced his guilt, I would have to act, but I didn't want to get to the time when the words that might condemn him were released.

I was not going far, just to the village that had grown outside the garrison. Once there, I decided to take my relaxation seriously, and sat down in the small tavern, calling out to Barris, the landlord, for some wine. There were few other customers at this hour, after breakfast, but not yet midday and I was able to sit near the brazier, well sheltered, with a partial view of the street. Barris brought over a jug and cup, and we exchanged a few words, before a call came from the living quarters behind the bar, and he hurried off. I smiled, knowing from experience what some women are like when soon to produce their first child, and indeed, how worried many husbands can be. I poured my wine, and idly let my eyes wander, catching a glimpse of a familiar figure outside, but I must have been mistaken. Gallius would have no need to be in the village at this time in the morning. He would be in the infirmary checking on his patients, or in the dispensary, making up poultices, infusions or ointments.

The heat from the charcoal helped dry the mud on my damp cloak and sent warmth seeping into my feet. I was comfortable sitting there, with my glass of wine, observing the comings and goings of people in the street, picking odd figures out at random to follow with my eyes.

In this way I watched a woman, swathed in a cloak like the many others. She had walked across the door of the tavern, and was now slowly moving back in the opposite direction. Was she waiting for someone by design? Maybe she was hoping for a chance meeting? Had she lost something in the mud? Who could tell?

My idle curiosity was rewarded when she stopped just at the edge of my view, talking to an unseen figure. Others walking about in the street moved around these two, who stood still, until a package was hastily passed to the woman. This movement brought her companion partially into view, revealing a glimpse of the familiar figure I had half-seen earlier. But what was Gallius doing here? If indeed it was him. I might be mistaken in my identification. As I watched from the gloom of the tavern interior, out into the now bright sunlight, it seemed that the transaction had been completed. The woman slowly retraced her steps across the front of the tavern, and I could see she was smiling to herself.

Leaving the inn, I started back to the garrison, anticipating that I would catch Gallius up, but he was nowhere to be seen. Either I had been mistaken and it was not Gallius, or he had returned to the camp with some speed, more than I could match.

I stopped off at the infirmary, finding that the attendant had not seen him for some time. Well, I would talk to him later, and so I headed for Memno's quarters.

'Memno, my friend. I'm pleased to see you looking so good. Do you feel as well as you seem?'

He was sitting in a chair facing the window. There was a rosy hue in his face that had been missing just two days previously. His weakness was still evident in the lethargic arm he raised, and quickly dropped, at my entrance.

'Tiberius. It's good to see you. I was starting to think you had abandoned me.'

'I have been ... tired. Working too many hours. Yes, I ... need a rest.'

'I know,' Memno said. 'Gallius told me. He's a good doctor, and will make a worthy successor to you.'

I sat down next to him, so that I could see his profile, but avoid his eyes. For a few moments, we both looked out at the courtyard where soldiers cautiously picked their way across the slippery surface. The many feet threw mud up into the air, to besmirch leggings, tunics, and, occasionally, a face. It was a scene that invited me to linger and just observe. But to do that meant further procrastination, and I had already put off this task once, with my walk to the village.

Ignoring the reluctance that I felt, I broke the silence, 'You seem to be recovering well from your attack.'

'Thanks to your skills. It must have been fate that directed my steps to your quarters that night.'

Again I hesitated. A laugh rang out from my companion as, outside, the inevitable happened. A soldier slipped in the mud, landing heavily on his side, before he scrambled onto his hands and knees, in preparation for standing up. The chuckles of his compatriots filled the air, before they condescended to assist him. Moving off, the soldier who had fallen tried vainly to brush the wet dirt off his clothing.

'Memno.' I kept my gaze fixed ahead, watching the now deserted courtyard. 'The night you had your attack, you came to my quarters to see me. You seemed to want to tell me something. What was it?'

I held my breath making the pause before he answered appear endless.

'Did I?' he said, his casual words as odds with his suddenly tense hand, where he gripped the arm of the chair. 'I don't remember. It can't have been important.'

'It seemed very important at the time. You wanted to speak to me. You wanted to … confess something. What was it?'

Again there was a gap, a hesitation. Or was my imagination playing tricks? I found it difficult to believe that I had suspicions about Memno's motives. He could not possibly be involved in the death of our mutual friend, could he?

'I think I just wanted to consult you on something,' he said. 'Yes, that was it. I wasn't feeling well, and I needed to see you about that. That must have been it.'

'No, there was something else as well.' My throat was tight and I mentally struggled to articulate the words. 'You may have come to see me about not feeling well, but then you wanted to say something else. After your attack, when you were unwell.'

'If I was unwell, then surely anything I said couldn't be taken as having any meaning. As you said, I was unwell. My words would've had no sense.'

I sat gazing at nothing. The rain had ceased completely leaving a fresh blue sky, full of white, fluffy clouds, tinged with a grey promise of further precipitation to come. The clash and clunk of wood on metal drifted across from the training ground, where new recruits were occupied in sword drill. Later there would be a queue at the infirmary for attention to battered knuckles and bruised bodies.

I glanced over at my companion. Maybe my silence would encourage the speech I was seeking from Memno. My words had manifestly failed to achieve the objective I had set myself. I needed to find out what Memno had wanted to confess.

My treatment worked. After a short time, Memno seemed to want to fill the quietness. He sat motionless, his hands gripping the arms of the chair.

'Trust me, Tiberius. That which I may have indicated, has nothing to do with that which you are investigating.'

So he had wanted to tell me something, despite his protestations. I sensed him move his head, and I turned to look at his face. His eyes held mine, and I could see nothing of complicity in them.

He continued speaking. 'There is a … matter I would wish to discuss with you, when this … this business is concluded. But it has no bearing on your investigation.'

While part of me longed to force the information from him, I succumbed to that part that shouted 'you know Memno to be truthful.' As we were thus sat, the unannounced entry of Gallius broke our eye contact.

'Tiberius, Master. I didn't expect to find you here. I came to give Memno his draught. Shall I come back later?'

'Carry on Gallius. Memno and I had finished our talk.' I swivelled my chair to face into the room. Gallius moved about, carefully preparing the medicine for Memno. I watched as he completed his ministrations, measuring and re-measuring the doses. Once he had settled Memno back into bed for a rest, I felt able to speak.

'How are things in the infirmary?'

'They … are fine. There are no new patients.'

'Not yet, but you may well be busy soon.'

Gallius looked at me, with an expression of incomprehension on his face, and I hastened to explain. 'The new recruits. They were training this morning.'

Relief flooded his features. 'Of course. I'll need to prepare some poultices.' He dropped his head, flicking glances up at me from his lowered eyes. 'Some of the cuts may be deep. Some might need stitching. It may be better if … perhaps you might … stitching wounds can be …'

I smiled to myself as I finished his sentence. 'Stitching wounds can be tricky for one person. I'd be glad to assist you, if you'd like.'

'Thank you. I'd appreciate your … your assistance.'

'Come on, we'd better make a start on those poultices.'

Putting my arm around his shoulders, I indicated the doorway and the muddy courtyard. Behind us Memno's breathing turned into gentle snoring. I surveyed the treacherous surface we would have to traverse and grimaced.

'What was it like when you came over from the infirmary, Gallius? Was the ground very slippery? It looks as if we could fall within two or three steps, unless we are very careful.'

There was a sudden tenseness about his neck and shoulders, and Gallius was very quick to answer. 'I have not been in the infirmary, at least I did not come from there. I have been in the dispensary, after being in the infirmary this morning.' As he spoke he moved back into the room, and picked up the tray of ampoules, boxes and spoons. 'I didn't come across the courtyard. I went the long way, via the storerooms. I thought the mud too difficult to cross when I had so much to carry.' He held out the tray, as if presenting the confirming evidence for his case, and I stood to one side to allow him to precede me out of the door. As he walked in front of me, I noticed the back of his tunic and legs. Mud had splashed up, creating a pattern of spots and streaks that could not possibly have come from the infirmary, dispensary or storeroom passageway.

As I caught up with him to walk together down the corridor, Gallius continued speaking. 'I've been busy most of the morning, cleaning out some of the old stock in the dispensary.'

I frowned, 'Surely there was no need to do that again so soon. It could only have been two or three months since we last did it.'

Gallius looked straight ahead as we passed down the cold passageways, past rooms keeping their promise of a comfortable winter. Some of the wooden boards we walked along were uneven and warped with the seemingly continuous wet weather. There were creaks and groans as we placed our feet.

'I needed to discard some drugs, as they were spoilt.' Gallius' voice was slow, and as he finished speaking, I saw him bite his bottom lip.

'Spoiled? In what way? Had they got damp? Was it a mouse?'

'Yes, yes.' Gallius' reply appeared almost before I had finished. 'A mouse. It was a mouse that had got in and eaten some of the herbs.'

'Gallius, I'm very disappointed that you could have allowed that to happen. You need to take more care. You must remember to always close the boxes after use.'

'Yes Master. I will take more care in future.'

His shoulders dropped and I became conscious of his even breathing. We reached the dispensary, and I unlocked and opened the door. Gallius entered, put down his tray and started to replace the items on it, in their various positions. I looked around, as if with new eyes. The mixed aroma of fragrant and pungent plants infused the room, so that breathing in was like a cure in itself. Gallius had been in charge of this area for so long that I almost felt like an intruder. He had managed my dispensaries for some years in various locations. The order and arrangement of the leaves, powders and seeds was his. Of course I knew what was here, and it was my decision as to whether or not the specific ingredient was stocked, but Gallius then gave it its allotted space. He could have completed a prescription blindfolded, which made it all the more surprising that he'd allowed a mouse access to the stock.

'I think I'd better check the spoiled drugs. They may not be as bad as you think.'

Gallius whirled round to face me. 'No.' His voice was high and his wide eyes locked contact with mine. He swallowed, and his breathing slowed as he did so. 'No,' he repeated in a normal tone, 'there's no need for you to worry.'

'I'd like to check the damaged herbs.' I continued to gaze directly into Gallius' eyes, as if by that invisible thread I could draw the truth from him.

'I have ...' He paused and made as if to turn away, but my look held him. 'I have ... you can't,' he continued. 'I have already ... destroyed them.'

I don't know how long we might have stood there if Belbo hadn't come running into the room. 'Master, sir, quick. Gallius, sir, come, please.' He was about to speed out again when I caught him by the arm. Reluctantly dragging my attention from Gallius, I looked at the boy.

'What are you talking about?' I demanded.

Belbo took a deep breath, expelling the words in one exhalation. 'Master, the infirmary, come quick,' and he started to pull me towards the door. I allowed Belbo to lead me out of the room, accepting it was probably quicker for him to take us than for me to delay and question the white-faced child. With Belbo leading and Gallius following we processed down to the infirmary and into the operating room.

At the entrance, I felt as if time had reversed itself. As I looked into the room, the walls threatened to dissolve into memory, and it was only the contact between my arm and the doorframe that kept my feet on solid ground.

I heard a sharp intake of breath that had to have come from Gallius, as I slowly released the air my lungs had held on to. A shape lay on the table in front of me, illuminated by a thin light from the afternoon sun, slanting in from the high windows.

Water from the wet cloths that covered the shape dripped onto the floor. The fall of the drops seemed to echo my heart beat. Drip, splash, drip, splash, drip, splash. The small pool of water that was being formed seemed to suck any light into itself, showing black and deep. Drip, splash, drip, splash, drip, splash. One rivulet reached out like a tentacle, feeling its way across the cold floor, feeling for life and warmth.

I was back, looking at the body of Lucius - but I wasn't. My eyes told one story, but the assault on my nostrils told another. Instinctively I put my hand to my face to block out the stench, while beside me Gallius backed away and turned to lean on the balustrade of the inner courtyard.

Belbo had disappeared, and part of me was glad. The boy was too young to be confronted with that which lay under the sheet.

Fighting both my reluctance and the almost palpable smell, I advanced step by step by step. Drip, splash, drip, splash, drip, splash. The sound that had risen from the darkness in so many of my dreams, transforming them into nightmares, was once again solid. Would that drip, drip, drip haunt me forever? I reached the table where the wet cloth emptied its burden down onto my feet. My hand hesitated to reveal the hidden shape, but slowly I picked up one corner, the texture of the fabric smooth and cold between my fingers and thumb. Slowly I exposed the body that I knew would be there.

Drip, splash, drip, splash, drip, splash. Unbidden my eyes superimposed the image of Lucius. I wasn't sure if I was in my operating room, or some fantastic land, where demons could create images to taunt me. But this was no dream. The floor was solid under my feet, the table cold under my hand, the smell acrid in my nostrils. There was the same stump of bone where once a head had been, but instead of smooth skin and well-defined musculature, there was a putrid mass of flesh. Any scars or marks to help identification had long since been hidden by decomposition. The room began to revolve around me, as formless bodies and faceless heads swirled past my eyes.

'How long ...?' Gallius' voice seemed to come from a distance. I had to turn to look at him, stood by my side to convince myself he was actually in the room.

'How long has he been dead?' he continued.

'Some weeks.' I replaced the cloth and turned, indicating the door where outside the sun shone, and a gentle breeze stirred the last few leaves on the trees. I could not remain further in that room where death hung in the air. To speak meant pulling lungfuls of decay into my breast. Gallius made a hasty exit, out to lean over the balustrade, where he violently expelled the remains of his last meal. Raising his head up, he breathed deeply several times.

I glanced back at the room I was leaving before turning towards my quarters. Later, I would come back and examine the remains, but not now. It would have to be later.

Entering my room, as I dropped heavily into a chair, Gallius headed for the window and gulped down more chunks of air, freshly washed by the recent rain. He then left and I could hear him, in the passageway, calling for refreshments.

As he re-entered, I indicated a seat, into which he sank. A slave quickly followed him, bearing a bowl of water and some cloths. I washed my face and hands, relishing the cool water and rough material on my skin. The smell that clung to my body dissipated somewhat, but there was still a hint from the fibres of my tunic. As Gallius also took advantage of the opportunity to freshen himself, I sat down again and drank deeply from one of the ready filled goblets of wine that had been placed on the table.

'We'll need to burn some incense in the air, before I can even look at ... before we can do an examination.' Gallius nodded in agreement, and I continued, 'I must find out who found ... the body, and where.' A further nod was elicited from Gallius who was taking almost continuous small sips from his goblet. I took a long draught of wine and leant back in my chair, my hands cradling the cup. Gallius' voice broke the short silence.

'Why, Master? Why?'

'The coming of death is never easy, Gallius. It is fate and the gods who decide how we meet our end.'

'But this was not the gods. This must have been the hand of a man or men.'

'I agree.' I looked up at the ceiling, noting a cobweb that hung down, fluttering in a gentle air. It may have been fate that decreed this ... I paused in my thoughts. My very brief examination of the remains had been so cursory that I could not say with certainty whether it was a man or a woman that lay on the table. This ... person might have died in this way, but it was also fate that put me here to bring the perpetrators to justice. I drained my cup and refilled it from the now half-empty jug.

'How long?' Gallius repeated his question of earlier.

'I'm not sure. Some weeks judging from the amount of decomposition.'

'The smell, it was ...'

I looked at him, his face still drained of colour. Maybe I had been too careful in his training, screening what he was exposed to. Previous cases of black rot, which gave off the same putrefaction as this body, had been heavily masked with incense and other strong smelling oils and herbs. Gallius had seen death in many guises, but not the decay that comes from prolonged exposure to the elements. The skill of a doctor is in keeping his patients alive and well, not dead and rotting. Having finished my wine, I emptied the jug into our cups, while I considered ways to distract him from the alley into which he was talking himself.

'Who bought the remains in? Does Belbo know?' I was not aware I had spoken aloud until Gallius called out to the slave standing by the doorway to fetch the boy, who quickly appeared. I asked him to find those who had brought the body and placed it on the operating table and he rapidly ran off, the activity seeming to help restore his balance and humour. Gallius and I both sat waiting, as a silence descended on the room. The sounds of a bird singing outside mingled with shouts and calls from people going about their business, as the routine of the garrison continued around us.

The body that lay on the operating table had disturbed the flow of normality no more than a rock thrown into a river. The splashes and ripples caused would affect some more than others, but the impact would soon fade. One rock would make no difference. But this was not one incident. Already there had been two murders. A river can accept one rock without alteration from its normal course, but if two, three or more rocks were added, how soon before the riverbed is raised, and the flow blocked.

A river can only take so much debris before it is damned and overflows, spreading havoc, misery and ruin to the surrounding fields, towns and villages. Could this be the cause for this mystery? Was it in some way related to the unrest in the East?

But how? How would the murder of one, possibly two, Romans help a Celtic leader in a distant uprising? Probably very little, but what if more deaths were planned, to spread revolt and insurrection here. Then our forces would be split, and diminished, fighting on two or more fronts at the same time.

But I was getting ahead of myself. I didn't know for certain if this body belonged to a Roman. It could have been someone local, caught in a private personal dispute, now settled and finalised. Even as I thought it, I knew that I was fooling myself. Something connected the death of Lucius with this new discovery, and in the same way I knew that I was the one fated to clear the secrecy and restore the smooth flow of life.

'Tiberius, Belbo is here, Master.' There was a slightly slurred sound to Gallius' words that made me cast a quick look at him before I concentrated on the figures that had just entered the room.

'Yes, Belbo, what is it?'

He did not speak, but indicated the accompanying people with his hand. I remembered now, I had asked him to find those who had discovered the body.

'Thank you, Belbo. You may go now.' The boy had regained his colour but still had a wide-eyed and haunted look that foretold of disturbed dreams in nights to come. He backed timidly out of the room, leaving a decurion and a soldier standing stiffly to attention.

'Please, be seated,' and I indicated the remaining chairs. As they sat, I continued, 'I need to know everything about the body that was brought in.'

The soldier looked to his decurion for reassurance, who began speaking. 'We were repairing the road up to Aquae Sulis. One of the sections had been damaged. The rain, sir. It had washed part of the road away … We were repairing the damage …' As he paused, seemingly reluctant to continue, I felt the need to prompt him.

'Where exactly was this?' I asked.

'Just before the third bridge from here.'

'You were repairing the road, and then what happened?'

Words burst from the soldier. 'It was a body, a headless body. I pulled it out of the river.' He gripped the arms of the chair, his knuckles turning white, and his breathing rapid and shallow.

His leader reached out to place a hand on his colleague's arm. The contact afforded them a private moment of communion and I allowed a short time before gently starting to draw the story from them again.

'You found the body in the river? Was it floating down with the current or at the side, on the bank?'

'What does it matter? What does any of it matter?' Gallius spoke, then picked up his empty goblet as if to drink. On realising it needed replenishment, he put it back on the table stretching out his hand for the jug. I reached out to stop his movements. As our flesh touched, he looked at me with wet and pain-filled eyes.

'Gallius, would you go and arrange for some incense to be burnt in the operating room?' I wanted to reassure and comfort him, but I could not allow him to be inebriated in my company. Certainly not now, when I was trying to elicit information. He dropped his gaze down to the floor, before standing and hurrying out, nearly colliding with the doorframe as he went.

Leaving my elbow resting on the smooth, level wood on the table, I looked down at the close grain, seeing the lines and knots flowing and merging, before nodding at the decurion to continue.

'Sir, the body was floating. The river was running fast and very high, after the recent rain.'

I tried to stop my own mouth muttering, 'That's all it ever does here, rain.' Focusing my attention on the two sitting opposite, I asked, 'How did you ...? If it was floating down the fast-flowing river?'

The soldier appeared to have gained more control over his emotions and his voice was firmer. 'The body got lodged against the pillars of the bridge. I didn't realise it was a body at first. It was just a bundle, a bundle wrapped in a cloth.' He swallowed hard. 'It was only when we bought it on to the bank, and I ... we ...'

The decurion finished his sentence. 'I ordered that the bundle be investigated, but as soon as the cloth was opened ...' He, too, trailed off into silence and shuddered. I didn't press them as to the details. If the decomposed body affected me, how much more it must have had an effect on the soldiers? Like Gallius, they were hardened to injury and death, but would seldom have come across this level of putrefaction.

'Would you be able to guide me to the place again?' I looked from one to the other as I spoke.

The leader nodded, adding, 'The surveyor, Agricola, would also be able to show you. He was there when we … were repairing the road. Will that be all, sir?'

'Yes, thank you.' As they left, I shouted to the slave still waiting at the doorway. 'Get me some more wine, now.' I needed to drown out some of my emotions in the pale, pink liquid.

The dullness of the day and the lateness of the hour meant that there would not be enough light for me to fully undertake any examination today. By tomorrow, the oils and incense would have started to mask the odour, and I would be more mentally prepared. I traced my finger along the table, following the flowing lines. The artisan, who had made it, had done well. He must have worked with the wood, not allowing the knots to dictate the future form, except to add to its beauty. The craftsman had shaped this table out of a larger plank. At what point did the object become more than just a vision, an idea in the creative mind, and result in a reality? At what point will my formless thoughts and ideas take shape and become solid? Soon. I was sure that I would soon have some of the answers. Very soon.

Heading to the bathhouse, I immersed myself in the water letting my worries and concerns seep out of my mind along with the steam from the hot water. Now I could shed the clinging smell of death as the strigil scraped off the oil and sweat.

Day Fourteen

I entered the operating room, the following morning, with a heavy step. Gallius had been waiting outside, apparently loath, as I was, to enter. His blood-shot eyes stood out clearly in his pallid face. Distributed around the room were several burners, emitting scented smoke, along with faint crackles. If I only took shallow breaths, I could convince myself I was breathing in a pleasant mixture of incense and perfumed oils. I could almost ignore the underlying tang of the malodorous stench from the body on the table. Almost, but not quite. Neither Gallius nor I were inclined to speak. To do that meant taking deeper breaths, which I certainly wanted to avoid.

The degree of decomposition was such that I could ascertain little, other than it was a man who'd been decapitated.

That which he had been found in, gave more information. Like Lucius, he was attired in a long tunic, which appeared to have originally been white. The body had then been wrapped in a white cloth, which revealed itself to be a toga. Either the dead man was a Roman, or those who killed him wanted it to appear as if he were.

We spent as little time in the operating room as possible, and on emerging I leant against a pillar bordering the inner courtyard of the infirmary. The whitewashed stone was cold and rough. It felt reassuringly solid and bland after the texture of the flesh I had just handled. The air was fresh with hints of wet grass, which was a welcome change from the heavily scented atmosphere I had just left. My eyes drank in the greens and golds of the autumnal plants, leaving behind the brown and red of a decayed body.

Soon my nostrils no longer detected any lingering odour of death, and I left Gallius, as I headed for the surveyors' office. The day, though dry was cold, and I was wrapped in both a cloak and my own thoughts. I was entering the door when a sound that I had been hearing behind me, over the last few moments, resolved into something I could recognise - my name being called out.

'Tiberius. I thought you'd never stop. Didn't you hear me, or were you trying to avoid me?'

I turned to see Corolius standing a few feet away. He was breathing heavily, as if he'd been running.

'I'm sorry, Corolius. I didn't hear you. I was deep in thought, and to tell the truth, I didn't expect to see you here.'

'What, a doctor not expect to see his patient? Either you must be very sure of your treatments, and thus all your patients are cured, or you must have so little faith in them, that you expect all your patients to die. Come, tell me which it is? But first, I suggest we go inside, out of this biting wind.'

I nodded in agreement, and we both entered the room, where Agricola was standing, poring over some maps and scrolls. He looked up at our entrance, and a thin smile of welcome appeared on his lips.

'Tiberius, Corolius. I did not expect you, but it is good to see you.'

His words jarred on my ears. Surely he must have been anticipating my visit. He had been there when the soldiers discovered the body now resting in my operating room. I looked at Agricola carefully. There seemed to be a look of wariness or distrust around the corners of his eyes, or maybe it was just a shadow cast by the shifting light.

Of course he would not have been expecting Corolius, who had now seated himself and appeared to have little intention of moving. I felt I could not discuss Agricola taking me to the site of the discovery, in front of Corolius. Agricola seemed ill at ease beside, casting glances between us, his hands toying with a stylus that he had been using. Neither he, nor Corolius, appeared inclined to break the silence, but I needed interaction with people, breathing, talking, alive people.

'Corolius, what brings you so far from your farm?' I asked. 'And in such weather as well.'

Corolius leant back in the chair, balancing on the back two legs and stretched his arms above his head. 'Business. I have several loose ends to tie up. Things were rather neglected during my recent illness, as I'm sure you can imagine.'

'I'm surprised you are out in this weather. I wouldn't wish you to get ill again, travelling in the cold and wet.'

'Oh, I am well looked after, by my … business acquaintances. I don't think you need worry on my account. Certainly nothing to lose your head over.' He smiled as he brought the front legs of the chair back down onto the floor with a soft thump, and leaned forward. 'But I hear you have matters much closer to home to attend to.'

Agricola looked up suddenly and dropped his stylus on the floor. As he bent to pick it up, I could see that he swivelled his body so he could continue looking at Corolius with wide eyes and a furrowed brow.

'I'm not sure I follow your meaning.' I, too, was now watching the seated man, who seemed to be the only one at ease.

'I'm sure you do,' Corolius said.

'There are always matters here that require attention.'

'Perhaps more so at present?'

'Maybe you should elaborate.' Our words circled the room, parrying and testing for weaknesses, when Corolius appeared to concede his advantage. He stood up and moved over to the table, idly glancing at the map that Agricola had been working on.

'I meant Memno's illness, of course. I hear he has not been well, although you were able to ...' Corolius paused, before continuing, 'well, shall we say, treat him.'

'Memno is recovering well.' My voice was cold and the words had an unintended edge to them.

'I am sure he is. I believe Gallius is looking after him. Is that wise, to hand over so much responsibility to one who is still a slave?'

He traced a line on the parchment spread out on the table, then looked up. 'But I'm sure you know what you're doing.' A weak smile showed itself on his mouth. 'Actually, that was the reason for my visit here, to see Memno, so that is what I shall now do, and leave you to your business without further interruptions.' He walked out of the door and was gone before I could say anything else.

I wanted to run after him, establish what his business with Memno was, find out where he had been. I was certain there was something behind his regular absences from his farm that was … suspicious, unexplained, mysterious. Of course Corolius may well be able to fully satisfy my curiosity. He knew I was investigating Lucius' death, and he appeared to know about the unknown body that had been found. I had no real reason to suspect him of anything, but he had done nothing to justify himself either.

Why did he seem determined to arouse suspicion by his actions and words? He was almost teasing me. I was sure that Corolius was guilty, either by direct action or by indirect withholding of knowledge. But which was it, and what was the nature of his guilt?

I also needed to speak to Agricola, who gave no indication of wanting to communicate with me. He had turned his back and was, even now, packing his writing implements away and picking up his cloak. Agricola was my friend. Why would he not wish to talk to me? He had been there when the soldiers had found the body. He knew I would want to discuss it with him, but here he was, seemingly trying to escape me.

My moment of indecision meant that the choice was made. Corolius disappeared round a corner while I still stood in the surveyors' office. I was left with Agricola who could not leave the room while I was in the doorway.

'Agricola, must you go?' I put my hand on his shoulder and guided him back into the office and to a chair. He sat down dutifully, as I continued, 'I was hoping we might talk about the body that the soldiers found.'

'I don't know anything about it. The soldiers found it. They fished it out of the river. That's all I know.' His words came out fast, spilling over themselves in their haste to be uttered.

I seated myself beside him, my hand still resting on his arm, where I could feel the tense muscles bunch and relax. 'I just wanted to hear your version of events, that's …'

'My version. I don't have a version. I don't know anything else. The soldiers found a bundle in the river. They fished it out. It was a body. That's all I know. If they say otherwise, they're lying.' His sentences were punctuated by shallow inspirations, and his voice was high.

'It's all right, calm down. I didn't mean to imply anything. I just thought you might remember things better than the soldiers did.' My smile seemed to do nothing to comfort him as he alternated between gazing down at the floor and out of the window. I continued, feeling that filling the silence would be more beneficial than leaving a chasm in the air. 'You are more skilled at noticing detail, much more used to remembering specifics then the soldiers are. I thought you might be able to help resolve the puzzle with your skills and knowledge.'

'I don't remember anything more than I've said.' He appeared to be slightly mollified as he made eye contact for a few brief moments.

'Would you be able to guide me to the place? I do need to see the area for myself, and I would prefer to do that as soon as possible.'

He jerked his arm away and stood up, to perch on the edge of the table. 'Why? Why do you need to go there?'

'There may be some clue as to who this person is.'

'No, I'm sure there was nothing. It had been raining heavily and the ground was muddy. The river was swollen and overflowing in places. Any clue would have been washed away.' He gripped the table and I could see his knuckles starting to show white. 'I'm sure there was nothing.'

'Still, I'd like to go. I was hoping to go today. There's still plenty of light left.'

'It wouldn't be a good idea. I'm very busy at the moment. I couldn't show you. Why not leave it a few days? We could go then.'

'I'd like to go today.' I repeated my statement, and watched as Agricola moved over to stand at the window, his arms wrapped round himself.

'There's no hurry, surely. The man's been dead for some time. There'd be no trace left there now.'

I looked at him. Why was he so reluctant to show me the site of discovery? 'Why don't you want to go? Why won't you show me?'

Agricola turned away to look out of the window. 'I'm scared,' he finally said, in a small voice that seemed to shrink him. 'I'm scared to return to that place, where a man has died. His spirit will still be there. Please don't make me go.'

His voice had the edge of tears mixed with the nightmares of a child. I could no more force him to take me to the third bridge from the garrison on the road to Aquae Sulis, than I could have made my sons put their hands in a fire.

'I won't make you go. Thank you, Agricola.' With that I left the room, so that he could recover his composure in solitude. Death may indeed come to us all, but we are each so very different in how we react in life.

Leaving Agricola alone, I headed for the stables. There was probably no need for him to show me the area, as the description from the soldiers was sufficient for me to find the spot without further assistance. The warm, earthy aromas of the livestock reached out to me and I breathed in deeply. There was something very comforting about the animals. They did not have secrets from each other, they were not violent to their fellow beast, they did not play games with lives as the stake. They just were.

Mounting my horse, I rode slowly out of the garrison. The sun was reaching up towards its zenith, soon to begin its journey down, when it would be replaced by the less bright, but more mysterious moon.

My spirits were light as I moved down the road, and I had the sense of shedding some heavy weight. I was active once more, going out to find and explore, not becoming mired in the machinations of people or poking at putrefied flesh. Maybe I had become too involved in the mystery, too close to the puzzle. I needed some space to step back. Some time on my own. Some time to think. Some time to put some pieces together.

For I was sure that I had many of the threads in my hand. I just needed to put them together in order to see the pattern that they made. A memory of childhood slid into my mind. My mother sitting at her loom, weaving an intricate hanging whilst my brother and I played hide and seek. From my chosen spot, I could see nothing but a mixed swirl of bright colours that made my eyes water to look at. When I expressed my disgust, my mother gently drew me round to the other side, and made me step back. As I did so, Hercules himself jumped out at me, stealing the apples of the Hesperides, with the dragon curled round the base of a tree. Right now I felt more like I was battling the hydra, but like Hercules, I, too, would overcome and emerge victorious. All I needed to do was step back and view things from a different angle.

And so I made my way down the road, towards the third bridge. There was little traffic today and I made good, steady progress. A few carts taking the final harvest to market and some travellers, trudging along, were all I passed. As I approached my destination, I could see where the soldiers had repaired the road, building up the bank and securing it against a further watery onslaught.

Dismounting, I tied my horse to a tree at the side of the road, where he could reach the river, and I stood on the bridge looking down at the swirling, brown water. The current seemed fast and unstoppable. As I watched, a large branch, denuded of leaves, hurtled down, spinning and turning, now showing this aspect, now another. It seemed to reach an arm up to the parapet, searching for a handhold, before succumbing to the pressure and sinking under the bridge. Who knew where it would end up?

Making my way carefully down the slippery bank, I could see gashes in the soil, where sandaled feet had struggled for grip. A smooth furrow indicated where they had pulled a wrapped bundle out to be examined.

Had they wondered what it contained? Had there been anticipation of goods to be shared? Had they mentally spent their findings before the bundle was even on solid ground?

I smiled. Of course they had. Few soldiers would voluntarily venture into the cold water for no reward.

I looked around, seeing willow and alder trees delineating the usual course of the river, their feet now standing in the water. Ferns, brown and crinkled, blanketed the ground, intermingled with brambles to catch the unwary. The gushing water provided a bass note for the bird song that was scattered in the air. I was certain that this was purely the temporary destination of the unknown man, now lying back on that cold table, and that he had started his penultimate journey further up this watery road. He had floated down one river, but his travelling was soon to end by crossing the Styx in Charon's boat.

Reaching out to the trees for support, I made my way up, going against the flow. I could feel the bark rough under my hands, enough to scratch and draw a network of red lines.

At times it felt as if the very plants were hindering my progress, as in some places I had to force the unyielding stems to allow my body access. In others, the branches snapped at the slightest pressure, leaving me teetering on the edge of being soaked. But my will prevailed, and I moved up the bank.

Twice I needed a detour, to find a place to wade across ankle-deep tributaries, usually little more than small streams that normally would have tumbled along their rocky beds. Many times the trees stretched themselves up, to create a tunnel down which I slowly crept. In summer, the canopy would block out the sun and sky. In their present stripped state, the branches made a mesh overhead, as if to catch the unwary.

I had travelled some distance, and was considering turning back, when as I emerged from one stand of trees, I saw in front, further up the bank, a third stream feeding into the larger river. It issued from a wood of beech, oak and birch, which I recognised. Part of me rejoiced that I was indeed correct in assuming the two deaths were linked, although I had little doubt that they were. But now, I had not only the manner of their death, but also the place. I had been here before.

I was standing on the bank of a stream, with a ridge on my right. Beyond which, on the far side there would be a burnt out village, the ribs of the roundhouses standing up like grave markers. In front of me, in amongst the trees and ferns, was the spot where Lucius' body had been pulled from the water. It could not be coincidence. The unknown man had been killed in the same way, and in the same place as Lucius.

Part of me wanted to turn back, to depart this place. It had been the scene of at least two violent deaths. Had there been others? Would there be more in the future? I am not a superstitious man. I do not expect the gods to concern themselves with my worries.

But as I moved forward, into the tightly packed trees, it seemed as if a door was closed behind me, with unseen forces hindering my progress. The sun did not penetrate more than a few paces, and in the dull light, I quickly lost sight of open ground.

Previously the ferns had been broken and bruised by the passage of man. This time they were dying down from the natural forces of time and nature. Then there had been sweetness in the swollen fruits of the brambles. Now there were only thorns and rotting berries. The bright mauve of the late foxgloves was replaced with the dull burgundy of the last battered remnants clinging to the stems. Many more leaves and rain had erased all signs of previous visitations, and the whole was a dull grey and brown. I stood still, and a squirrel jumped down in front of me, chattering in its vain quest for beech masts or acorns. A leaf that had hung on through the wind and rain now relinquished its hold and fluttered down at the edge of my sight, making me start, and the squirrel fled in a flicker of red.

I continued on, much further than I had ventured on my previous visit, to where I could see a dark green that spoke of a solid stand of holly, flecked with red. My imagination gave a different view of the innocent berries, as I edged round the armoured trees. The ground was still damp underfoot, but with less of a coating of leaves. Or was it that they were more trodden into the earth? I could easily visualise many feet having walked to this spot.

At first I thought the grove was impenetrable, but as I moved round the edges, I found a section where the trees were thinned, whether by nature or man, I could not tell. I was loath to enter. The unseen sky must have darkened, as the still air turned to gloom. I could either give up my quest now, and return to the garrison, knowing that I had failed, and I would never avenge Lucius' death, or I could go on. Some of the answers I sought lay ahead of me, of that I was certain. I had to go on. Easing my body between the trunks, I could feel the barbed leaves catch hold of my cloak. As I turned and pulled myself free, I caught a glimpse of white, almost glowing in the dull air. It was a piece of fabric, clean and pure, which I removed from the branch on which it had been impaled.

Pushing it deep into the bag tied at my waist, I continued through the trees, soon to come out into an opening. The ground was clear from ferns, brambles or seedlings, yet the canopy opened to reveal an overcast and dull sky. Around the edge of the clearing grew six oak trees that had the look of careful nurturing. The earth was impacted, and there was a smell of ...? Something I could not at first identify, yet knew.

I was reluctant to step into the open, and edged along the perimeter hiding myself from unseen eyes. A soft and gentle breeze stirred the leaves and brought knowledge of the odour - a mix of sandalwood, incense, hemlock ... and stale blood. As my eyes located the source, my mouth became dry, at odds with my sweating palms. Identification seemed to strengthen the smell until it swirled and leapt from tree to tree, pursuing me.

I backed away, feeling the rough bark of an oak against my spine. The solidity was reassuring and I kept in contact with it as I edged round the tree. With the bulk of the trunk between the clearing and me, I paused, trying to force air into my lungs, and calm the rapid beating of my heart.

I needed to get away, as far as possible from this place. I must not be found here. But at present my head was swimming and my legs felt shaky. They would not support me … but they had to. I had to get away from here.

For this was no ordinary glade. This was, without doubt, a sacred grove of the druids. That which I had smelt had been the remains of the offerings and sacrifices made. There had been a small forest of stakes around one of the trees, with heads for adornment.

I had not stayed long enough to establish the number or source, for I didn't wish to be among them. If I were found here, the next investigation might be into my death, although there would be no-one to pursue the case. No-one knew where I was, so no-one would know where to look.

I eased my way into the thick cover of the holly, grateful now for its evergreen foliage, which provided shelter. The gloom meant that I was only able to distinguish shapes and movements. My ears were alert for the sounds of others, magnifying every creak and groan into an army of potential pursuers.

I had almost reached the edge of the wood when I could not ignore or misinterpret the crack of a foot breaking a branch. Or was it just a badger coming out for its evening feed? The sound was behind and to my right. Or maybe not? I caught a movement to my left. Was it a person, or a bird flying home to roost? Was that a fox barking out, or a call from a human throat? I had no options left but to run, and I did so.

I ran, moving across the uneven ground towards the scant security of some trees I could just distinguish in front of me. The gasping of my breath was matched by the pounding in my chest and ears. I could no longer hear sounds of pursuit behind me, but that did not mean I was safe.

Reaching the first rank of bushes, I pushed through, regardless of the thorns that made no allowances for my flesh, tearing it and my robe alike. My outstretched hand felt rough bark and I pulled myself round behind the protective tree. But I knew this sanctuary was only transient.

The brambles that had ambushed parts of my clothing now laid a clear trail for my enemies. Pushing against the wood, I started off again, only to feel the ground dip down sharply. The covering of wet leaves on mud gave no purchase for my leather sandals and I had no choice, but to abandon myself to the inevitable. I slid, rolled and tumbled, finally coming to rest beside a gentle stream.

In other circumstances this would have been an idyllic spot. The trees cast their gentle shade, the grass was soft and the stream whispered quiet music. In my overwrought state, the trees concealed unknown menace, the grass was too alluring and the stream went on its way, uncaring of those around it.

Scrambling to my feet, I staggered into the current, feeling the cold against my legs. The unseen surface was rocky and blood from my quickly cut knees was soon erased by the flowing water. Making my way across, I hoped to escape from my would-be captors.

Looking behind me for the space of a heartbeat, I saw shadowy shapes spread out, shifting and changing with the light, merging into the shadows to re-appear at different points. I could not stand still. I could not wait to establish their source.

Their intentions might be friendly or hostile, but I could not pause to check. I needed to keep moving. On and on, until I had the opportunity to lose myself in the friendly darkness.

I turned and continued my flight onwards, scrambling up the bank out of the streambed. My feet fought for purchase on the mud and long grass. My fingers groped wildly to find a friendly handhold amongst the overhanging branches. But I was deceived. The shrub I grasped came away from its anchorage and I was falling. Falling, into the stream I had just crossed. Falling down much further than I had climbed. The rocks I had just stepped on came up to meet me, and the coldness overwhelmed me totally.

I drifted, unknowing, unaware, floating down, now tossed and tumbled, now gently cocooned. Thoughts and patterns merged and coalesced, then dissipated to reform into new shapes, all without meaning or understanding. Holly leaves became ferocious, taloned hands, reaching out to grab and entwine the rocks, which melted into pink and yellow water, to turn blood red.

White shapes emerged, some mainly animal, some almost human, dancing around a mound of severed heads, out of which grew a tree with acorns and heavily indented, feathery leaves. The white shapes revolved faster and faster, spinning into a blur of smoky swirls, which gradually darkened, except for a bright red heart.

The coldness that I had felt earlier was still present, but it had retreated to my inner core. My skin now burned with a fire that would never provide true heat or comfort. The flexibility of the water gave way to an unexpected softness with none of the rocky hardness I was anticipating. For the moment I felt safe. Safe and secure in this soft and silky setting.

The air that I breathed ... I was breathing. The thought trickled through to my consciousness. If I was breathing, I must be alive. I was not dead.

The air that I was breathing was heavy with smoke, hanging in the stillness like garlands, shifting and scattering, being continually supplied from a seemingly endless source. My eyes, which were now open, perceived little, other than an overhead intricacy of wood. The ruddy glow that had intruded into my dreams - or was it delirium? - revealed itself to be a fire.

The logs crackled and spat, creating the festoons of smoke that writhed above, riding the thermals, seeking an exit out through the overhead covering. My skin now gave meaningful feedback as to the surface I was lying on, which was a skin, a pelt with thick, luxurious hair.

The particles in the air irritated my lungs, causing a cough, which created multiple lances of agony. Head, chest, arms, legs, back. All contributed their individual notes to the overall harmonic of misery. Once initiated the pain seemed to multiply rather than ease. However much I shifted, I could not find a position of comfort, as that which reduced the ache in my back caused sudden stabs in my knees. Moving my legs so that they were eased meant setting off the soreness around my shoulders. And nothing stopped the burning in my ribs, other than not breathing, and that was not an option. Now that I realised I was alive, I wanted to stay that way. All the time the pounding in my head created a background, highlighting everything else.

For some moments I was engulfed in an internal and private world, unable to focus fully on anything external. But then a movement diverted me back to the outside environment.

A shape shifting and moving on the far side of the flickering fire. My breath quickened, fear overriding my natural curiosity. Was I still in danger? And almost immediately after came the realisation that if I was, I could do nothing about it. I was helpless and could only wait for the figure to make its move.

It approached me and the person spoke, but I could not understand the words, which sounded harsh and cold, although uttered in a soft, melodic voice. It was a girl or woman, for I could now see the details more clearly. The long, dark woollen tunic was topped with a paler, striped cloak, pinned at the shoulders. A necklace and bracelets gave soft chinks as she moved. The glow from the fire reflected in the braids of her red hair hanging down either side of her face. She spoke the words again, and this time supplemented her speech by proffering a bowl towards me.

In my weakened state I could do nothing other than passive acceptance. Whatever this woman intended, whether good or evil, I could not prevent. She knelt down and put the bowl by her side. Putting one hand under my head to raise it, she spooned a little liquid into my mouth.

It was warm, slightly salty, and tasted of vegetables and barley. Once my taste buds had been engaged, I could not prevent myself from swallowing.

Several mouthfuls followed, before the bowl was empty and the woman withdrew her hand. Her actions, though apparently caring, were none too gentle, and a sudden throb as my head fell back onto the pillow made me close my eyes and grimace, as I waited for the pain to subside. The memory came into my brain of another woman, who had been soft and gentle, who had tenderly caressed my body, easing my aches away. And then the darkness reached out and claimed me.

Day Fifteen

When next I looked about me, the quality of the light indicated it was mid-morning, but of which day? Had I been here a few hours or a few days? Now I could see that I was lying on a raised dais, covered with skins, inside a roundhouse. In the centre the red embers of a slumbering fire gave little light, but the open doorways provided just enough illumination to see the thatch of the high, conical roof, supported on the mud and stone walls. As far as I could see, I was alone, but voices were discernible outside. One high and one low.

Summoning my strength, I shifted, rolled and raised myself up on one elbow, gritting my teeth, to prevent the searing pain in my side from taking over. I swung my legs round so that I was now sitting on the side of the low platform and could see the interior from the correct angle.

The effort had used my small reserves of energy and I had none left to reach my sandals that I could see were at the end of the bed. The clothes I was dressed in were my own, no longer wet but torn and stained with green, brown, and red.

A figure entered, stooping slightly to avoid the low lintel. I recognised the red-haired woman who had fed me - was it yesterday? My body told me it was only a few hours since I had eaten. With only the briefest glance in my direction, she headed for the fire to waken it. As she moved about, feeding the flames, preparing food, tidying the area, I could only guess at many of her activities as her face was turned away from me. Her movements were brisk and spare, and soon she hurried out again.

I watched her go, and as she disappeared out of the doorway, a silence descended, punctuated only by the crackle of the fire sending its sporadic heat out into the space. Where was I? In a normal village there would be laughter and cries from children, the snuffling of pigs and the yelping of dogs. Where was the chattering of women? The thud of wood being chopped? The regular clunks of the loom? While the thoughts spinned in my head, my body recovered some of its strength, and I shuffled and slid along the bed to reach my footwear.

If I did not bend much, or breathe too deeply, the pain in my side remained a constant, dull ache, rather than a burning throb. Having reached my shoes, I contemplated how to do them up, and then whether I would be able to attain, and keep, an upright position. The doorway darkened again and the woman returned, going straight to the fire. There she sat, watching me with dark and wary eyes. My attention was not on her for long, as a second figure entered. This person came up to me, standing in front of me. I had to look up to see him, the movement causing a stab of pain from my neck.

'Tiberius, you have recovered better than I expected.'

The voice was well known to me, but belonged to almost the last person I was expecting.

'Agricola? Is that you?' I could not fully trust the evidence of my ears, and my vision was not clear enough in the interior gloom.

'Of course it's me.' He sat down beside me. 'How are you?'

'I … I am …' I was unsure, myself. I was better than a few hours ago, but not as well as I had been a few days previously. 'I'll be fine. But you? Why …? How…?' I seemed unable to articulate my thoughts and questions.

'Don't try to talk too much. You fell and must have hit your head.

I had memories of a chase, rocks, flowing water, white shapes and dark green leaves. I reached up to touch the back of my head, and shuddered as the soreness confirmed the story.

Agricola continued, 'You must have knocked yourself out. I was unsure if you were alive or dead, so I brought you here.'

'But where is here? And how did you know where I was?' I had so many questions, so many gaps in my recollection.

The voice of the woman broke into our conversation, her words directed at us from the fire. I could only guess at her meaning from the way she tilted her head and curled her upper-lip. She sat on a low stool with her hands on her hips. I looked at Agricola, as, to my surprise, he answered her, in short sharp sounds. My incomprehension grew, as she then stood and walked towards the opening, glaring at me as she went.

At the doorway she paused and delivered a parting shot, her arm pointed at Agricola and then me, as if to emphasise the tone of her voice. Without waiting for an answer she turned and left, letting the door curtain fall down, intermittently blocking some of the light as it swung to and fro for a few moments.

'Don't worry about Etain. She … I had to use a lot of persuasion to get her to help.' Agricola's words had a comforting sound and the semi-darkness meant that was all I could go on.

'Who is she? How do you know her?' I was full of questions, but Agricola's hand on my arm silenced me.

'That can all wait. What we need to do now is get you back to the garrison. I'll fasten your sandals. There we go, all done. Now, do you think you can walk if I help you up? That's it, heading for the door.' Agricola's constant flow of words and active assistance meant that I was soon standing at the entrance, blinking in the sudden daylight. The roundhouse was one of a group of six or seven, in various states of disrepair. The others seemed deserted, with the sun slanting down through gaps in the thatch and walls, showing their internal structure.

'How …?' I was finding it difficult to talk and move at the same time. 'How are we going to get back …?'

Agricola ushered me outside where I could see two horses, calmly shortening the grass on the ground, and on the thatch.

'My horse?' I ventured.

'I brought it down from where you'd left it, at the roadside. Now, can you ride, if I help you up?' Agricola was already cupping his hands to assist me up into the saddle.

'I can't,' I protested.

'You must.' Agricola's words were sharp, and he paused, before continuing. 'You can do it. I'll help. Now put your foot in here, that's it. Up you go.'

Again I was in place without realising what I was doing. It was easier to allow myself to be directed and ordered, than to think about self-choice. If someone else made the decisions, all I needed to do was obey and trust. Then I could even abdicate responsibility for the increase in my pain. Someone else was doing it to me, and I could concentrate on managing the stabbing, aching and burning.

The journey back to the garrison was a long, drawn-out agony of jolts and movements. I truly don't know how I managed to stay upright.

Cuts on my knee started to ooze blood that trickled down my leg. My head was being pounded by the relentless autumn sun and every stride the horse made, nailed the pain from my ribs along my entire spine. Despite the sun and warm cloak I was wearing, I felt as cold as if I had been soaked in water.

A shout from Agricola as we arrived at the garrison brought three or four slaves running to meet us, and to catch me as I half dismounted, half fell from my horse. With maximum assistance I stumbled to my quarters, finding Gallius there to fuss over me.

I only partially listened to his utterances of concern, disapproval and worry. I was more interested in reaching my bed and the comfort it held. Once there, enveloped in clean sheets, I would be able to succumb to the arms of Morpheus, but Gallius had other ideas. He looked at me, his eyes scanning quickly from my head to my feet, before he turned and issued orders to a hovering slave.

'Tiberius, where have you been?' he said, as he turned his attention back to me. 'I waited for you, but no-one seemed to know where you'd gone, and now look at you. Sit down, so that I can start by sorting out that knee.'

I did as I was told, sitting on the edge of my bed, so near and yet still distant from its promise of relief. A slave brought in a tray that I could see held a bowl, as well as cloths, and other items I hadn't the energy to identify.

Gallius knelt down, saying, 'This cut is full of mud. It should have been cleaned before. How could you let it get in such a state?' He dipped a cloth in the bowl of warm water and started on my knee. 'Don't pull away. I can't clean it properly unless you keep still.'

'It stings,' was my curt reply. I tried to maintain a dignified pose, which was lost on Gallius, as his head was bent, concentrating on my leg.

'That's better. It's bleeding again.' He paused to pick up another cloth, dipping it in the water, before scrubbing at my knee again. 'How did you manage to get yourself in this state? I thought you were going to look after yourself.'

'I went out to see where the second body was found. I'm sure I was being watched. I felt I was being hunted.' My words meant I had his full attention now, as he gazed up at me, his hand arrested in mid movement. Blood ran unheeded down my shin.

'But who? Why? What happened?' Concern, astonishment and surprise ran across his face, each emotion fighting for supremacy.

'I don't really know … I can't recall properly. There was a grove, a druids' grove. I remember some shapes, noises, a chase … but that's about all. Thank the gods that Agricola found me, before …' As I spoke, Gallius bent down again to place some foxglove leaves on the cuts, holding them in place with a soft pad and bandage. While he was doing so, two slaves entered, one laden with pillows and the other carrying a tray with a bowl full of liquid.

I was grateful for the pillows, as it meant I would be able to sleep. Sleep, that was what I longed for, what my body cried out for. Sleep. My eyes started to close, to open with a jerk as Gallius stood up, and I registered the end of his sentence.

'…dangerous. You must go back to Aurelius now.'

'With what?' was my reply. 'I don't have anything definite to give him yet.'

'Of course you have. You've just told me you were chased away from a druids' grove. You must send a message to Aurelius.'

'I'll think about it, when I've had some sleep … or you could do it.'

'I will, when you've eaten this.' Gallius stood rigidly holding the bowl and a spoon.

'No, I'm not hungry. After I've had some sleep.'

My protestations were ignored as Gallius insisted.
'You're not going to sleep until you've eaten, so the sooner
you do, the better.'

I gave in. If Gallius was going to stand there until I'd
had something to eat, it was easier and quicker to obey. I took
a small amount, ready to refuse the rest, but once my body
had been given a meagre mouthful, it demanded more. My
unrealised desire for fluid overtook my need for sleep, and I
drained the bowl. Gallius smiled as he watched me, and then
assisted me to lie down, re-arranging my pillows until I, and
he, were satisfied. I closed my eyes and fell asleep so quickly,
I didn't hear him leave.

When I woke, the evening sun was casting long
shadows, which were eclipsed by those thrown by the lamp in
the corner of the room. Belbo sat on the floor near the door,
playing with a small stick of charcoal. The brazier, from
which it must have fallen, was providing the welcome
warmth. As I shifted my position, a pillow fell to the floor and
the boy jumped up and disappeared.

I stayed where I was. I was warm, relatively clean and
safe. Many of my aches and pains seemed to have eased, and
the sound sleep I had just enjoyed appeared to have cleared
my head.

I had had few dreams, so few that I suspected Gallius had added a little something to the broth I had eaten. I knew that had he asked or suggested that course of action, I would have refused. Of course, had the roles been reversed, I would have insisted he take some medication to aid sleep and recovery. Why is it that we doctors never seem to accept for ourselves, that which we know will be beneficial for others? As I contemplated, Gallius entered.

'Tiberius, I'm glad to see you looking better, almost your old self again. Did you sleep well?'

'Gallius, you know perfectly well that I did. Not only did you drug my food, you also left Belbo on guard to report back to you.'

He grinned and appeared to be thinking of an excuse, when I forestalled him, 'Which is almost exactly what I would have done.' Gallius' grin encompassed his entire face as I continued, 'So what was it you used, to speed my rest and ease my aches?'

'Just your standard sleeping draught, but you said it was not quite what you would have done.' Professional curiosity made a faint frown appear. 'Where did I go wrong?'

I hastened to reassure him. 'No, your choice of medications was fine, but I would have trusted them to do the job. I don't think Belbo was impressed with his duties this afternoon.' I pointed at the floor, and Gallius' eyes followed my finger, to where there were several charcoal designs and shapes, evidence of a dull few hours for a young boy.

Gallius nodded. 'Maybe next time I'll have more faith in my preparations, but now, here's your next dose.'

'I don't suppose it's any good asking you to leave it, and I'll take it later?' I wasn't sure I wanted to sleep again yet. I needed time to think, to consider the events of the last hours and days.

In answer, Gallius picked up the cup and handed it to me, standing over me until I had drained it. The wine tasted sweet, and this time I could distinguish the flavours of poppy, camomile and knapweed.

Day Sixteen

Before I knew it, the dawn was peeking in through a gap in the window shutters. The excess of sleep over the past hours meant I was now wide-awake in both mind and body. The previous doses of poppy that I had imbibed had worn off, a fact I became acutely aware of when, as I moved to sit on the edge of the bed, many of my pains returned. The glow that heralded a new day outside, was just enough for me to find a clean tunic, and to avoid stepping on the sleeping shape of Belbo, snoring gently, curled up in the corner of the room.

Putting my sandals on proved more difficult, and I contemplated waking the boy, but I gritted my teeth and persevered. Movements in my sleep had started to unravel the bandage that held the foxglove leaves in place around my leg. Bending my knee further loosed the dressing, which was now threatening to slip down to my ankle.

I mentally added the leaves to the poppy, knapweed and camomile I wanted to ease my pains again. Melilot was also on my list to aid my remembrance and recollection.

The sound of birds starting their day's song filtered through as I picked up my cloak and stepped out of the door. Moving slowly, with a decided limp, I made my way to the dispensary. I leant against the door, catching my breath, while I pulled out the small group of keys hanging from my belt. Selecting one, I inserted it into the lock. It turned stiffly, the mechanism more used to Gallius' touch. Once inside the room, I opened the shutters, letting the wooden bolt drop with a dull thud. The light from the just-risen sun reached in to chase away shadows. I breathed in the heady mixture of herbs, forgetting for a moment the reason for my visit, but as I twisted away from the window, a sharp twinge reminded me of my mission.

The foxglove leaves were easy to locate and, sitting on a low stool, I untied the wrinkled bandage around my leg. Removing the stained and crumpled dressing, I placed some new leaves over the cuts and rewound the strip of cloth as neatly as I could.

I then started searching amongst the boxes, vials and pots for the knapweed root and camomile oil. The first came to hand quickly and I put a piece to one side, ready to be boiled to produce the decoction I required. Whilst rummaging through the many vials and bottles to find the melilot and camomile oil, I noted some that were empty. I had thought to try some hemlock leaves over my eyes as they were somewhat sore and inflamed, but that was one container that was bare, as was the borage and stonecrop.

The distillation of melilot was on a low shelf, and I had a struggle to reach it. Sitting on the stool, I picked up the bottle and was about to get up when there was a rustle of clothing behind me. I could not turn quickly, and I heard a woman's voice before I saw her form. For a few moments, moments which showed my need for the potions I was seeking, I thought it was Lydia, although I quickly realised that this wishful thinking was not to be.

'Please, I could not wait. Forgive me, but I ...' Her breathy words trailed off as I turned to look at her. 'Oh sir, I did not ... oh please ... I came to ask for help.'

The young woman looked at me with red-rimmed eyes, as she leant against the doorjamb.

I scrambled awkwardly to my feet, feeling that I had left my dignity on the floor by the stool, but the woman in front of me appeared not to notice. Her brown woollen cloak was held tightly, wrapped around her body and her rough hair displayed evidence of haste.

'Why are you here? Why do you need help?' I demanded, receiving no reply.

She half-turned as if to disappear, but something held her in the room. I could see tears starting to trickle down her face, the drops catching the sunlight to sparkle briefly, before they faded and fell.

'What help do you need?' I repeated in a softer voice.

Still there was no reply as she fixed her gaze on me, lifting her hand from where it had grasped her cloak, to roughly wipe her eyes. Her long tunic was creased and showed evidence of heavy wear in the expert patches and mends.

'If you don't tell me, I can't help you. You came here for a reason.' I smiled at her and extended my hands towards her. 'Let me see if I can help.'

She moistened her dry lips, and then spoke, 'My son, he's not well. I thought, I needed ...' The words tumbled out, then trailed off as she ended with a barely audible, 'Please don't let him die.'

'Why do you think he'll die?' I asked, 'What's the matter with him?'

She wiped her nose with the back of one hand, before saying, 'He can't breathe very well, and he feels so hot. Hamia said I shouldn't come, but I couldn't help it. I couldn't wait.' She started to back away, easing her body through the doorway.

Despite my own aches, the pain that emanated from the figure in front of me meant I could not turn her away. I was trained to help others, and if I walked away now, the distress I had failed to address would always be with me. However, it was obvious to me, though not to her, that I was not the one she had anticipated finding here. I didn't want her to flee which is what I felt her actions might be, should she discover I was the surgeon rather than a mere dispenser of cures. If she ran away I would be totally unable to catch her, and her son might suffer because of it.

'I'm sure I can help you.' I pointed at the array of shelves behind me. 'I have some skill with herbs and healing.' The wary look on her face led me to further justify myself. 'I wouldn't be in here otherwise, would I? Now, why don't you show me, your son, did you say?'

She nodded, and turned to lead the way out of the door, pausing to allow me to replace the wooden shutters on the windows, and lock the door. These actions appeared to strengthen her shaky faith in me, as she smiled briefly. She then set off at a fast walk, a pace I had difficulty keeping up with. Twice I had to ask her to stop, and I certainly had no extra breath left for conversation. It soon became obvious that we were heading for the village, making for a building facing onto the main thoroughfare. There were few others moving about, as it was still early, although there were signs that activity would soon bring life to the collection of dwellings. I could smell the aroma of hot charcoal and fresh bread. Tavern doors were pushed open, with a thud, and the stale dregs of wine flung out to sink into the mud.

My companion suddenly slipped down a narrow alleyway, barely wide enough to allow us passage. The wooden walls on either side blocked the light, and I only realised the woman had stopped when I walked into her. She opened a door and we entered an unexpectedly bright room. I was out of breath yet again, and leant against the wall, feeling the rough texture of sawn wood. My perusal of the area was interrupted by a strident call.

'Who's that? Why did you bring him? Where's the other one, the young one?'

As I located the source, my erstwhile companion answered, 'He was in the room that you told me to go to. He said he would help.' She took three or four paces over to where an older woman sat. 'How is he? Is he any better?'

She knelt down by a bed, stroking the hair of a young boy who lay there. As my breathing eased from the exertion of walking, I could hear a harsh, regular rasp emanate from the child. I went to step forward, but the older woman blocked my path.

'Who are you? You're not the usual one. I don't know you.'

'Hamia, he said he would help. I trust him.' The voice of the younger woman appeared before I could answer, but Hamia was not convinced. Standing in front of me, she had to tilt her head back to look at me. With one hand on her ample hip, she punctuated her sentences by jabbing her right index finger at my chest.

'Where's the young one? What can you do? I've not seen you before?'

'Hamia, I came to help the boy. Please let me see what I can do.'

Hamia didn't move except to cross her arms.

A lock of white hair, with traces of dark, fell over her face, and she brushed it back, tucking it behind her ear, without taking her eyes off me. A fit of coughing from the corner caused us both to look over.

'Please, let me see him.' Without waiting for a reply, I gently pushed past Hamia to sit down on the edge of the bed. A boy of about ten lay there, his face flushed. The dark hair that the young woman had been stroking was plastered to his head. At my approach the mother stood up to allow me room to examine her son.

'What's his name?' I asked, as I lifted up his hand, feeling for his pulse, rapid under my fingers.

'Rufus, his name is Rufus. Will he recover? Can you make him better?'

'I'll try. And your name is?' Putting down Rufus' hand, I gently palpated round his neck.

'Melita.'

'Now Melita, what treatment have you given him so far?'

The reply came from Hamia, 'A mustard poultice to the feet, of course, to draw his fever. Some lungwort, mullein and balm for his breathing.'

Her voice carelessly tossed the words over, almost daring me to deny the effectiveness of her care. I nodded in confirmation and approval as I gently moved my fingers over Rufus' soft abdomen, while he lay semi-slumbering.

'You're very skilled with herbs, Hamia. Melita did well when she called you.'

'I was the natural choice. Everyone comes to me. Few others know the secrets of healing like I do.'

Moving my attention back to the boy's throat, I depressed his jaw, so I could see inside his mouth. 'But even with your skills, he does not recover.'

'I wasn't allowed enough time. Melita wanted instant results. If she'd given me another day, I would have driven the fever from him.' Hamia's words sounded in my ear as her shadow fell across the sick child. 'But no, she insisted on asking the one at the garrison to help. Maybe next time I'll be too busy to come, since she doesn't trust me.'

I only half listened to her mutterings as I concentrated on the breath sounds the boy made. 'Hamia, if Melita had not called at the garrison, there may not have been a next time.'

On hearing this, a sob escaped from Melita, who pushed me out of the way so she could clasp her son's form to her.

As she sat there, rocking forwards and back, I continued, 'His condition is serious, but not beyond saving, and to do that, I need your help.' There was clearly no use in sending Melita, and I hadn't the energy for a further walk yet. The distance from the garrison here had almost exhausted me, and there was no way I could get there, and back, again.

'I want you to go to the garrison and ...' I paused, sending a silent prayer to any and all gods that my hunch was correct. 'When Melita brought me here, you were expecting someone else. Do you know the other one? Would you recognise him?'

I almost held my breath, despite my own pain, as she contemplated her answer. I saw her eyes narrow, before she looked away from me. When finally her words appeared, they seemed to bridge a great gulf. Suddenly we were both on the same side, that of healing.

'Yes, I know him, but only by sight. He never told us his name.'

'You must find him, and tell him to bring the wooden case of instruments that is in the infirmary office. Also I need some poppy syrup.'

I paused, trying to pull my reluctant memory into focus. Why was I finding it so hard to concentrate? Why was I here? What was I trying to do? My voice sounded again, almost to my surprise, 'Poppy syrup, Damask rose and elecampine. Mind he brings the syrup of root, not the dried elecampine. Tell him I need them, and him, here, as quickly as possible.'

Instead of donning her cloak and leaving, Hamia stood still looking out of the window and frowning. 'It's daylight, sir. I ... we ... he said never to come in daylight. It would be dangerous, and he would have to stop. Only at dawn, or evening, were we to go to him, and then only if very urgent. Never at this time. Usually he would meet us, here in the town.'

I glanced round the room at the few possessions it contained. There was nothing which I could use to write with, or on. Hamia was right. She would find it difficult to openly enter the garrison in daylight, whereas the comings and goings of a cloaked woman at night-time would easily be given a different interpretation. As I thought, I suddenly realised the answer lay in my own hands. I could not go myself, but I could give credence to Hamia's errand.

Slipping my seal ring from my finger, I handed it to her, saying, 'Take this. If anyone stops you, show them this, and say you have an urgent message for Gallius, at the infirmary. Say that Tiberius Sextus Valerius has sent you. You'll recognise Gallius, he's the man you've seen before. Now go, please.'

Clutching her promise of unhindered entry, she wrapped herself in her cloak, and gave me one last gaze full of fear and courage. Then the door closed behind her, and I was left with the quietly weeping woman and the sick child.

'Master, Hamia said you needed me.' Gallius put the instrument case down on a low table. Opening it, he made a careful study of the contents he knew so well, and continued, 'I hadn't expected to find you here.' His gaze swept the room, encompassing everything except me.

'We can discuss the reasons I am here later. Right now, it is Rufus who needs our attention.'

Gallius looked over at the bed where I was sat. Melita had laid the boy back down and was now sitting holding his unresisting hand.

'But from what Hamia said, it appears to be a simple case of fever. Why...?' Gallius completed his unfinished question by indicating the case he had brought. 'The boy developed a chill after being out in the rain. Surely that requires a poultice to draw the fever, and a cure such as Hamia has already given, not these.'

Hamia stood near the door, watching us both, as she slowly removed her cloak. When she did speak, her words were directed at me. 'What do you intend? These things, what are they for?' She edged round the room to the bed, keeping the maximum distance between herself and the table which held the case.

Mentally cursing myself for having come on this mission without making adequate provision for my own pain relief, I levered myself to my feet. 'Hamia, Rufus has a fever, that is clear to us all, but I must remove the source of the fever, otherwise he may well die. I need your help, your assistance, please.' I could hear Melita renew her weeping, but my attention was focussed on Hamia.

Nervously she nodded, 'What must I do, sir?'

'Right now, I need some boiling water, and then I'll need you to look after Melita, so that Gallius and I can treat the boy.'

233

Again she nodded, and smiled reassurance back at me.
'Melita, we need some hot water. There's a little here, but we
need more.' Her voice had regained the strident edge I had
originally heard, which spurred the younger woman into
movement. 'You must get some more from the well. Now!'

She held out a leather bucket, which Melita reluctantly
took, with a look that spoke of surprise at her own actions.
When there was no further movement from her, Hamia took
her by the shoulders and almost pushed her out of the room. I
could hear voices for some moments, before Hamia re-entered
the room alone. She then fiercely coaxed the fire into a
brighter blaze, causing the water in the pot to jump and steam.

Meanwhile I took some of the poppy infusion, and,
sitting on the edge of the boy's bed, eased open his mouth,
and dripped some liquid onto his tongue. I then stroked his
throat, to encourage him to swallow, repeating my actions
three or four times. When I felt he had taken enough, I moved
back to the table, where I selected several instruments from
the case, handing them to Gallius, who briefly immersed the
ends in the water. Hamia, Gallius and I then approached the
bed, where Rufus lay in sacrificial stillness, his sterterous
breathing providing a counterpoint to the intermittent crackle
of the fire.

'Hamia, could you hold his head still … that's fine, now just make sure that his mouth is open … Gallius, could you come round here … no, further over, otherwise you block the light, and then hold this here. Pass me the clamp and, Hamia, try not to let his head move … Now, Gallius, can you then hold this clamp tight, that's it.'

As the swollen, inflamed mass at the back of the boy's throat was held firm, I gently cut it away, finally removing it totally. As I did so, the harsh rasp emanating from the child, became a soft snore. At that moment, the door re-opened and Melita stood there. After a moment of hesitation, she dropped the leather bucket, drenching one side of her cloak and tunic, and sending water splashing onto the earth floor. An attempt to reach her son was thwarted by Hamia who caught hold of her, abandoning the boy to our care.

'Should I release the clamp yet, Master?' Gallius' voice was soft, as if he dared not disturb the child.

I wrapped some soft cloth around the end of one of the probes, and used it to mop the excess blood from Rufus' mouth, before answering Gallius' question. 'Very slowly, and be ready to tighten it again, should the bleeding become profuse.'

As his slightly shaking hand gently released the pressure, notch by notch, I was pleased to see that the wound held, and appeared to have sealed. He withdrew the clamp from the child's mouth and laid it down. Behind me I could hear voices hissing and the rustle of clothing. Melita managed to break Hamia's hold, and threw herself at the bed, pushing Gallius out of the way. The relaxed breathing of Rufus appeared to reassure her, and her shoulders dropped as her own expirations slowed and deepened. The shy smile she flashed at Gallius seemed wasted, as he collected together the instruments, washing them and re-packing the case.

'Please, sir, Rufus,' Hamia approached Gallius, and waved an arm in the general direction of the bed. 'What care does he need now? Will you return to look after him?'

In reply Gallius looked at me. I still stood near the foot of the bed, and I could feel the ache in my chest settle deep into my inner core. I gazed back at him, with bleary eyes, as if through seawater. I knew I was being asked a question, but I was unable to formulate any answer or even to comprehend the meaning.

'Master.'

The voice I heard came from Gallius' lips, but it seemed too far away for my ears to recognise it.

I sat down heavily on the end of the bed. I felt as if standing and thinking and speaking, all at the same time, would overwhelm me. The noise that I could hear then coalesced into words, understandable words, meaningful words. Words that required attention.

'… care does Rufus need now?'

'I'm sorry, Gallius, what did you say?'

'How should Rufus be looked after now? Is there anything in particular that needs to be done?'

I tried to think logically. 'No food, only drink for three days. Not hot, only cold water. You must keep a check on the boy's throat, and send word immediately, day or night, if any bleeding occurs. Keep him in bed, and continue this,' as I indicated the two bottles on the table, 'three times a day, for three days. He will need more poppy syrup to make sure he sleeps.'

Poppy, that was what I needed now, but that which Gallius had brought had only been sufficient to sedate the boy.

I stood up and, on heavy limbs, crossed the room to the door, supporting myself against one rough upright as I fumbled with the catch.

The simple mechanism eluded my surgeon's fingers for several moments, moments when I thought I was trapped in this room for ever.

'Come, Gallius, we must return to the garrison. Other patients need our attention,' and I needed to rest in a drug induced stupor. Behind me I heard Gallius talking to Hamia, his voice hurried, his words following each other with barely a pause between them. I finally mastered the skill involved in opening the door, and stepped out into the narrow alleyway, heading for the slit of brightness and activity I could discern. Gallius caught up with me and attempted to support me, but I resisted. I would not be shown up as some invalid to be escorted to his dotage.

Summoning all my depleted reserves of pride and strength, I used them to brace my back and shoulders. Instead of sagging muscles and drooping joints, I held my head high, pulling the rest of my body up, and in this way I stepped out into the bustle and jostle of the daily activities of the village.

The dullness of thought that I had felt earlier was partially eased by more rest, some wine and one of my own potions. I tried reading, but the words would not stay still upon the page, and the volume seemed too heavy to hold.

Instead I lay back, with eyes closed, considering what I should do about Gallius. I was too tired and muddled to scold him and in some ways his actions were admirable, in extending the facilities of the garrison to benefit local villagers - but not every one would see it in that light. I was an army surgeon, contracted to provide services primarily for the soldiers where I was stationed. The dispensary was there to enable me to carry out those duties, and while I had considerable leeway in how I treated my patients, that did not include unauthorised disposal of state property.

The dispensary, and all its contents, legally belonged to the army, and I had a responsibility to protect and maintain those resources. And here was Gallius, who I had trusted to oversee and manage the dispensary, letting stocks run down, apparently giving cures away, and all for no discernible benefits.

As I sat thinking about it, I felt disappointed and betrayed. Was that because he had not justified the faith I had in him? Or was it envy and jealousy I felt, that Gallius had worked on his own initiative, in seeking out knowledge from local healers, whereas I had sat back, content with my expertise?

Would I have felt this way if I had found the leaves I had been looking for that morning? Had the fall, and blow to the head, caused me more confusion that I would admit to? Who could say?

A thought pushed its way into the morass of feelings. No soldiers had suffered as a result of this sideline, so there probably hadn't been any harm done. Surely it was better to forget the past and move forward to utilise this new avenue of learning. But no. Punishment and retribution must follow. Gallius had been wrong, had been doing wrong, had known he was doing wrong, although maybe from the best intentions. As I was pondering on his future, Gallius announced that my meal was ready, and from the fragrant smells drifting in, I could tell he had made a special effort.

I sat down, ready to eat, my elbows supported on the wooden table in front of me. An aroma of roasted pigeon in vine leaves lifted from the plate and mingled with coriander and aniseed. A bowl of olives sat where my hand would automatically reach, tempting me with their plump shininess. Gallius stretched out to refill my goblet, adjusting its position close to where my hand could easily grasp it. He then carefully replaced the jug on the table, without it making a sound.

He said very little, other than, 'Master, I sometimes exchange the herbs in the dispensary with some that grow locally, that Hamia knows. In this way, knowledge is shared and expanded, and we both benefit. Sometimes Hamia asks if I would see someone, if their condition surpasses her skills.' He stayed standing in front of me, his eyes examining the floor in great detail.

I had already heard Gallius say the same words three times so far, in various arrangements. The rehearsed feel to his voice was not surprising. I sighed and leant back in my chair, wincing slightly as its firmness met my ribs. Picking up an olive, I slipped it into my mouth, relishing the smooth, oily taste. Gallius stood the other side of the table, in an attitude that he must have thought would appeal to the forgiving part of my nature. Maybe he knew me too well? Maybe we knew each other too well? He must guess that I would be reluctant to hand him over to the garrison commander for punishment. Our relationship was too long and deep for me to easily take that step. Something we both knew.

Sitting here now, I was replete, satisfied and almost benign. I could easily have admonished Gallius, telling him off with a request not to repeat the actions, but I knew in my heart that he had been doing far more than barter and the occasional consultation.

Maybe with hindsight, I would be able to analyse my feelings better, but not now, not here in this room.

Finding the goblet at my hand, I lifted it, letting the rich fluid swirl around my mouth, appreciating the fruity fullness, before swallowing. Looking at Gallius over the lip of the cup, I reached a decision.

'Gallius, come and sit down.'

At least that brought his attention away from the floor as he raised wary and wide eyes to mine. 'Sit down, now,' I repeated. 'I'm getting a crick in my neck looking up at you.'

Gallius lifted a chair to set it by the table and sat down, upright and symmetrical.

'Hamia seems very knowledgeable and skilled in healing.' I said.

A slow nod was elicited from across the table.

'How did you first meet her?'

I took another long sip of my wine, and as I swallowed, Gallius mimicked my action. But his mouth was dry and he ran his tongue over slightly parted lips. I pushed the dish of olives over to him, the bottom of the pottery bowl rasping on the wooden surface.

'She sells cures and ointments, in the market. I met her when I needed some supplies.' Gallius' voice was cracked and dry. 'You've always said we should make use of locally available herbs.'

It was true that I had always encouraged Gallius in the procurement and use of native plants that had healing properties. Why should I now be annoyed that he had continued and expanded that process on his own initiative? In many ways, I had no right to accuse him of anything wrong, except that there were no stocks in the dispensary of certain herbs.

'She seems a good person to know. Have you learnt much from her?' As I spoke, I sensed rather than saw Gallius start.

Leaning back in the chair, I studied the ceiling, before sweeping my gaze round to the open window, where the colours showed that the sun was just setting. A soft breeze caused the door curtain to swing with a gentle flap.

'Yes, Master. She's taught me several new cures and ointments.' Gallius' voice was still precise, but his tone was becoming less monotone. 'The poultice that I used on Carinius' foot was one of hers.'

'And I thought it was my skill in stitching that made the difference,' I remarked, dryly.

Gallius' eyes widened, and he dropped the olive he had just lifted. 'No, I didn't mean that.' The fruit rolled unevenly across the table to fall onto the floor. 'Of course it was your expertise, all I meant was I ... I tried to enhance your work by ensuring that the wound healed quickly. That's all. I didn't mean to criticise your work.'

I smiled at his discomfort, knowing that I could never be angry or annoyed with him for long. We had been through too much and been together too long for that. I did a few mental calculations, and, to my surprise, found that some twenty-five years had passed since that day when I walked through the slave market. The hot, dry Athens sun had been remorseless, beating wave after wave of intense heat.

My wife had indicated her need for a new girl, to help with our two sons. Once that item had been selected and purchased, I had continued wandering, idly viewing the different merchandise on offer. I paused every so often, long enough to note the different skin textures and colours, brief enough not to become entangled in the mire of negotiation.

Did these slaves look at us, their prospective owners, with as much interest as we observed them? Did they mentally mark out their preferences? Were they disappointed or pleased with the choices that had been made without their involvement?

I fancied that this one stood taller, when a rich lady walked past. That one slumped down, to appear aged in front of a galley captain. Or had their spirits been so broken that they accepted any lot that came their way?

While I was thus musing, I found I had stopped in front of a group, who lacked the dark hair and bronzed skin that spoke of sunny climes. My attention was caught by a boy of nine or ten, whose alert manner and bright eyes made him stand out from the rest. Even though I had not been specifically looking for a future assistant, I felt the lad in front of me had the potential I would be seeking. And so on a whim I bought him. Now a quarter of a century later, we were sat opposite each other, in a land neither of us had imagined would become part of the Empire. A cold, often wet country, far from those sunny shores of our first meeting. A land that was becoming less foreign, where we were both likely to spend many, if not all, of our remaining years.

I picked up some more olives, letting them ooze their reminders of sunshine into my mouth. 'We've been together a long time.'

Gallius looked up, lines creasing his brow, as he nodded slowly.

'How often have you been treating the local villagers?'
I took some more of my wine, letting the flavours mingle
together.

'Fairly often,' he replied, watching me as he took some
olives, eating them one by one.

'Which means very, doesn't it?' I didn't wait for his
confirmatory nod or attempted denial as I continued, 'Is that
what you were doing in the village the other day, just after
Memno had his attack?'

Gallius glanced at me, biting the edge of his lower lip,
and nodded slowly, his eyes watchful and wary. 'How did
you know I was there?'

'I saw you.' I lifted the jug to replenish my cup. 'I was
sitting in the tavern, and I could see you.'

'I had an urgent message. Usually I would only meet
people in the early morning or evening.' He smiled brightly
at me, as if to gain credit with his words. 'That way, I could
be sure that no-one in the garrison would suffer from lack of
attention. But that morning I had a request that couldn't wait,
so I slipped out. I didn't think anyone had missed me.'

At least now I had an explanation for Gallius' strange
behaviour of a few days previously. 'What payment basis
have you been using?' I asked.

'Usually, it was in exchange for new herbs and cures.'

'And the rest of the time?'

Gallius paused before answering, his eyes apparently studying the grain on the table in detail. 'They will pay me, when they can,' was his eventual reply.

'It's as good a way as any to build up a practice.' I lifted my hand to prevent any interruptions, and continued, 'You know I've been with the army for twenty years now. It's time I retired, from the army at least.'

I thought about all the countries and regions I had lived in during that time. This was as pleasant a place as any to settle down, certainly better than dusty Judea or the baking temperatures of Athens. My sons and their wives were here, and I had hopes of further grandchildren, especially from my younger son. 'You know that I've always said when I do, you would be free, and since you've already started to become known in the area, you would do well to set up your practice here.'

A smile started to define itself around the edges of Gallius' mouth. 'I really feel you're too young to consider retirement yet.'

'I need to clear up this business about Lucius first, but then I shall seriously consider it. Mind you, remember what I said about those girls.' I could see a blank look come into his eyes, as I enlightened him, with a grin. 'Big breasts and wide hips are much better than a pretty face. You'll need a son to carry on your business.'

His smile was fully formed now, as he replied, 'I shall consider your advice, and reserve the right to name my firstborn after you.'

'As your patron, I shall expect it.' I flinched as a twinge from my ribs reminded me of my concerns over the dispensary.

Gallius must have noted my changed expression, as he asked, 'Are you all right? Do you need anything?'

I shook my head, and drank the rest of my wine, cradling the glass in my hands. 'When I was in the dispensary this morning, I noticed that some of the boxes were empty.'

Gallius was quick to respond, 'Yes, I know. I was intending to refill them today or tomorrow. There had been many illnesses and injuries in the village recently ...' His words petered out as I waved my hand.

'I can understand the borage and stonecrop, from what you've just said, but why is there no hemlock?'

'That can't be right? I have used a lot of borage and stonecrop, to stay the fevers,' he shook his head vigorously, 'but I haven't used hemlock for some months. I had no idea it was empty. Could someone else have taken it?'

'But how?' I asked, even as I was considering the idea. I was fairly sure that Corolius had been poisoned with a dose of hemlock. Could it have come from my own dispensary? But no, the room was always kept locked, as there were far too many dangerous drugs in there for it to be otherwise. And why would anyone at the garrison want to poison Corolius? There were other places to obtain the plant, not least the local woods.

'There are only two keys. You have one, and I have the other,' I said, as I produced mine from its attachment at my belt.

Gallius fumbled at his waist for a moment before holding up his iron bounty to match mine. As I gazed at the dull metal, I yawned, suddenly aware of how long it had been since I had used my key to unlock the dispensary that morning.

An insistent knock at the door intruded into our discussion.

Every fibre of my being wanted to ignore it, so that I could once again sleep even though it was still early. Even my doctor's training and need for response at whatever hour was necessary, was subdued. Gallius got to his feet and walked over to see who required attention. In the few moments of muffled speech that transpired, I pushed back my chair and stood up, ready to retire for the night.

My anticipation of a deep sleep was delayed, as Gallius re-entered the room, closely followed by a tall man in a thick cloak, spattered with mud. For a few moments I felt that I was unable to think properly, as I sat back down in my seat. Victor and Lachlan had only recently left. They weren't due back at the garrison for some weeks, so why was Lachlan standing in my doorway, and where was Victor?

Gallius, too, seemed stunned, and not totally sure of himself. 'You need to come and see.'

I sagged against the back support of the chair. Surely Gallius or Victor could not expect me to look at merchandise at this hour. I started to wave my hands in denial, when Lachlan strode to my side. Taking hold of my arm he pulled me to my feet, and pointed me at the door. The dried blood on the side of his face, from a wound three or four days old, suddenly caught my attention.

With a sense of foreboding, I asked, 'What do I need to see?' Somehow I knew it would not be beautiful blue glass bowls, cooking pots and pans or thick cloaks from Gaul, that would keep out the wind and rain.

The reply came from Lachlan, who uttered a series of incomprehensible sounds from his mouth, given meaning by the tears running down his face. He wiped one scabbed hand across his eyes, and pointed to the door again.

I went outside, to see the large covered wagon standing at the infirmary door. Shadows jumped and skittered across the ground from the lamp that Gallius held. As if frustrated by my tardiness, Lachlan pushed past me, reaching in through the canvas opening, to pull out a large shape. Staggering slightly, from both the bulk and weight, he hoisted it up, until it was cradled in his arms. Again the sounds came from his mouth, and at last I understood.

Standing to one side, I motioned him into the infirmary, opening the door of the operating room so he could enter. He laid his burden down on the table, where it lay at a slight angle. Lachlan's breathing was laboured, whether from the effort or sorrow, I could not tell.

He looked over his shoulder to where I was standing in the doorway, and reached out his arm to me. His other hand was hovering over the concealed shape, and his eyes directed their gaze to me, then the table, to me, the table.

Gallius brought the lamp in, which merely highlighted the sorrow on Lachlan's face. I stepped up to him, standing beside him as he un-peeled the blanket from the body, to once again display the sight this room was coming to know. A headless corpse, dressed in a long white tunic, stretched tightly over the distended abdomen. I lifted my hands to my head, rubbing my face and eyes. The shadows from the corners of the room were invading my mind, making my thinking dull, my eyes ache and my body weary. I could do nothing, but turn away. I would be more refreshed in the morning. Hands would be steadier, minds would be sharper, eyes would be more alert.

Lachlan must have misinterpreted my actions, for he caught hold of my arm, refusing to allow me to walk away. I looked up into his face and gently disentangled his fingers from my tunic sleeve. He looked many years older than he had just five days ago.

I shook my head, saying, 'I can't do anything tonight, Lachlan. It'll have to wait until morning, when there's more light.' Another few hours would make no difference to a corpse a few days old. 'Gallius, would you arrange for Lachlan to sleep in the infirmary tonight.'

'Of course,' Gallius replied, and with that I moved my feet and legs, which propelled me towards the door, and my bed.

Day Seventeen

I did indeed, feel better when I woke the next morning, but at the same time, I felt worse. My mind was alert, my eyesight was steady and sharp and my body had shed its weariness. But alongside these was running the thought that if I'd been quicker at solving Lucius' murder, then maybe I wouldn't also be investigating a third case. The second body had obviously been dead for some weeks before being found, but could I have prevented …

I paused. I was assuming that the body brought in by Lachlan was Victor. Part of me hoped it was, not that I wished his death, far from it. But something had happened to Victor, for Lachlan to think he had carried his partner from the wagon. I would be certain of the identity very soon. Could I have prevented this murder? Should I have warned him in stronger terms?

But if we all hid away, fearing to go out, scared to conduct our business or meet with friends, then surely the murderers would have gained. They would have killed our liberty and taken away our rights and we would have allowed them to do it.

I walked over to the infirmary, to find Gallius already there.

'Lachlan slept in the second room, Master.' His voice was low, as if he feared to wake those around us.

I nodded to him and made my way down the corridor, lifting up the curtain at the appropriate doorway. I could see Lachlan sat on a bed, his back towards me as he gazed out of the window.

'I going to examine …' I paused. I had to assume that Lachlan knew who he had brought in. '… Victor's body. Did you want to be present?' When there was no response or acknowledgement, I repeated my question. 'Lachlan, did you want to watch when I look at Victor?' Still he sat, his back to me, silent and unmoving. As I walked into the room, my foot caught the leg of a chair, scraping it across the floor, but it was not until I reached him, and touched his shoulder, that Lachlan responded.

'How are you this morning?' When I spoke this time, he looked at me, before standing up, and pointing towards the door. I nodded, feeling tears welling up in my eyes. How could I have been so blind as to not realise why Victor always did the talking? Lachlan didn't speak, because Lachlan couldn't speak. He was deaf, living in a private world of silence, and the one person who he had communicated with, was lying dead on a table in the operating room.

And now I was once again standing in that operating room, with a body draped in a long white tunic in front of me. I needed to establish that it was Victor, and find any clues as to his killer. Lachlan might be able to give us some information, but it would be scanty and difficult to obtain. Gallius had already removed the blanket that had been wrapped round the victim, and was stood on the far side of the table, Lachlan at his side. Taking a deep breath, I cut away the tunic, already torn and ripped in places, revealing the bloated body. A quick look around the neck confirmed what I already thought – the head had been severed with one blow from a sharp blade, giving a clean cut.

'How long ago do you think it happened? Lachlan, when did he die?' Gallius words were directed initially at me, then at his companion.

'Gallius,' I said, shaking my head, 'Lachlan won't be able to tell us anything. He can't hear anything.'

Gallius' mouth and eyes momentarily widened in surprise. 'What, nothing?'

'I think he's totally deaf, and dumb.' I looked up at Lachlan, who was gazing at the table, as I continued, 'So we'll have to see what this body can tell us about his murderers.'

Gallius swallowed, then repeated his earlier question, 'So how long has he been dead?'

I responded with my own query, 'What do you think?'

Gallius looked down, laying his hand on the cold flesh. He lifted one lifeless arm, now free from the enclosing garment, bending and straightening the elbow, wrist and hand. Moving to the end of the table, he lifted a leg, heavy and cumbersome, flexing the knee and hip, before replacing it on the table.

'The stiffness of death appears to have gone, so that would be at least two or three days.' He traced his finger down the greenish purple blotches and streaks that clearly marked the abdomen, the trunk and limbs, less so. 'The abdomen is distended, but then Victor was …' He paused, apparently searching for the correct words. 'Was well built.'

'Victor may have been on the large side, but he was not as fat as this. The decomposition of the body has started, which means he probably died four, maybe five days ago.' I thought back to the last time I saw him, lying on this same table, only six days ago. His amulet had not protected him for very long. 'But Gallius, we are ahead of ourselves. How do we know this is Victor?'

Gallius lifted his hands. 'Of course it's Victor. Lachlan brought him in. Who else could it be?'

'Let's suppose we don't know who it is. What about the body? What information is it giving us about its identity?' I could see Gallius trying to switch from concerned friend to impartial investigator.

'Marks, scars, injuries to the body. The height and weight. The condition of the hands, and also the feet.' Gallius looked over at me.

'Carry on. Are there any injuries?'

He looked over the torso and limbs again, peering at different aspects, before saying, 'It's difficult to be certain. The blotches tend to mask everything, but I think there are bruises to both upper arms, here,' as he pointed to an area just above the elbow, 'and here.'

I lifted up the dead man's arm, looking at his hands. The podgy digits were bruised, with broken skin around the joints. Gallius saw what I was looking at, and came round to my side of the table. 'Look,' I said. 'You can see indentations in the fingers where his rings have been, and the damage caused probably when they were ripped off.' Gallius and I looked at each other. Were we both sharing a memory of seeing the sun glinting off the gems that adorned Victor's hands?

'Of course,' I said, 'there is one way of knowing for certain whether this is Victor or not, and that's to see his back.'

Gallius started to lift the bulk of the abdomen, ready to turn him over, when I stopped him.

'I think you might find he'd roll off the table. I only need to see his back.' I looked at Lachlan. Reaching over, I took one of his hands, and placed it at Victor's shoulder. I then positioned his other hand on the body's pelvis. Lifting my own hands up and away from me, I hoped Lachlan would understand. He did, pulling the corpse towards him, while his own body prevented it from rolling too far. I bent down and quickly found what I was looking for, the site of the boil I had so recently lanced. As I straightened up, Lachlan laid Victor down again, with a reverential tenderness.

Gallius picked up the blanket, and laid it over Victor, while I indicated to Lachlan that we should move to my quarters. On the way I pondered the difficult task of eliciting information, possibly vital information, from this man who could neither hear my questions nor utter a response.

Once we were seated, Gallius brought some wine. I certainly felt I needed something to wash away the taste of death. Lachlan drained his cup in one, as soon as I handed it to him.

'Don't go, Gallius, I might need you,' I said, as he appeared to head for the door. He turned round and sat down next to me, and I leaned across the table to Lachlan, wondering how to begin. He seemed as eager to tell his story, as we were to listen. Standing up, he began to act out the events of the previous six days.

Pointing towards the infirmary, and then in the direction of the main gate, he sat on the chair, bouncing up and down, while his fists were held out in front of him. Then he stopped, lifted one hand to his eyes, and peered ahead. Standing up, he made some shapes in the air, with his arms, before bending down to kneel on the floor. Reaching out, he lifted an armful of air, moving it to one side. Still kneeling, he jabbed a finger at the back of his head, keeling over to lie prostrate on the ground.

Clambering back onto his feet, he went round the room, peering in corners and under furniture. As we swivelled round in our chairs to watch, he stood in the centre of the room, shrugging his shoulders. Suddenly he pointed, and despite ourselves, both Gallius and I looked at the blank space he indicated. Again he collected together a bundle of nothing, carrying it back to his chair, before repeating his bobbing movement. Finally he pointed over at the infirmary and then at me, jabbing his finger towards my chest repeatedly, before banging his fist down on the table.

Reaching out his hand for the jug of wine, he poured a generous amount into his cup. Drinking it down in one go, he suddenly hurled the vessel at the wall, where it clattered to lie unheeded on the floor. In apparent frustration, the chair followed, bouncing off the plaster. Lachlan's hands opened and closed a few times, and then he was gone, the door slamming against the wall as he went.

'Gallius, make sure someone follows him.' I suspected his destination was the tavern, where he could drink away some of the memories he had so graphically described. 'If he goes to the tavern, then make sure Barris knows what has happened.' The landlord knew Lachlan and Victor, and would look after him. He, too, had been one of their customers.

As Gallius rapidly left the room, I replaced the cup on the table, dabbing at the small stain that was left on the wall. The chair was lying in three pieces, which I collected together. Maybe the carpenter could repair it, but it was more likely that a replacement would be required. As I was thus occupied, I must have missed the knock at the door. It was only when Gallius spoke, that I realised I was not alone.

'A messenger, from Aurelius,' he announced, before withdrawing, and leaving the two of us alone.

The courier stretched out his hand, which contained a scroll. I took it, resting the papyrus on the table as I fumbled to open it. For a short time I was bemused by the response, before recalling that Gallius had written, on my behalf, after my accident.

'But how?' I read the words again. 'What can have happened?' I threw the scroll down onto the table, where it unrolled, finally flopping to the floor. If this was the reply, I could not understand it. I was unable to reconcile the message it contained with my own experience, and was, therefore uncaring of its fate. The messenger who had brought it, slowly bent down and picked it up. He replaced it carefully on the table and then stood gently to attention. I sat drumming my fingers on the wood, as if I had the power, by mere sounds and thoughts, to change the content of the scroll.

'Is there a reply, sir?' The words slipped through the air, settling gently in my brain.

'Yes … no …' What reply could I possibly give? I wanted to say that there was something drastically wrong, that the message must have been false, that I had read the words incorrectly. I picked up the smooth papyrus to peruse the contents again, but the words stubbornly refused to rearrange themselves.

The messenger stood, silent and impassive, while I decided. I could see why he was entrusted with Aurelius' errands. Information, questions, requests, demands, all the paraphernalia of bureaucracy that would come from the office of the law, all would be delivered by this man. He had the knack of making himself appear part of the furniture, merging into the background. He could be comfortable and reassuring or sharp and insistent as the situation required, and able to report back all that had transpired.

'No, there's no reply … No, wait. Yes, there is.' I struggled for words that eluded me. 'Tell Aurelius that I have read his message, but would assure him that the…' I hesitated. I wanted to convey a communication that would be understood by the recipient, but that would not have meaning to others. 'Tell him, his experience differed from mine.'

'Yes, sir.' The messenger inclined his head, and left the room. I was in turmoil as once again I picked up the scroll. Two days previously a letter had been sent to Aurelius, advising him of my discovery of the druids' grove, and its likely link to the death of Lucius, and the unknown Roman. As expected, Aurelius had sent soldiers to investigate, and they had found nothing. Nothing, except a clearing in the woods that may possibly have been used as a sacred grove at some point, many months, if not years, ago. Nothing to indicate any recent use. Nothing, except a fine crop of mushrooms that may been mistaken in the half-light for more sinister objects.

In frustration I threw the entire parchment across the room, where it hit the wall, and dropped to lie like a slumbering snake. With part of my ire dispersed, I could think more clearly. And think I must. I felt as if the allotted time in which I would be able to solve this mystery was almost up. We doctors know that when the patient has reached crisis point, then the time in which a cure may be effected is limited. I was aware of my patient, the resolution of these murders, slipping away through my fingers.

I had been so sure of my conclusions, but now I must start again from the beginning. This avenue of exploration appeared to lead me into a stagnant backwater, but I felt sure my direction was correct. Was there an alternative solution? If so, what could it be? Lucius had been beheaded, as had Victor, and an unknown man. Two were Roman, the other was presumed to be, having been wrapped in a toga. That much was definite. They had been killed within a short space of time, the last two months. The first bodies had been found in locations, which were close enough to indicate a connection. I had no idea where Victor's body had been dumped. So far I was on certain ground, but then my thoughts started to sink into a quagmire of doubt.

There were strong rumours of a cult of druids who had gained strength in the area, with an active convert within the garrison. There was talk of local support for the revolt in the East, by this Iceni ruler, Boudicca. I had come across a sacred grove such as druids' use, near where the bodies were found. It was known that Boudicca and her followers, as well as druids, cut off the heads of their enemies, in order to gain power over them. My supposition was that the local druids had endeavoured to show support for Boudicca, and followed her example.

The believer within our own ranks must have betrayed the victims, and enabled their easy capture. How much simpler to lie in wait for a person you know will pass by, rather than hoping to surprise someone on the busy open road. By murdering Romans and beheading them, they could lend their vicarious power to the uprising, or even cause enough insurrection in this area to divide the army, and enable an easier victory for the Iceni.

That had been my conclusion, which was apparently erroneous. Only three days had passed since Gallius' message to Aurelius, on my behalf, only four days since I had stumbled across the site. Four days. Less than an hour ago, I had pronounced Victor as having died four days ago. Was that the answer to the shadowy shapes that had chased me? Had they been gathering for a sacrifice? However the soldiers had found the grove long since abandoned, and not having been used for several months. Could I have been that mistaken? I have to admit that the details are difficult to recall, but whether because of the injuries I sustained or because my eyes saw what I wanted to see, I am, at present, unable to say. My heart says I saw and remembered true, and while my head must believe Aurelius' message, there was something lurking at the perimeter of both. Something that would mean my heart was right, but I could not pin it down.

I stood up, turning away from the traitorous scroll to lean on the windowsill, bracing my elbows. My hands could feel the rough plaster covering the wooden structure. It felt real and solid, not like the phantoms of truth I was chasing.

How many times had I vowed vengeance for Lucius, in this room? Shadows, caused by clouds chasing each other across the sky, multiplied behind me, hiding in the corners. It needed little to imagine the spirit of Lucius, now joined by Victor's, standing there, a sad and questioning look in their eyes. They would not have accused me in words, but every fibre of their beings would reach out to me. I kept my gaze fixed ahead, but even there I could see their faces, their features, their faith in me.

My concentration was broken by a movement at the edge of my sight, providing a welcome distraction. A young slave girl picked her way across the courtyard, with the elegance and grace of a deer, her movements lithe and sinuous. A memory thrust a tentative shoot up from the morass of thoughts, images, ideas. A woman walking, a courtyard, a man leaning on a balustrade. Then there had been a ceiling of grey wetness; now the sun was playing hide and seek with the clouds.

I allowed the emerging memory to develop, recollecting a face that had been turned up to mine, eyes full of questions, a body full of promise. Lydia. Would our paths cross again? This time both my head and my heart agreed. I wanted to meet her again. We would meet again. Once this mystery was solved, I would seek her out, persuade Corolius to sell her, so that she would belong to me.

With pleasant memories of Lydia swirling round and banishing some of the spectres, I sat down in a more relaxed mood. I was about to pour some more wine, when I recalled what had eluded me before. Shouting out for Gallius, I started rummaging through the tunics in my cupboard.

'What is it? What's wrong?' Gallius stopped to catch his breath, after running in response to my summons.

'The tunic, where is it?' I turned to look at him, and was struck by his bemused face. I sat down on the edge of the bed, as I said, 'The tunic I was wearing, when I came back from my accident, where is it?'

Gallius continued to look at me, before asking, 'Why do you need it now? Are you feeling all right? I think you need some rest.'

I shook my head, 'No, I don't need to rest, or rather I will, when I've found the tunic I was wearing then. I left something tied at the waist.'

'But the garment has been cleaned, and is now being mended.' Gallius spread his hands out in front of him. 'It was badly stained and torn. I didn't realise you would want it back.'

I slumped down on the bed. Of course, the clothes I had been wearing would have been taken away for washing. I could not imagine that anything could have remained in the waist bag, and the washing girls would not have recognised the significance of the scrap of white cloth. Cloth that I had taken from a holly leaf in a grove. Cloth that was white, clean and dry. Cloth that could not have been there for more than a day or two at the most. Cloth that would have proved the grove had been used recently. While I did not have the evidence in my hands, at least I had the reassurance of the memory in my mind. I wasn't sure how to explain or reconcile it, but I was certain that the grove I had seen, had been in, was in use.

I dismissed Gallius, and he hurried out again. Resting my elbows on my knees, I rubbed my temples. The events of the past few hours had affected me deeply, and I knew the cure that would partially restore me. Now that the cuts I had sustained in the apparently abortive expedition along the riverbank were healed enough, I could take full advantage of the warm restorative powers of the waters.

With my body submerged, I watched the steam coiling and rising from the surface and let my troubles be wiped, temporarily, from my mind. I fancied I could see shapes in the vapours, which quickly shifted and changed, a game I had played with my sons, when we were all younger. We would lie down, gazing up at the clouds, finding a fortress, boat, tiger, elephant, gladiator, shouting out the visions as soon as possible, before the shapes changed mid-description. But that was half a lifetime and an entire world away.

My reveries were broken by the entry of another person into the water, sending small waves that disturbed the surface and splashed against the side. Focussing my eyes, I smiled a greeting at Agricola, as he settled into a comfortable position.

'Tiberius, it's good to see you up and about again. I trust you have no ill effects from your injuries.'

'None that are lasting, thank you.'

I shut my eyes and leant my head back against the edge of the pool, but I could sense, through the continued agitation of the water, that Agricola was moving.

'How is the investigation going?' he asked.

'Fine, fine. I believe we shall soon be in a position to bring Lucius' murderer to justice.'

I kept my eyes closed and hoped the steam would mask any guilt that might show on my face. I felt I was further than ever from uncovering the truth, but did not wish to admit it. There are few people who will happily admit to total failure until they also have a partial success to report. Agricola moved again and a water droplet splashed onto my face.

'That's good.' His voice seemed curiously flat, as if the water absorbed the emotion. 'I thought the soldiers didn't find anything.

'Which soldiers do you mean?'

Agricola's reply appeared hasty and half-thought out. 'Didn't Aurelius, didn't he send some soldiers. You said about some grove you thought you'd found. You said when we were travelling back, after you fell. I thought the soldiers didn't find anything.'

'Is that what you'd heard? Of course that isn't the only line of investigation, you understand.' I glanced over at him, hazy through the steam, before standing up to move out of the pool. The heat was starting to make my head spin, and I needed to cool down. Agricola followed, seemingly eager to continue the conversation.

'So who do you suspect? You can tell me.'

I turned to look at him as he stood, his arms wide and ready to embrace the truth. Water ran off his limbs onto the tiled floor, creating a second pool to mirror the one at my feet. Something was eluding me. The harder I attempted to grasp it, the more it slipped away, like trying to capture and hold steam.

'How did you know?' I asked.

'Know what?'

'Where I was.'

Agricola looked at me, a frown ruffling his brow. When he didn't answer I repeated my question, 'How did you know where I was? When you found me, after I had … fallen.'

'Oh, then. You told me, remember?'

Now it was my turn to be silent.

'Don't you recall, we were talking about the body that the soldiers found? It was in my office. We discussed visiting the area where it was discovered.' Agricola wrapped his arm round my shoulders, guiding me into the cool bathroom. The boundary was immediately evident as the tiles underfoot changed from warm to cold.

'I couldn't go with you that morning, due to work,' Agricola continued. 'Since Memno's illness and Lucius' death, I have been busy, very busy. But I manage, especially since he's never around when you need him. Then when you can find Memno, he's always defensive, seems to think he's the only one who can do the job.'

Plunging into the cold water caused us both to gasp, almost in unison. Quickly removing ourselves from the pool, Agricola resumed the conversation. 'Yes, I manage, even though I am doing the work of three people at the moment. Sometimes I'm not too sure what took Memno so long on his surveys.' He lifted his hand as I started to speak. 'Oh, I'm sure he did a good enough job, but I have managed to keep the road building programme on track, and on time, even though I am effectively working by myself. In fact I have come across certain inefficiencies, in the way things were done, which naturally I have corrected.'

I took the towel that the attendant was holding out, feeling the rough texture on my skin, as it dried. Sitting down, I rested back against the smoothness of the tiled walls. I looked up at Agricola, as he stood in front of me. His chin was tilted up, and he appeared poised for activity.

'That's good,' I said. 'I'm sure Memno will appreciate the ...' I paused, searching for the right words, 'Improvements that you've made when he returns to work. Have you discussed it with him yet?'

'Humph. Of course.' Agricola threw his towel at the slave. 'I tried, but he adamantly refused to listen. Said I wasn't experienced enough, and that I hadn't taken various aspects into account. But we shall see.' He grabbed his clothing from the rack and started to dress. 'When my work is noticed by those in power, as I'm sure it will, then we shall see who assumes their rightful places in society. It's time for the ancients to give way to those with the vision and strength to forge ahead. We will not be held back.' He finished dressing and stood to leave, but then he turned to me, saying, 'Tiberius, you would do well to consider your own future. Think about where your loyalties should be,' and with that, he left the room.

Agricola's words reminded me that it had been some days since I visited Memno, and it was with a guilty step that I headed towards his rooms. Around me the daily life of the garrison continued.

Soldiers hurried or dawdled across the courtyard, some late for training, duty or lunch, others contemplating how to spend their rest period. The semi-visible network of slaves moved around and amongst them - the two streams of people never quite fused together. In between, a figure ran, as only the young can run, with pure exuberance and joy at just being outside. I recognised Belbo, just before he darted into the bathhouse, and I entered Memno's rooms.

'Tiberius, it's good to see you,' Memno looked bright and alert as I entered, but his smile quickly turned to a frown, 'but you must sit down. Are you fully recovered?'

'I'm fine, really I am. And it's good to see you so well now.' I sat down across the table from him.

'Are you sure you're fine? Your face is still bruised, and ... yes, what is it?' As Memno had been speaking, a slave had entered in some hurry, hesitating just at Memno's shoulder.

'Sir, there is an urgent message for Tiberius Valerius.'

'What is it?' I asked.

The slave turned to me, 'Sir, Gallius says there is news from Corolius' farm, and that you are needed there. He would like you to meet him there as soon as possible.'

I frowned. I hadn't been aware that Gallius had gone out to Corolius' farm. He must have gone just after he left me this morning, as I went for my leisurely bath. But why should Gallius request my presence there, when he had authority to act in any medical matters? 'Is that the whole message? What has happened?'

The slave hesitated, and glanced at Memno. 'There has been an accident, sir.' He paused, and licked his lips, before continuing, 'There was an accident at Corolius' farm, and you are needed there, sir.'

'An accident? Has someone been injured? Why do they need Tiberius?' Memno had risen from his chair, only to sit back heavily as the slave replied.

'Sir, there's been a serious accident, sir. That's all I know. That's all the message, sir.' The slave stepped back, out of reach of Memno as he uttered the words.

'I'll ride out. Get my horse ready,' I said, as I looked over at Memno, 'but, first, get some wine.'

The slave hurried out, and I could hear him relaying the request to others in the hallway.

'Memno, are you feeling alright?' I asked.

Memno raised both his hands to wave me back into my seat. His eyes were closed as he spoke, 'I'm … It was just a shock, that's all. I wasn't expecting it.'

I silently echoed his words. I, too, was shocked, for if someone on Corolius' farm had been seriously injured, and there was a message requesting my presence, then it must have been Corolius or his family. None of the slaves would be valued enough to request the presence of a surgeon. I wondered what had caused such a major accident that my skills were required.

The sun was preparing to set by the time I reached the farm. As I rode up the slope, I could see the house outlined black against the red smear of the sky. On my previous visits there had been a warm welcome, slaves had run out to hold the horses, the master of the house had appeared. Now the blank windows seemed to stare out into the night as if brooding and hurt. No lights were visible, and only one elderly slave stood up from his post near the front entrance. He hobbled over to me, each step giving an almost audible creak, to catch the reins so that I could dismount. Before I could demand he take me to his master, the front door opened, and a woman stood there. There was a light behind her, which streamed out either side, throwing her shadow long onto the ground, reaching to my feet. Her face was shrouded in darkness, and I could not identify her, until she spoke in her familiar, husky voice.

'Tiberius, thank the gods you came. I could not think who else to call on, or trust.'

'Julia, of course I came. Gallius indicated there was some urgency in his message. Maybe I should see him immediately, as well as Corolius.'

Julia came down the shallow steps, as I went towards her. She reached out her hands, which I took in mine.

'But you should not be out here,' I said. 'It's cold, and your hands are icy.'

She allowed me to guide her back into the house, leaning her head on my shoulder as we went.

Entering the sitting room, I escorted Julia over to the charcoal brazier that was sending its soothing heat out into the room. As we sat, I again suggested that Corolius be told of my arrival. Her reaction was unexpected.

'Tiberius, I cannot call Corolius.' She suddenly dropped her head, her hands covering her face.

'Is he away again? But I thought he sent for me. Julia, what has happened?'

'Julia, you should be resting. I could have watched for our visitor.' The arrival of Germanicus had gone unnoticed until his words sounded in the room. He stood in the doorway for a few moments, before coming to kneel in front of Julia.

She lifted her head and looked at him, as she murmured, 'Of course. I'll go and rest.'

I watched her as she swept out of the room.

'Germanicus, I have received an urgent summons from Corolius via my assistant, Gallius, yet he is not here to see me. I have ridden far, and in some discomfort, in answer to his request, and I'd like to discuss the matter with him now.' As I spoke, I noticed that Gallius had entered the room to seat himself to my right.

Germanicus stood up and moved over to the window, speaking out into the night. 'Corolius did not send for you.'

I glanced over at Gallius, who was sitting silent and still. I felt as if I were feeling my way through fog, with no signposts to direct my route. 'What's going on?' I asked. 'I was told there had been an accident, and that my presence here was needed.'

'Corolius cannot see you, because ...' Germanicus paused, and moved to the brazier, reaching out his hands to the warmth.

'He is dead.' The words came from Gallius, whose hands were nervously picking at a loose thread on his tunic.

'But how? Are you sure he's dead?'

Germanicus finally turned to look at me. 'We found him today, this morning, in one of the fields. His head had been severed from his body.'

Attached to the end of his words was a train of silence that gradually filled the room. I looked around me. Gallius was sitting on the edge of his seat, his hands now resting on the arms of the chair, ready for either action or rest. Germanicus was standing in front of the charcoal brazier, his hands clasped behind his back.

The entry of two slaves into the room broke the quietness, as they moved round, tending to the oil lamps that would provide illumination. They seemed to need each other to complete their duties, one to fill the containers, the other to mop up the many spills. After each task they glanced at Germanicus from under lowered heads.

'Germanicus, where are the house slaves? These two would seem to be more at home on the farm.' As the slaves paused near me in their circumnavigation of the room, I could see the broken fingernails and work-hardened calluses that spoke of time spent in the fields.

'Where do you think? Locked in the barn with the rest of them. That will do. Leave us now.'

Germanicus' words seemed to reduce the limited dexterity of the slaves still further, and they rapidly obeyed his instructions. As they left the room with rigid backs and tense shoulders, I caught a glimpse of redness around the neck of one. Germanicus continued, 'Naturally they have all been flogged until they confessed.'

I closed my eyes, to rapidly open them again. I could almost hear Lydia crying out in pain as the whip drew vivid marks across the skin of her back. If I concentrated on the room, I would not imagine the tears running down her face, or the blood dripping onto the floor.

'Isn't that a little soon? Shouldn't you have waited until you knew who was involved?' I asked in a cracked voice.

'It needed to be done as soon as possible, so that we could find out who was guilty, which I have established.'

'But to whip every one, why did you need to do that?' Gallius' voice was high and his words rushed out, speeded by indignation.

Germanicus turned to face him. 'Because I had to. I, Julia has that right. I do not have to answer to you for how I treat my slaves, especially after one of them has been instrumental in murdering the master of this house.'

He looked at me, saying, 'Tiberius, I'm sure you'll agree with me and the way I've handled this, once you've checked the details.'

I felt a need to separate Gallius and Germanicus, before words were exchanged that could not be retracted. I didn't know what might have happened earlier in the day, between Gallius' arrival and mine.

'Gallius, could you see to the slaves in the barn now.' I felt slightly nauseated as I smiled at Germanicus, adding, 'It may be necessary to question them further, in which case some treatment now may speed up the process.'

Germanicus nodded, and as I watched Gallius leaving the room, I will admit to a strong desire to go with him. Gallius, naturally, felt aggrieved for the workers, but Germanicus was perfectly within his rights. Or rather, Julia, who presumably was now the owner of the estate, was legally permitted, and encouraged, to flog slaves to obtain accurate information. The evidence of a slave in any trial would be inadmissible unless they had been adequately tortured.

There were currents of conflicting motives within the room, and I found myself longing to move out of the deep waters of investigation, and into the shallows of the simple treatment of injuries.

But no, I had set a course, and I must steer my way to the finish, negotiating such rapids as I might encounter.

I turned back to my host, 'When can I see the body?' I asked, trying not to let my reluctance show. I was not at all keen on examining a second body that day. The memory of Victor was still fresh in my mind, but I had to do my duty.

He moved back to the window, remarking, 'The light's going now. Tomorrow would be better.'

'Then I think it would help if you told me what has been happening here, Germanicus. And maybe the story would be better told with some wine and food.'

Germanicus looked at me through narrowed eyes, then strode to the door, calling out for refreshments. As he seated himself in the chair that Gallius had vacated, he leaned back, stretching his legs out in front. Putting his hands to his face, he ran his fingers through his short, fair hair before starting to speak.

'As you know, Corolius has had several episodes of general malaise over the past months. Indeed, he has consulted you on many occasions.'

I nodded assent, remembering the last time I had visited the farm, finding Corolius in his bed, lethargic and paralysed. I had been fairly certain then that his illnesses were the work of poison, and Germanicus seemed of the same opinion as he continued.

'I've had my suspicions over the nature and cause of these bouts, given that Corolius is ... was such a healthy man, apparently in favour with the gods. But that all appears to have changed. I believe I told you of his many recent absences from the farm, when no-one seemed to know where he had gone. Only last week he returned from a trip of some days.'

'Yes, I remember seeing him at the garrison, but that must have been ten days ago.'

Germanicus shifted position so that he was facing me, and seemed to be about to reply, when the elderly slave, who had initially met me, appeared, carrying a tray with a jug, cups, bread and fruit. His aged bones creaked and groaned their way across the room as he headed for a small table on which to deposit his load. Once this was done, he levered himself upright and, taking a deep breath, set off for the return journey.

'Please, Tiberius, help yourself.' Germanicus waved at the table, and waited for me to pour a cup of wine, and take some olives, apples and bread. He then continued speaking, 'I didn't know he had visited the garrison. Was that to see you?'

'We spoke briefly.' I felt a reluctance to discuss my actions and conversations, with the man sat in front of me.

'As I was saying, Corolius returned a few days ago, but was very edgy and withdrawn. He seemed to be anxious, as if he was afraid of something or someone, but he wouldn't tell us. Julia was very worried about him.' Germanicus took a sip of his wine, and three or four olives.

I did likewise, waiting for him to resume speaking. I did not want to interrupt the narrative. All my training was telling me to listen not only to what was said, but also to what, either by accident or design, was left unsaid. There was much that was being omitted.

So far the information that Germanicus was giving was little different to the story I had heard on previous occasions. The frequent absences from the farm, the secrecy over his destination, the unexplained illness. Which part should I be focussing on – all or none of it?

Putting down his cup, Germanicus continued, 'I tried to get him to tell us what the matter was, but all he said was that he was in fear of his life. Yesterday he went out for a short time. On his return, he retired early, after checking the doors were bolted securely, as usual. This morning, when the slave went to rouse him, he wasn't in his room, and couldn't be found in the house. We searched the house, then the farm buildings, and eventually found his body in one of the fields.'

'This morning, you found him dead this morning?' I was surprised as the message for me from Gallius had only arrived at the garrison in the early afternoon. Gallius must have received a summons in the late morning, which would have been some hours after the discovery. A messenger, riding in haste, would have only taken one, or at the most, two hours to get to the garrison.

Germanicus continued smoothly, without pausing, 'Yes, it was mid morning by the time we found him, and then, of course, Julia was in a state of collapse. For some time, there was no authority, no-one seemed to know what to do. I felt that it was my duty, as Julia's friend as well as tutor to her son, to assume the mantle of responsibility and so I sent for Gallius, and he sent for you.'

'Why didn't you ask for me?'

Germanicus continued smoothly, 'I actually asked for the doctor, not the assistant. I was very surprised when your slave turned up, so I was rather thankful that he realised this might be out of his jurisdiction, and told me he had already sent for you.'

'I see.' I took some more bread, eating slowly, before asking, 'Has the body been moved?'

'Yes. I arranged for it to be moved to the stables.'

'Good.' I paused, thinking over the conversation. 'You said Corolius had been beheaded. How do you know it is Corolius, and not someone else?'

Again Germanicus replied quickly, saying, 'Who else could it be? I think that I could be trusted to know my own master, and Julia recognised his ring.' He took another handful of olives, slipping them into his mouth as he continued, 'I thought … that is, Julia and I thought that it might be related to these other bodies you've been investigating. The coincidence would indicate that the same people are responsible, wouldn't you say?' He leant forward to expand his point. 'Corolius was certainly involved in something that he kept very secret, and he returned home last night very worried. I think he might have had a suspicion that he was to be the next victim, don't you think?'

My slow and careful non-committal nod seemed to be taken as encouragement by Germanicus as he continued, 'It would all fit. I've heard these rumours about druids in the area, and how they meet in secret. Well, Corolius was certainly having covert meetings, and visitors. If it was related to his business, there wouldn't have been a need to hide the details.' Germanicus shook his head, before concluding his argument. 'No, he must have been involved in some cult, which means he must have been a druid. For some reason, they decided he was to be the next sacrifice.'

I hesitated before answering, 'There are some similarities from what you say. However I'll need to examine the body before I can be certain.'

'Of course. That's why I gave orders that no-one was to enter the stables. The murdering slaves are now locked up in the barn, with only a few that can be trusted to provide for our needs, here in the house.'

My mouth felt suddenly dry, and I took some wine, forcing myself to swallow, before asking, 'You seem to know who was involved in this murder. Do you have a suspect?'

'Yes ... that is, I'm fairly sure. She denies anything to do with this, of course, but after a long and appropriate beating, she confessed.' Germanicus gave a smile that I could not echo. 'One of the house slaves, can't remember her name. Used to be one of Corolius' favourites, until Julia reminded him who is mistress of this house.'

His words fell onto my ears, like stones into a deep lake. Germanicus might pretend to forget her name, but I was certain I knew who he meant. Lydia had told me how scared she was of Julia. Maybe she had reason, and my counselling, given one long week ago in the cart, had been to no avail. I yawned, and suddenly realised how tired I was.

'Forgive me, Germanicus, but I have ridden far, and I'm not yet fully recovered from a fall I sustained a few days ago. I must excuse myself now.'

'Of course. It's been a long day for us all. I'll show you to your room, but as I said, I'm afraid there will be few slaves to attend to any needs you may have. This way.' Germanicus rose to his feet and indicated the door. I stood up and we walked out of the room, along the corridor, to one of the bedrooms. Here he left me, and I sat down heavily on the bed. My body may have been tired, but my mind was fully active.

Very little in what Germanicus had said was making sense. He felt that Corolius' death was at the hands of the same people who had killed Lucius, but the circumstances were so totally different. At least the version I had heard so far did not fit with what I knew about the previous three murders.

Lucius' body had been found, and he had been killed, in a specific place, next to a river. A place that obviously had some special meaning for his murderers. The second body that had been found, was also in the same area, or at least washed downstream, after a period of heavy rain. Lucius certainly, had been kidnapped, presumable during the day, somewhere on the open road, when he was taking a message. If it had been during the night, the owner of the lodgings he would have used, would surely have raised the alarm.

Victor was attacked when he was driving his cart along a lonely stretch of road, having stopped for Lechlan to clear something, possibly a fallen tree, from the route, and they would not have been travelling at night.

Corolius, on the other hand, was attacked either in his own house, or certainly on his estate. He appeared to have been killed during the night, and then left in the fields.

But yet if it was a different murderer, a different reason, a different place, then who, and why? I could go round in circles for all eternity, thinking about possibilities when what I needed was something concrete in this miasma of half-truths and semi-lies. When the morning came I would be able to examine the body, to see what evidence the dead man himself could provide.

Lying down, I rested my head back on the pillow, gazing up at the ceiling, as if seeking the future in the cracks and discolour of the plaster. I could easily believe that there was a portal through to some darker world, which issued forth demons to haunt my days. Demons which invaded my sleep at night and dogged my steps in daylight. Shadows flickered across the room, chased by lights I could not identify. Was this to be my future, forever sharing my life with evil spirits?

The tap, tap, tap of a loose shutter turned into the drip, drip, drip of water from a shroud. I shook my head and smiled to myself.

It had been a long day. Did I believe I was a soothsayer, divining destiny from the flight of birds or the fall of a group of stones? I am just a surgeon, trying to do his best in solving a mystery by using his skills and knowledge.

But then, maybe fortune tellers had the easy option. They gave their predictions from their observations of the natural world around them, and left the interpretation to the client. I worked with what I could see and deduce from man, that most fickle and inconsistent of omens. With these thoughts, I allowed my eyes to rest, while I ran over the recent conversation with Germanicus. Not to sleep, I didn't want to sleep just yet, only rest my eyes.

Day Eighteen

When I woke up, it was still early. Light crept silently into the room, through the gaps in the window shutters and distributed itself round the room. It was not bright enough to give colour and substance to the objects around me, but I could see the shape of Gallius, curled up and motionless on the floor at the side of the bed. Straightening my crumpled tunic, I carefully stepped over him and quietly opened the wooden shutters. Outside the sky was clear, a pale, turquoise blue, with hints of the rising sun evident in the streaks of coral pink. The air was fresh, and my breath hung like a puff of smoke before dissipating.

'Good morning, Master.' The sudden inrush of cool air must have woken Gallius, who was now clambering to his feet.

'Good morning, Gallius. I can't believe you slept well, with just the floor as your bed.'

'No, but it seemed the … safest place to sleep.' He stifled a yawn, before continuing, 'The household is in some disarray, but I'm sure I can find some bread, and wine. If you'll excuse me, I'll see what I can do.'

'Yes, that would be fine, but before you go, how were the slaves? Were there many injuries?'

'I treated some. Maybe once I've found us some breakfast, we should enjoy the fresh air and eat outside.'

'Outside?'

Gallius was persistent, 'I really do think the open air would do us both good, and help to wake us up. We need to be alert when examining Corolius' body.'

The cool air on my cheeks and in my lungs was, at last, starting to enliven me and clear my head of the fog of sleep, and I acknowledged Gallius' caution. 'I'll bring the cloaks, and meet you out in the courtyard.'

He left the room, and I put on my cloak. The day promised to be fine and dry, but it was late into autumn. In this distant part of the Empire, the winds would be cold, the air chill and the ground damp.

Picking up Gallius' cloak, I went out into the courtyard. Standing there, I could discern few stirrings of life.

In front of me, within the house, slept Julia, now the owner, and her son Petronus, now presumably heir of this large estate. What part did Germanicus play? Was he hopeful that now the estate had a new owner, he would rise from tutor to master?

Away to the left, set back out of view, were the barns, usually stocked with animals or produce. Now there was a different commodity stored there. What were the thoughts of the slaves, locked up for the night? Were they even now plotting to provide a scapegoat? Someone to admit culpability, allowing the rest to return to their usual labour? Did they realise there was already a suspect? Would it concern them whether that person be innocent or guilty? Or were they all taking advantage of extended sleep and rest, when usually they would already be at work?

If I turned round, near the barns I would be able to see the stables. Long, low buildings that, for the past night had housed an unexpected visitor. I suspected that this might have been the first time that Corolius had spent more than a few moments inside the stables. He certainly struck me as someone who would always have his horse brought to him, and taken away again as he dismounted, at the front door of his house.

I turned my thoughts back to the barn. I wondered what information Gallius was to impart, together with the victuals that he was procuring. How brutal had Germanicus been in his floggings? Common sense would veer towards a light beating. After all, they were not his property, and he must surely want to retain their value, to keep in favour with Julia. Slaves with obvious scars did not fetch a high price. And Lydia, what of her fate? Out here in the bright light of day, I could not fool myself. If either Germanicus, or Julia, had chosen a scapegoat, then the flogging would be more brutal. There would be no need to worry about scars and a drop in value.

Part of me yearned to break down the barn doors, find and comfort her. I wanted to touch her soft skin, feel her silky hair and hear her gentle voice. I wanted my dreams to become real and gain substance and longevity. But I am no longer a young man, and maybe I must content myself with visions, and memories.

As Gallius reappeared, bearing a tray, I found a low wall that we could both sit on. It was sheltered from the fitful breeze that had sprung up, and that was playing with dead leaves and handfuls of dust, but provided a vantage point from which I could see anyone approaching.

Putting the tray down, Gallius handed me a cup, saying, 'I've added some poppy to this one for you.' When I frowned slightly, he continued, 'Don't worry. It's a very small dose, just enough to ease your pain, but not enough to dull your senses.'

I drank it down, grateful for the relief it would bring, and there we sat, dipping our slightly stale bread in the wine, before eating.

'Now, Gallius, tell me what you found out,' I said.

He glanced round, as if to reassure himself that we could not be overhead. 'I got a message saying that there had been a serious accident, and that the doctor was required. Naturally, I assumed that I should answer the request.' He looked to me for reassurance, which I gave with a nod. 'I sent Belbo to find you. I was hoping you'd be able to ride out with me. The message seemed ...' He gazed up at the sky, before shrugging. 'The messenger seemed edgy. I was suspicious, and had a hunch there was more to this than a simple accident. When Belbo couldn't find you straight away, I rode out here.'

He paused, before continuing, 'When I got here, I found Germanicus acting as master of the estate. He wasn't too pleased when he saw me, and it was obvious he was expecting you. Luckily you arrived quickly.'

He broke off some bread, holding it in his hand for a few moments, before dipping it in the wine and biting.

'What explanation did Germanicus give you?' I asked, as I, too, ate.

Swallowing what must have been only partially chewed bread, he said, 'Nothing. He told me nothing, except that Corolius was dead. I wasn't allowed to see anyone or speak to anyone, until you came. Now you can see why I felt it safer to sleep in your room last night.'

'I think you made the right decision.' I picked up a few crumbs of bread, throwing them to the sparrows that were hopping about the courtyard, watching them argue over their newly found wealth. 'What about last night, after you left us?'

'Virtually all the slaves were in the barn,' said Gallius, 'but most had only been lightly beaten, and there were few cuts deep enough to warrant dressings. They were all very scared, and most would not talk to me at all, but one of the house slaves, Alena, told me what had happened the evening and night before last.'

'Germanicus told me that Corolius went to bed early, but was missing in the morning, which is when the search was started.' I broke off some bread, holding it in my wine, before eating.

'No, Alena told a different story.' Gallius shook his head, emphasising his point. 'She said that Corolius and Julia were arguing and shouting at each other. Late on, in the evening. She didn't know what it was about, only that their voices were raised.' Gallius took a mouthful of wine, quickly swallowing it, as if eager to give me the information he had. 'Afterwards Julia complained of a headache and she ordered Alena to get a poultice. One of the other slaves, Zera, also heard an argument, but she thought it was between Corolius and Germanicus.'

I frowned. 'Germanicus didn't say there had been any disputes. Almost the opposite.' I cradled my cup, sipping and appreciating the flavour. 'He indicated that Corolius had been very withdrawn, refusing to discuss anything.'

'Alena also says that after she had prepared the poultice and was applying it, Germanicus came in to speak with Julia. Julia ordered Alena away, and didn't call her back until she was ready to retire, much later than usual.'

'But Julia has the right to have her slaves come and go as she wishes. I can't see that there's much suspicious in that.'

'But apparently it was so out of character. Previously when Julia has had a headache, which are fairly frequent, she has insisted on Alena staying with her, to renew the poultice, shade the windows, open the windows, get something to drink.' By now Gallius was on his feet and waving his hands about as he spoke.

'Umm, I see.' I stood up, and tried to rub some relief into my partially numb buttocks. 'Well, Gallius, I'm getting too old to sit on cold, hard walls. I think we need to look at Corolius and then where he was found. Let's see if we can make more sense of this, with what he has to tell us.' I stretched up and then back. 'No, leave the tray. Someone else can return it. I need you with me. I need you to observe and notice anything I might miss. Don't forget your cloak.'

He took the garment from my outstretched hand, throwing it round his shoulders, and together we headed for the stables.

'Which block is it, Master?'

We had a choice of two. On one side the doors stood open and inviting, showing glimpses of movement within.

I could hear the elderly slave muttering to himself, as he slowly and methodically went up and down the length, tending to his charges. The other building was quiet and closed, and we headed towards it.

As we opened the doors, the dark, warm aromas that had been imprisoned for the night, escaped out into the daytime. We waited until most had gone, before venturing inside. The interior had no lights, and illumination from the door was meagre. We stood, listening. Normally, there would be the stamp of impatient hooves, the occasional whinny, and the rustle of large and small bodies moving in the straw. Here there was silence. All the animals that would usually be housed here had been moved. I felt along the wall, running my hand along the rough plaster until my fingers located the grain of wood. Throwing open the shutters caused a dull thud to break into the gloom, bringing the new day with it. Gallius followed my example and soon we were in brightness.

We walked down the length of the building, peering into hastily cleared stalls until the occupied one was found. A bundle tightly wrapped in cloth lay at an angle. As I bent down I could see where tiny, sharp teeth had attempted to gain entry, but had been foiled by the double thickness.

'Is this how he was found?' As he spoke, Gallius knelt down, moving about to peer closely at different angles.

'If he'd been found like this, then how could they have known it was a body? No, someone has wrapped the cloth round after he was identified.'

'Well done, Tiberius. You are, of course, perfectly correct.'

I stood up to see Germanicus walking towards us.

'I didn't realise you would be up so early, or I would have joined you sooner.' He pointed down at the bundle lying on the floor between us. 'I ordered that the body be wrapped and moved in here. Otherwise, there would be nothing left for you to examine, and we would have had very fat rats.' His thin, short laugh was not echoed by either myself or Gallius.

'But the position, on his back, is identical to the way he was found?' I asked.

'Yes, yes. When I was informed of the discovery and went to see, Corolius was lying on his back, with his arms at his side, just as he is now.'

'Who normally sleeps in the stables? Don't the stable boys stay here over night?'

I moved along, looking in the other stalls, leaving my questions to hang in the air behind me. Piles of roughly raked straw adorned the floor of most sections, while bits of harness hung from the walls.

'Normally, yes, but they are in the barn at present.' Germanicus kept pace with me.

'What about the other block? That's in use?'

'Of course. The animals from here were moved over there, but Titus uses that one, and he won't allow anyone else to sleep in there with him. He didn't hear anything, but not only is he deaf, he's also a very sound sleeper.'

'Titus?'

'The old slave, you saw him when you arrived last night.' Germanicus moved to one of the windows, nodding outside. 'He's over there now.'

'I know the one you mean.' I bent down by the side of the wrapped corpse. 'I think I've seen all I need to here. I will need to look at Corolius, but not here.' I straightened up, and looked at Germanicus. 'I need him placed on a large table.'

'What about one of the carpentry tables? Would that do?'

'Yes, perfect. Would you arrange for the body to be moved, while Gallius and I look at where he was found?'

'Of course. Shall I show you?'

I shook my head, 'Thanks, but there's no need. If you could just tell us where to go.'

Germanicus walked over to the nearest window, and pointed out, across the fields. 'You see that hedgerow, with the large tree. Just past there is a ditch. Corolius was found there, but there isn't really anything to see. It's just a ditch.'

'All the same, I would like to see everything.'

'While you're looking over there, I'll get Corolius' body moved to the carpentry workshop, just next to the farthest barn.' At this Germanicus walked away, and I could hear him shouting as he did so.

It was a relief to walk out across the fields, away from the tight cluster of buildings that formed the hub of the farm. The ground was firm and dry, with the dying stalks of harvested crops crackling underfoot. To our right, some distance away, a fox emerged from the boundary bushes and matched our pace for a few yards, before abruptly disappearing. Some deer that had ventured into the field in search of missed treasure, took fright and bounced away. Our arrival at the hedge was noted by a robin, perched on a branch, ready to examine us. He displayed his jaunty, red breast like a badge of office, as if over-brimming with the power to permit or deny us access.

'Well, Gallius, what do you make of it?'

'This … well, it's a ditch, just a ditch, that's all. As Germanicus said, there's nothing to see here.'

'See how far it goes that way, will you? I'll go this way.' I set off to trace the course of the shallow, muddy hollow. There was only a stretch of stagnant water in a series of puddles lining the bottom. Ferns and moss clung to the sides, lying mangled and torn in one area. I got down into the depression, mud oozing over my sandals and between my toes, but I gained nothing else from my efforts.

If Germanicus had not pointed out the locality, I could not even have been certain of being in the right place. Struggling out again, after wiping most of the earth off with some leaves, I continued on, but had not gone more than a score of paces before the ditch petered out in a low-lying area of mud. Turning, I could see that Gallius had gone further, but he, too, soon turned and retraced his steps.

'It just ended. Nothing there.'

'So did this end, Gallius. As you so rightly said, it is indeed, just a ditch.'

I paused, looking round, rubbing my chin and frowning, before continuing, 'Gallius, I know I said that I wanted you with me when examining Corolius' body. However, I think your time might be better spent in talking to the slaves again, but don't make it obvious. Now let's get back to the farm, and I'll see Corolius' body.' As I spoke, I could see the robin bobbing up and down, as if to say, I told you there was nothing here.

'But why? Why don't you want me to help you?'

'Because ...' I paused, unsure how to justify the request. Normally I would insist on Gallius being present, but this time was different. 'I want to be out of here as soon as possible, and the quickest way is if I examine the body and you see to the slaves again. They won't trust me, so you need to do that.'

He appeared slightly appeased, as we headed back, retracing our steps across the field, until parting at the edge of the buildings. Gallius went back into the house, to collect his case of ointments, dressings and cures.

I entered the carpentry workshop, where I could see that the wrapped bundle had been placed on the large table in the centre of the room.

The artisan's tools were arranged on racks hung on the walls, each with its own space. Two or three partially completed projects were evident. New shutters for a window, a chair needing a replacement leg, a plough in for repair. In one corner was a pile of rejected lumber, either too short or too knotty to be of use, and next to it, a jumble of broken blades, chipped chisels and bent sickles. The smell of newly cut and shaped wood hung in the air, partially masking any malodorous emanations from the table. The only other occupant was Germanicus, who was leaning against a bench, idly playing with a short length of timber. As I entered, he straightened up.

'Was your trip useful?' he enquired.

'Not really,' I replied.

His mouth formed a thin smile, as he said, 'As I said, there was nothing to find.'

'I agree. The ditch is just a ditch. Now, let's see Corolius.' As I spoke, I began to un-wrap the bundle, revealing the naked body.

There was extensive damage to the neck, where the head had been severed. Such force had been used that the bone showed several deep cuts, while the skin displayed many savage gashes. Other than this, there appeared to be few injuries.

In common with the previous corpses, there was extensive bruising, but this time it involved the chest as well, and only one upper arm. In places it was difficult to clearly trace the margins of the contusions, due to a red discoloration, broken by some small, regular white squares, that ran down the right side of the body.

'How could you be sure this is Corolius?' I asked, rolling the dead man onto one side so that I could see his back, where again the bruising merged and blended with the redness on the right of his torso.

'As I said, I am sure this is Corolius, unless you wish to put Julia through the anguish of seeing the body again? A wife would surely recognise her husband, don't you think?' Germanicus' voice came from across the table, where he was closely observing my examination.

I quickly shook my head. No woman should have to endure the ordeal of looking at and then identifying the remains that lay on the table. It was beyond their capabilities; they are much weaker than we are. It was a job that should only fall to men, who were much stronger in mind and spirit.

'Besides, that's his ring.' He pointed to the man's left hand, where a gold and red signet ring adorned his finger. 'Who else could it be?' Germanicus continued, 'No-one else is missing. Are those bruises on his body?'

I nodded, as I laid Corolius onto his back again. I, too, was certain this was Corolius. Remembering back to the time when I had bled him, in my infirmary, I checked his right arm, finding the small scar that I had inflicted.

'They must have been caused when he was abducted,' he said. 'The murderers must have beaten him first. How else would they have got him out of the house?'

Lifting my head, I turned and smiled brightly at Germanicus, hoping my face did not reveal my inner emotions. Making a conscious effort to control my voice, I replied, 'It certainly seems that way, but I'm surprised no-one else was woken with the noise of a struggle. And even so, how did the murderers get into the house?'

'It was that slave, remember? I told you that one of the house slaves was guilty.' Germanicus' words jumped out enthusiastically, as he continued, 'She must have let them in.' He walked about, one hand cradling his chin.

'I sleep on the other side of the house, so I wouldn't have heard anything, and Julia may well have taken something to help her rest. I know she had a headache that night.' He came up to me, and his hands suddenly gripped my shoulders. 'We could all have been killed in our sleep. Thank the gods that the rest of us were spared.'

'Thank the gods indeed, Germanicus.' While it seemed that the dead body had given up most of its information, there were many more secrets waiting to be exposed, but I would make better progress by myself. The answers I was looking for would not be revealed unless I were able to seek them out alone. 'And we must also be thankful for Julia's headache, or she might have woken and investigated.'

Germanicus' hands dropped from my shoulders and he took a step backwards.

'She must have been worried,' I continued, giving a quick glance round the room. 'Still be worried. I think I've finished here. Maybe you should check on how she's feeling this morning.'

Germanicus' gaze flickered between me, Corolius' body and the direction of the house, unseen through the wooden wall. When he spoke his voice was hesitant and uneven, 'I wouldn't want her to be concerned, but …'

'I'm sure she would appreciate some company. I just need to complete a few checks, then I'll join you.'

As Germanicus still seemed reluctant to leave me, I continued, 'You've been a great help to me here. I don't think I'd have resolved this mystery so quickly without your help.'

'So you know what happened here?'

'Yes, Germanicus, I do. Now, as I said, I just need to tidy up here, then I'll join you and Julia, and we can decide what action needs to be taken.'

He turned and left the building. The breath I had been unconsciously holding escaped from my lungs, causing my shoulders to sag. Quickly I returned to the table, and the previous master of the estate. Lifting up his right arm, I once again examined the limb and his torso, tracing the pattern of regular white shapes with my finger. There was something familiar about them, a design that I had seen before, in a different place, a different setting.

Leaving the body, I knelt down by the pile of discarded tools, rummaging through for what I thought I might find. Pushed down at the back, hidden from first and second view, was a chipped, blunt and discoloured chisel. I stood up and went to the door, both so that I could see more clearly and also to ensure that Germanicus did not return to surprise me.

The clear, sharp light revealed that the rusty stains on the tool had not come from the action of water on iron, but from cleaving through flesh. Moving back to the body lying on the table, I looked down at the damage around his neck. If I was right, this corpse had one more thing to say. Carefully I tried the blade in my hand against the cuts that had severed Corolius' head.

I weighed the heavy implement in my hand for a few moments, before tying it to my belt with a length of cloth I found in the workshop. I could feel it at my left hip, hidden from view where my tunic concealed it. Turning round, I took a last look at the former owner of the estate, only to find a hand touching my elbow from behind. Whirling round, I confronted my potential assailant.

'Tiberius. Are you alright?' The enquiry came from Gallius, who was now in front of me, framed by the light from the open door.

Within my breast I could feel the rapid beating of my heart under my open palm. 'I wasn't expecting anyone. You startled me.'

'I'm sorry. You seemed to be concentrating. I didn't want to disturb your thoughts.' Concern was evident on Gallius' face as he stepped forward, briefly resting one hand on my arm.

I reached to silently communicate through touch, before enquiring, 'What did you find out?'

Gallius glanced round before replying. 'The majority of the cuts and bruises that I treated yesterday are healing well. I have no worries on that part.'

'Most, but not all …?'

'One of the house slaves, Lydia, has a few, deep lacerations that could cause a problem if not looked after.'

My throat was dry, and for a few moments, the pounding in my ears blocked out Gallius' voice.

'… as to the care she needs, but Germanicus does consider her guilty, so I'm not sure how much treatment he'll allow her to receive.'

'She's innocent.' My words came out quicker than I had intended and I stopped, lifting my hands to my head, then dropping them to slow myself down. 'I don't think the situation is that simple.'

'I agree. From what the other slaves are saying, Lydia appears innocent and …'

'Stop. Don't say anymore at present.' I looked around me, to check that I had not missed anything in the room. The late-morning sun shone in, casting our shadows over the table and its burden. The air was not cold, but I felt suddenly chilled.

'Let's go outside. If you can creep up on me unnoticed, then so might others.'

I headed for the doorway and into the open air, without waiting to see if Gallius followed. Once there I took three or four deep breaths, pulling the peace and calm of the surrounding countryside deep within my soul.

By the time Gallius joined me, I felt more able to objectively discuss the information that he had. I selected the same spot to sit which we had previously used for breakfast, with its view of the villa entrance.

'What were you saying about the other slaves?' I asked, as we sat down.

'I was talking to some of the house slaves, as you asked me. Alena, Zera as well as some of the others. Lydia is also one of the house slaves.'

'Yes, I know that. What were they saying?'

Gallius looked sideways at me before continuing, 'They - Alena, Zera and Lydia - share a room in the house, with another girl, Thalia. She has had, has still got, a bad cough, which kept both her, and the others, awake most of the night. They are all certain that Lydia never left the room. Germanicus is saying she did.'

I gripped the cold stone that we were sitting on. 'Are you sure?' My fingers tried to force their way through the resisting rock as I waited for his reply.

'Of course I'm sure. At least I'm sure of what I heard. That's what the slaves told me. I have no proof that any of them are telling me the truth.' He paused, and started to examine some dead leaves that had blown onto the stone wall. 'Master, you seem very ... concerned about this Lydia.'

I pushed myself upright. 'I'm concerned about justice. Now, was there anything else you found out?'

He was about to reply when a figure appeared at the door of the main house. I held up my hand to silence Gallius. He stood up by my side, and we both watched Titus move slowly, but purposefully towards us. Heavy, lumbering steps soon brought the elderly trustee into calling range.

'Mistress wants you in the house,' he wheezed, his words interspersed with a hacking cough. He tossed the phrase, 'Wants you now,' over his shoulder as he turned to shuffle back to the building.

'I think it would be best to see Julia now, and not keep her waiting. Was there anything else I need to know now, Gallius?'

He hesitated, apparently thinking, then slowly shook his head, his lips pursed.

I quickly started towards the house, initially leaving Gallius standing. I wanted to finish this business and vacate the farm as soon as possible. The many pieces of this puzzle were slotting into place, and revealing a picture I had no desire to see. But look at it I must. I had started on this path, and I had to follow it through to the end, regardless of the repulsion I might feel.

For I was almost certain that I knew who had killed Corolius. Why, at this particular time was unclear, although I could see the reason behind the murder. The position and location of the body, the regular, white lines on the torso, the story that the slaves told, even the chisel still hanging heavily at my hip, all pointed unerringly in one direction. All I needed was one or two further elements to confirm my conclusions, and those I would find within the house itself. My feet seemed to know the pace with which my mind was working, and matched the sense of urgency, such that I almost ran to the main door of the villa. It was here that Gallius finally caught up with me.

'I don't understand what's going on.' His voice came in gasps, evidence of the speed he had needed. 'I feel there's something you're not telling me.'

I was too engrossed in the moment to delay. Later, I could explain later, but not now. I stood in the portal, the heavy entrance door half-open in front of me, to either admit or deny passage. The iron lock and hinges looked black against the smooth, weathered wood.

'Gallius, I must speak with Julia. The lady, and owner of this property, has issued a summons, which must be answered.' I turned to enter the gloom of the interior, and headed for the reception room that I had been in before, guessing that Julia would want to discuss matters in comfort. I was not mistaken. As I entered I could see her semi-reclining on a couch, her head resting back on a cushion. She raised a languid hand as I approached.

'Tiberius, thank you for coming. Germanicus tells me that you are close to confirming the identities of the cruel murderers who robbed me of a husband, and my son of a father. Please, be seated and tell me.' She shifted position, causing the cushion to fall to the floor. It was retrieved by Germanicus, who left his post by the window, to take the chair nearest Julia. I sat opposite them, while Gallius came to stand at my shoulder.

'I am indeed close,' I said, 'but first, I must ask you to tell me your recollection of that night.'

'I have already told you what happened.' The tones of Germanicus cut in, his voice initially rough, then speaking more smoothly. 'Surely there's no need to put Julia through this torment, when I've told you all that happened?'

I gazed steadfastly at him, my eyes connecting with his. 'But you haven't told me everything that happened, have you Germanicus?'

'I don't understand. I told you everything.' His gaze dropped and he leant down to brush an unseen mote of dust off his tunic. As he looked up his mouth stretched into a smile. 'What are you saying?'

'That other things happened that you have not told me about.' I leant back in my chair and shifted my surveillance to the ceiling and the walls, before finally resting back on Julia, who had laid one hand on Germanicus' arm. 'Germanicus, you could not tell me what transpired between Julia and Corolius.'

Julia sat up and leant towards me, her outstretched hand just able to touch my knee. Her melodic voice still had the power to delight my ears.

'Of course I'll tell you what I remember, if you think it will help.'

She turned to the man sitting at her side. 'You shouldn't be so brusque. We ... I asked Tiberius here to investigate this atrocity. He has a right to ask any questions he likes.' Her gaze was re-directed at me, and she smiled. 'How else could you ensure that the guilty are brought to justice and punished?'

'That is what I intend to do,' was my response.

Julia re-arranged herself so that she was, again, semi-recumbent and gave a long sigh. 'I've tried so hard to forget, tried to imagine it was all a dream, a nightmare. You do understand that, don't you?' and she again stretched out a hand that, in her present position, only reached part-way to me. Letting her arm fall, she continued, 'Corolius had been so withdrawn and edgy of late. I've been so worried about him. You know how unwell he'd been.'

I supplied the expected confirmation, 'Yes, he's consulted me on several occasions.'

'I think he'd been travelling about too much, that's what'd been making him ill. I told him as much that night, and he agreed with me.' Julia gave a single sob and paused before continuing, 'That was the last conversation we had. He was going to spend more time on the farm, more time with me and Petronus, and then this happens.'

'I understand from Germanicus that Corolius retired early that night ...'

Julia gave a half sob, 'Yes ... no. He was tired and went to his bed, but found he couldn't sleep.'

I felt the need to gently probe deeper. 'So Corolius was in agreement with staying on the farm more? He didn't say why he had been away so much?'

'No. We were going to talk more, but I was so worried, that I developed a headache. Corolius left me so that I could rest.' She buried her face in her hands, almost wailing, 'It was so dreadful. How could that slave have done such a thing to my dear husband?'

Germanicus stood up and moved to stand behind the couch. Resting one hand on her shoulder, he said, 'Julia, you mustn't upset yourself so. I'm sure Tiberius has all the information he needs now.' His eyes stared into mine. 'Or do you need more?'

The look I returned was unfaltering, but inside my emotions were in turmoil. These were deep and dangerous waters I was traversing. One false move, one misguided turn might send me plunging down or leave me dashed upon rocks.

My heart was pounding in my breast as if trying to escape its imprisonment, pounding so hard I could be convinced that all in the room might see and hear it. My concentration was focused on the two people in front of me. The rest of the room receded, becoming merely a distraction, easily ignored.

Marshalling my thoughts, and choosing my words, I spoke. 'Germanicus, and of course you, Julia, have been instrumental in the solving of this case. Without your help, this would have remained just another mystery. Now I can safely assert that, not only will the perpetrators be punished for this crime, but also for others they have committed.'

Germanicus walked slowly back to sit down, resting one elbow on the arm of his chair. 'So you do think that Corolius' death is ...' He paused.

I hesitated before finishing his sentence, '... connected with those I have been investigating at the garrison? Yes, Germanicus, I do.' As I spoke I could see his clenched fists gradually open. 'You were quite right to call me,' I continued. 'The spirits of Lucius and Victor will also rest in peace.'

'So you really do think it was Lydia?' Germanicus had sat upright, his hands now gripping the seat of the chair.

'If that's the name of the house slave you told me about, then yes.'

'I can't quite believe it,' murmured Julia. 'Corolius was so fond of her, and so good to her, and this is how she repays him.' She rested her head back and closed her eyes. 'To think she could deliberately murder her master.'

A sudden noise behind me and a tap on my shoulder brought an awful realisation.

I looked round to find Gallius was speaking to me, loud enough for Germanicus and Julia to also hear. The gasp of in-drawn breath came to my ears over the words.

'But Master, you know she couldn't have done it. Remember? Zera and Alena said she never left the room that night?'

How could I have forgotten? I felt the rapids of defeat looming, rocks on every side to trap and crush me, shallows reaching up to snare me. How could I have forgotten? The presence of the man behind me had slipped out of my conscious thought. Gallius, the very person who had the unknown power to destroy all that I was working towards, to the detriment of us both. I needed to act quickly to save the situation. I roughly brushed his hand from my shoulder and turned away from him as my words snapped out.

'How dare you, Gallius? How dare you insult us with your slave market gossip? Be gone, before you demean me any further.' It was key to my plans that he now leave us.

I could not risk any further discussion with him. 'Go. You are not fit to be in this company,' I added, as I sensed him hesitating. Even now, I was rapidly cogitating on how to restore the situation.

Only when I felt a draught on the back of my neck from the carefully opened and then closed door, did I lean towards Julia, with what I hoped was a convincing look of concern and reassurance on my face.

'My lady, I hope that did not distress you.' I coated each word with honey. 'My slave has forgotten his place. What has happened here should be a lesson to us all.'

'I must say I have often found that your slave does not display the proper respect for you.' The speech was from Germanicus, and I turned towards him.

Pulling up the corners of my mouth, I gave a wry smile, 'I feel I have been rather too easy. I'll have to implement some changes.' I spread my hands wide, shrugging my shoulders. 'However, slave gossip it might be, but I fear there is some truth in Gallius' words.'

Julia's voice was higher than usual as she stated, 'Surely not. You said you believed … were certain that Lydia had done this.'

'And I still am certain,' I tried hard to get every word dripping with conviction, 'but it would seem she was not alone.'

Julia's hands flew to her mouth as indiscernible, whispered words emerged.

'Well, of course,' came the tones of Germanicus, 'she can't have been alone. She would not have been able to kill Corolius by herself. She betrayed him to the cult of druids. They were the others.'

'Yes, I agree with that, but what I meant was that Lydia was not the only occupant of the house who was involved.'

'Oh.'

'Other slaves must have been enmeshed in this evil plot. The three she slept with. Lydia could not have left the room without waking them, yet they deny this. Therefore they must all be guilty.' I leant back to assess the reactions of Julia and Germanicus. She was semi-lying, her hands now resting gently on a crumpled and maltreated cushion. He had his hands supporting his bowed head, which he lifted as I watched.

'So it runs deeper than we thought,' he half-whispered in a husky voice.

'It does, but you need have no worries.' I gave my words a ring of authority that I did not fully feel inside.

But I could not step aside from the route I had embarked on. The only way was forward. 'These four are all guilty, and they will be dealt with accordingly. The other slaves are all innocent.'

'What will happen to them?' The enquiry had come from Julia, who was now examining the nails of one manicured hand, while the other was playing with a loose tendril of hair.

'Obviously death. The exact manner will be for the courts to decide.' My words came out harsher then I had intended.

'Yes, of course,' she murmured.

I could sense my turbulent journey gradually becoming calmer. Most obstacles were passed, with just one more difficulty to negotiate, but if I grounded on this last rapid, then I would count everything as failed. Admittedly this had been complicated by Gallius' outburst, but having apparently sold my story successfully so far, I could adapt to allow for that.

'As I said, the other slaves are all innocent. However, as the legal owner, Julia, you have the right to have them all put to death.'

Her emphatic 'No!' came even as I pronounced the final word.

'I knew you would be just and merciful. A woman of your breeding and refinement could not be otherwise.'

She smiled and nodded at me, acknowledging the compliment, although the words felt thick and cloying in my throat.

I continued, 'Then you must now get back to your normal routine as soon as possible. You cannot continue to live without your slaves to attend to your needs.'

'That's true.' Germanicus took up the conversation after a wave of the hand from Julia. 'The estate will not run itself. But how can we resume our normal lives with four murderers on the grounds? It may take some time to arrange for their collection.'

'I agree,' I said, 'and keeping them on the estate may allow them to infect others with their evil ideas, or to communicate with their co-conspirators. There must be some way to take this burden away from you.'

We all sat for a few moments, mutually pondering the question of how to now deal with the situation. For the first time since entering the house, which seemed so long ago, I noticed the sun casting its light and shadows about the room. Our shapes were marked out clearly on the tiled floor, which was itself shown in a sharp relief of regular squares.

As if I had suddenly received a revelation, imparted through the shafts of light, I exclaimed, 'I think I may have the solution.' I stood up, both to stretch my legs, and to indicate my excitement. 'We are all agreed that the estate, and house, needs to have its slaves working again as soon as possible.'

There were confirmatory nods from my two companions.

'And that the presence of these criminals would impair the smooth running that is so important,' I continued.

Again the nods, slowly this time.

'I need to return to the garrison. Why don't I take them with me? The remaining slaves have been taught a lesson. They'll be much more compliant and in a proper frame of mind for work. The farm should quickly return to normal.' I paused to gauge the success of my proposal.

Julia was smiling, which I took to be approval. Germanicus, on the other hand, had a frown wrinkling his brow, and he almost immediately had an objection.

'How will you transport them back to the garrison?'

Julia supplied the answer. 'You can borrow one of the carts.'

Germanicus still had questions. 'But can you be sure that your slave will not assist them to escape? Maybe I should come with you.'

'I can vouch for Gallius. He may be insolent at times, but he is totally faithful to me.' I was sure Gallius would understand and forgive me for the slur on his character when I could explain. But that would be later, much later, when we were safely away from this place. 'As for you coming with me …' I paused, as if to consider the idea. It was definitely not part of my plan for Germanicus to accompany me. 'I thank you for the offer, but I feel you are needed here much more. Julia cannot be expected to manage by herself. She has need of your assistance and support at the moment.'

Germanicus seemed about to scatter more difficulties in my path, when Julia's voice cut through the air.

'If Tiberius thinks he can do this, then I think we should let him. I want those cursed slaves off my land as soon as possible. Use the cart, and tie them to it, so that I can rest in peace here.' With that declaration, she stood up. 'Tiberius, I want to thank you for your help. Any time that you are passing, you would be an honoured guest here. Good luck on your return journey.' With these parting words she walked out of the room, her head held high; the very picture of a woman who has suffered much, but who will survive. Both Germanicus and I watched her leave in silence.

Once she was out of earshot, Germanicus spoke, 'I'll arrange for the cart to be brought round. I think it would be best for you to start as soon as possible.' His voice was low, and I quickly agreed with him.

'I'm sure there will be no possibility of escape,' I continued, 'The … correction that you ordered will have subdued both their spirits and their flesh. If you hadn't done that, I would not have been able to suggest this course of action.' As he smiled at my false admiration of his beatings, I pressed home my point. 'Besides, if we leave now, there can be no possibility of any organised ambush. Her, their accomplices will not be able to help, if we take the initiative and act now.'

He appeared placated, standing and holding me by the shoulders. I returned his embrace, saying as I did so, 'You must now care for Julia. She's all alone, and will need a good friend, like yourself, to depend on.'

Germanicus' eyes mirrored the actions of his mouth in the first genuine smile I had seen that morning.

A short time later we were riding, in some discomfort, along the road leading away from the farm that had been the scene of such drama.

The day was dry, with a clear, cornflower-blue painted backdrop. The ground on either side of the route was clear, and we could see for some distance both in front and behind the cart, if any of the occupants had a mind to do so. Trees thrust their skeletal shapes up into the air, showing as black, grey and brown cut-outs, posted onto the flat heavens. Birds conducted their own private ballet, wheeling, spinning and separating, according to some exclusive score. All was clean, open and free. The air around us whispered tales of joy and happiness, echoed by the muffled clop of the horses' hooves and the rumble of the wheels. Everything that I could see, hear or smell was healthy and free. Breathing was a cure in itself, as if all of nature were successful in the pursuit of health, and wanted to share its prize. The only thing that didn't belong in that landscape was the cart, and its occupants.

Gallius was driving, sitting slumped and listless on the seat, his gaze shifting between the road ahead and the back of the horses, with only an occasional glance sideways, away from me. He had not initiated any conversation since I had ordered him from the room. The only noise from our human cargo was when the cart gave a particularly violent jolt, which was followed by suppressed sobs and moans. Otherwise they were as silent as when they were first loaded and secured.

I, too, made no effort to interrupt the quietness once we had left the farm behind. I could not relax until we were well out of sight of not only the buildings, but also the outlying estate. At length we had put three or four rolling hills between us, and the last fields of the late Corolius. Part of me realised that I was being over cautious, as the possibility of us being followed was remote, but I could not be otherwise. The tensions of the day so far meant my nerves were wound so tight, I would be unable to let go partially. It would be total release, or nothing.

Turning my head to scan the area behind us, looking beyond the back line of the cart, I checked the road was clear. I could see nothing at the sides or in front either, and at last I could ask Gallius to stop. The order elicited a puzzled look from him, and it was only when I repeated my request, that he followed it. He then sat in the motionless vehicle, the reins lying limp in his hands, for the time it took me to move my stiffened joints into the positions needed to get down and stand up.

'Master, what is going on? What are you doing?' Gallius' voice sounded, suddenly loud in that peaceful setting.

I looked around in apprehension, then smiled to myself. Was I imaging the birds would report my actions, or the trees spy on me?

'Gallius, please, get down, and I'll explain.' I continued speaking as he slowly started moving. If I stopped I could imagine his movements ceasing also. 'I've not gone mad, although it may look that way, and I need to apologise for speaking so abruptly, when you were only giving me accurate information. But I was more concerned with us both managing to leave the farm alive.'

He was now standing in front of me, a frown puckering his brow. 'I'm not sure I understand. One minute you seemed to be saying that Lydia couldn't have done anything wrong. The next you were agreeing that she was indeed guilty, and that the others were also involved.' He threw up his hands. 'I really don't understand.'

'I know. It was all so clear to me, that I completely forgot I hadn't explained things to you. Then, when we were in the house, in front of Julia and Germanicus, there was no way I could say anything. I just needed ... It was a dangerous game we were playing.' I leant heavily on the edge of the cart. 'I needed to make them believe that I thought Lydia, and, after your interjection, the other three slaves ... I had to make Germanicus and Julia believe I thought them guilty.'

I mentally reviewed my words, and rearranged them. 'I needed to make Germanicus and Julia think that I thought Lydia was guilty. Otherwise, there may well have been an accident, or ambush arranged for us.'

Gallius stood, opening and closing his mouth a few times, with no sound issuing forth. 'I still don't understand,' was his eventual offering.

'Lydia and the other three, they didn't have anything to do with Corolius' death, except to act as scapegoats. It was Germanicus and Julia who killed him, and might have killed us too. I'm sure of it.'

'But Master, surely not.'

'Which bit do you doubt? That they could have killed Corolius, or that they would have killed us?'

'Both.' Gallius turned away from me for a few seconds. Overhead, the birds in the aerial ballet appeared to reach their climax, before the performers moved on to another display. When he turned back, I could see that he had been thinking. The furrowed brow was replaced with an alertness and attention that was mirrored in his stance.

'Master, how can you be certain that Germanicus and Julia murdered Corolius? Surely they would not have called us to investigate if they had?'

I glanced back at the contents of the cart. 'I'll explain as we travel, but first I think we should untie these four, so that they can travel in a little more comfort.'

While Gallius wedged a large stone under the wheel of the cart, I climbed in the back. As I did so, eight eyes looked at me, directing hatred and distrust in my direction. Nothing was said.

'Please, I know you have no reason to trust me, but will you all promise to stay in the cart if I untie you. If you run away, I won't be able to help.'

One, either Alena or Zera, glanced at the others and then nodded slowly.

'I know you haven't done anything wrong.' I started to wrestle with the bonds that held the nearest girl firmly attached to the side of the cart. 'You won't be treated like criminals.' Germanicus had overseen the knots personally, and had insisted they be tight, which was now causing me problems. But this one was coming loose. 'You will be under my personal pro ... oof.'

As I had been speaking, the knot I had been fighting, suddenly became a tangle and then merely a rope.

The released girl, instead of sitting meekly or helping untie her friends, had bent her knee, and made contact with my groin, to the accompaniment of cheers and encouraging shouts from the other girls. I lay against the wooden side, unable to do any more than recover my lost breath. I was dimly aware of Gallius catching hold of her, before she could swing her fist at me as well. Above me, I could see the clear blue sky become streaked with white wisps, and I could feel the air grow turbulent. As my breathing returned to normal, it brought with it a release of emotion, and I found myself burst into laughter. So might Epimetheus have felt, after accepting Pandora and her jar of evil and sickness? A good deed done for others is not necessarily taken as such by them. We can never know how our actions may be interpreted. As my tension receded in humour, I felt more relaxed, and Gallius' voice registered on my ears.

'Master, are you all right? ... Why did you hit him like that? There was no call for that. He was only trying to help you ... Master, can you hear me?'

'Gallius, I'm fine.' I clambered back to my feet. 'I think you can let her go now. She won't try anything else.' I looked directly at the girl he was holding, who was struggling and still trying to lash out with her bare feet.

'If you try to run away, how far to do you think you'll get with these three?' as I pointed to the back of the cart. 'Or were you going to leave them to their own fates?'

The women looked at each other, eyes locked in silent communication.

'So,' I continued, sensing that my will had prevailed, 'Gallius I think you can let her go now. She's not going to try anything, are you?'

She looked defiantly back at me for a few moments, before dropping her gaze and shaking her head of golden, tangled hair. Gallius slowly and carefully released his grip, but in a way that meant he could rapidly restrain her again if necessary.

'Gallius, you undo her,' as I indicated the nearest to him. 'I can't remember who's who.'

'I'm Alena, that's Thalia, Zera and Lydia over there.' My would-be assailant matched her words to actions.

'Thank you, Alena. If you could untie Zera, I'll look after Lydia.' Again I struggled with bonds that had already cut deeply into flesh. As I did so, Lydia looked up at me, the hatred and fear in her eyes starting to melt away. She said nothing, but for a few brief heartbeats, no-one else existed, just the two of us, silently communicating.

As the ligature loosened, I let it fall, unheeded. Reaching out my finger, I gently traced the outline of a bruise around her right eye. She caught hold of my hand, as silent tears started to flow.

'So, are you going to tell us what's going on here?' The confident voice of Alena broke the silence, and as I looked up, a gust of wind caught her hair, sending golden threads whirling and spinning. With one hand, she captured the loose tendrils, and repeated her question. 'Are you going to tell us what's going on?'

I glanced up at the sky, where the streaks of white had arranged themselves into patches of greyness. The wind was rapidly marshalling more forces to join them, overwhelming the small amount of blue that was left.

'Can it wait until we're back at the garrison?' was my reply. 'I don't want to be caught out here if it starts raining.'

Alena shivered in response. 'It is getting a bit cold,' she conceded. 'I guess your story can wait.'

She was right. I, too, could feel the chill brought by the rising wind. Gallius and I had our cloaks, but our female companions wore only their tunics, scant protection against potentially vicious weather.

'Gallius, get the horses ready. We need to get back to
the garrison, preferably before it rains.' I indicated to Alena
and the others that they should make themselves as
comfortable as possible. My intention was to sit in the back
with them, using my cloak as a blanket for us all, but Gallius
had other ideas.

'Master, you had best drive, and I'll go in the back.'
The girls had already seated themselves on the floor, to take
advantage of any scant protection the wooden sides might
offer, and there were one or two giggles, when they realised
Gallius proposed to sit with them.

I was about to demur, when Gallius continued, 'It
wouldn't be right, you sat in the back with the slaves, and me
at the front. With you driving, we won't attract any attention.'

Conceding defeat, I wrapped my cloak round me, and
took my place at the reins. It felt lonely up there, when I
could hear chatter and an occasional laugh from the carriage
behind me. I could not distinguish words or even identify
voices, as the cruel zephyr took the sounds, mixed them up
and tossed them away. I concentrated on reaching the
garrison as soon as possible, letting the scenery slide past on
either side, unnoticed and unhindered.

Dusk had crept up on us while we were still travelling, causing the glow of the garrison to shine out like a beacon. The dim light acted as friend and aide, providing concealment for the passengers in the cart. While I knew them to be innocent, I did not want news of their arrival to be common gossip by morning, or Germanicus would have reason to demand a different destination for them. My representation on their behalf needed to be done quickly, before he felt impelled to do so. I made for the infirmary, where we could all alight in partial safety, out of sight of the main barracks.

As soon as we reached the door, Gallius jumped out of the cart, ready to assist the quartet as they made their descents. By the time I had made a slower and more laborious climb with my stiff and heavy joints, Alena and Zera were standing with their arms round Thalia, whose cough could now be clearly heard despite her best efforts to muffle it.

Lydia was still sitting on the back edge of the cart. Her back was bowed, and Gallius' arm appeared to be the only thing that prevented her from slumping to the floor. My immediate reaction was to displace him. I wanted to be the one giving her support, not Gallius. Why should he be assisting her?

As I reached them, Lydia had found her feet, and was being escorted inside on unsteady legs, by Gallius. The dim light could not prevent me from seeing the dark, uneven stripes that stood out clearly on the back of her light coloured tunic.

I stood, momentarily rooted to the spot. My heart wanted my feet to move, to run after her, to help bind her wounds, lay her down to rest. My head said I needed to go to my rooms, write out the account I would need to send to Aurelius, outlining all that I had found at Corolius' farm. Until that was done, and Aurelius convinced that my version was the most accurate, none of our four visitors was safe. Even now, Germanicus might be sending a messenger down to Durnovaria. I had to forestall him. And so it was with lethargic steps that I turned and headed for my quarters, there to pick up my pen and papyrus.

I was still writing when Gallius entered, bringing a large bowl of hot, steaming stew, and a very welcome flagon of wine. When I had first sat down, it was my knees and back that had cried out for relief, now it was the turn of my shoulders and fingers, as I forced them to complete the task.

While I finished, Gallius ladled a generous helping onto my plate. Sealing the scroll, I handed it to Gallius, with the instruction, 'That needs to go to Aurelius tonight. It must definitely be sent tonight. Could you see to it, and then come and sit here with me? I've some explanations for you.'

He returned in the space of one long-savoured mouthful of hot food, and seated himself at the table. I nodded at the large bowl, still well filled.

'Help yourself,' I said.

Smiling, he produced a second plate and cup. 'I thought you might say that, Master. I was prepared.'

'Gallius, you know me too well.' I took another mouthful, letting the warmth from the meat infuse my throat, stomach and body. 'How are our four passengers? Have you arranged for them to have food?'

'It's all sorted. They'll stay tonight in one of the rooms in the infirmary. That way, Alena and Zera can look after Thalia and Lydia, and as few people as possible will know they're there.' He forestalled my unspoken question. 'They'll all be fine, given a good night's sleep, a decent meal and the reassurance they won't face the arena.' He poured some wine and I watched the pale liquid transfer itself from the jug to my cup. 'Master, you, too, might be better for the same. Stories can wait until morning.'

'No, it's best told now.' I leant back in my chair. Even though I had resolved to explain my reasoning to Gallius, I felt reluctant to do so. What if my logic were in error? Could I have misinterpreted that which I thought I had seen? Was my chain of deduction from the evidence the only one possible, or had I assumed a link where none existed? By stating my understanding of the events on Corolius' farm, I lay myself open to criticism and possible censorship. Was this how an artist felt, on completion of a work, which he has yet to show his patron? Did writers of plays get nervous before the opening, fearful that no-one would come? But then I had already told others. The scroll was, even now, on its travels to Durnovaria. I could, at least, trust Gallius gently to point out any falseness in my reasoning.

'Gallius, what do you think happened at Corolius' farm?'

He sat back, cradling his cup in both hands. 'Corolius was killed, was beheaded, at some point during the night. His body was left in the ditch in the field. In the morning, the main door was still locked, and none of the slaves were missing.'

He frowned. 'Surely if any of them had been involved, they would have disappeared. No-one who had killed their master would have stayed.' He replaced his cup on the table, and leant forward to rest both elbows on the wooden surface. 'I can't see how or why any of the slaves would have wanted to hurt him. By all accounts, Corolius was a reasonable master, although Julia was often demanding and pernickety about things.' He paused in his summary, looking across the table at me. 'And you don't think any of the slaves were involved either, do you?'

'No, I don't.' I shook my head as I met his eyes.

'But you do think you know who did.'

This time I responded with a slow nod, before speaking. 'When I examined the body, I found that the right side was reddened, with some regular white squares. When we first saw how Corolius had been found, Germanicus said he was lying on his back. For Corolius to have that redness from the blood settling after death, he must have been lying on his side for some hours after he died. He couldn't have been in the position Germanicus said he was.'

'Yes, otherwise the redness would be on his back. But what about the white marks? What could they have been?' Gallius had picked up his cup again, and was swirling the pink fluid around, before taking a deep draught.

343

'I've been thinking about that, and I think I now have the answer.' I picked up the jug to replenish my glass. 'We know that if a body is lying on a smooth, hard surface for the hours after the person has died, then there may be patches of whiteness, where the pressure has stopped the blood.'

Gallius gave an affirmatory nod.

'Well,' I continued, 'what if a body were lying, not on a smooth surface, but one with a regular pattern of raised squares?'

This time Gallius just looked at me for a few moments, before saying, 'What sort of raised squares?'

I took a deep breath. This was my first link in the chain of events I had constructed. If this were false, then so might everything else be false. 'The sort you would get in a mosaic floor.'

Time seemed to stand still. The wind outside could be heard in the rattle of the wooden shutters. Was it trying to enter and blow away my imagined fortress of proof?

'You think Corolius was lying on a tiled floor for some hours after he died.' Gallius' words were slow and precise. 'It would certainly fit the picture, but that would mean he was in the main room of the house. I can't imagine Julia or Germanicus not noticing a dead body at their feet.'

'Neither can I, Gallius, neither can I.' The external air currents subsided, as did my fears. 'Corolius had to have been on the tiled floor, nothing else could have left those marks. Which means it's almost certain that the slaves weren't the culprits. They would not have killed their master, and then walked away leaving him on display.' I picked up a dried fig from the dish, holding it in my hand before continuing, 'Anyway, slaves would be more likely to poison his food, stab him in the back or throttle him, than hack off his head.' I bit into the fruit.

'But Germanicus or Julia could have done it.' Gallius slammed his cup back down, sending drops of wine splashing onto the table. He hid his face in his hands, causing his words to emerge muffled as he said, 'I can't believe I'm sitting here, accusing Julia of involvement in the murder of her own husband.' He dropped his hands back to the table, announcing, 'It must have been Germanicus, but why? Why would he kill his employer?'

'Maybe he no longer wished to be the employee? I suspect his designs on the fair Julia were reciprocated. You told me yourself, that they often spent the night together, when Corolius was away. Maybe there was an argument, which progressed to a fight?'

'Is that likely? Is that what you think?' asked Gallius.

'I know that Corolius had several bruises on his body, that could have come from a fight. In that household, only Germanicus would have had the strength to strike Corolius hard enough to give him the marks I saw. Remember Germanicus used to be a soldier.'

'So Corolius' death may have been accidental?'

I sat back down again, and refilled both my cup, and that of Gallius. 'It might have started out as an accident, but he then deliberately tried to make it look like murder, and as if the slaves, as if Lydia was guilty. If we accept that Germanicus killed Corolius in a fight, and the pattern of the bruises on the body would support that, then we must also accept that Germanicus then tried to make it look as if the death was part of the same sequence as that of Lucius and Victor.'

Gallius nodded slowly, and sipped his wine. 'But you have no proof of that. You can say how the injuries on Corolius were sustained, but you can't prove who inflicted them.'

I stood up again, and untied the chisel from my belt. There was a dull thud as I placed it on the table between us. 'That's my proof.'

'But it's just an old chisel. It can't prove anything.'

I took a deep draught of my wine, to moisten my drying throat. 'Whoever killed Corolius, also set up the scene to try to make it look like Lucius' and Victor's deaths. Would you agree with that?'

Gallius nodded, a frown on his face.

'So whoever set the scene and decapitated Corolius, must have been the person who killed him.'

'But that's what you've just said, only a different way round.'

'Gallius, the order of the words is important. I can prove who severed Corolius' head from his body, and therefore we can say who fought and killed him.'

Gallius started shaking his head, apparently at a loss for words. He did not need to say anything for me to know he did not believe me.

I picked up the chisel and continued speaking, 'I found this in the carpentry workshop, in a pile of discarded tools. This edge is chipped, as if used on something hard, like bone. The cut in Corolius' neck was not clean. It had been hacked at several times.' I brought the chisel up so I could see it more clearly. 'I matched the size and shape of this blade to many of those cuts.'

I turned the tool round in my fingers. 'I believe this is blood on the end as well as part way up the blade, and also here, on the handle. See, you can tell where a hand, covered in blood, has held this.' I passed it over to Gallius who peered closely at it for a few moments.

'I can see blood on the blade, and I can see a hand print on the handle, but it could have been anyone's hand print.'

'It could, except that if you look here,' leaning across the table, I pointed to one particular section, 'you can see that the man who held this had lost the tip of his third finger, his ring finger on the left hand.'

'The man …?'

'It must have been a man, Gallius. Look at the size. The impression is far too large for a woman.'

He measured the palm print against his own hand, finding that his was slightly smaller. 'I agree on the size, but the tip of his finger missing?'

I took the chisel again, pointing out the marks as I spoke. 'There you can see the ends of his other fingers, but here the finger seems shorter. He wouldn't be able to lift the end of that finger off the handle, especially as he would have needed to grip it tightly, so he must have lost the finger pad and nail.'

As I was speaking, Gallius had picked up his cup and was looking at how his digits made contact with it, trying to lift just the tip of his third finger, without success. I laid the chisel down on the table between us.

'Germanicus has lost the tip of his third finger on his left hand.' The words I uttered seemed hard and final. As I'd worked through my reasoning, I had half hoped that I would come to a different conclusion, but no. This was the same result I came to each time, the right result, the truth.

Gallius looked at me, and nodded. His voice was quiet. 'So Germanicus did kill his master.' He sat silent and still for a few moments, before questioning, 'If that's so, then why did he set it up to look like the other murders you're investigating?'

I picked up another fig, slowly chewing it and swallowing, before answering, 'I think that was a gamble, and the reason why I think Julia is as much involved as Germanicus.' I ignored the sharp intake of breath from Gallius. 'She must have known what happened - was happening - and saw it as an opportunity to get rid of Lydia. For some reason, Julia hated Lydia, but Corolius liked her. If they set up the body to look as if Lydia had conspired with the druids to kill Corolius, they would get rid of her at the same time as covering their own guilt.'

I looked up from my study of the grain of the table, to gaze at Gallius. 'I think they - Germanicus and Julia - thought I would take the evidence on face value, and confirm their story.'

'Which you did.' Gallius' words were still soft, but there was a hard edge to them. 'You told them that you thought Lydia, and Alena, Zera and Thalia were all guilty. They think you believe their story.'

'I know what I said, Gallius.' Suddenly I was cold at the memory of our close shave. A chill, straight from the Underworld, ran along my spine. 'Do you think we'd be sitting here, discussing it, if I'd told them what I really thought? I'm sure that Corolius' earlier illnesses were no accident. I think he was being poisoned, probably with hemlock, which would mean someone in that household has been plotting to get rid of him for some time. Saying what I said, meant we were able to leave in relative safety, otherwise there might well have been an accident along the way, or poison introduced into our food.'

Gallius' eyes suddenly widened, and his lower lip dropped. 'Then when I reminded you that ...'

'When you reminded me that Lydia couldn't possibly have had anything to do with the murder, I had to stop you saying anything else.'

'Or we might have been killed as well.' He took a gulp from his cup, holding it with hands that were shaking.

'But we're both here now and safe, as are our four passengers. I couldn't have left them there, or Germanicus might have decided to act as judge and executioner.'

Despite the mental and physical exertions of the day, my rest that night was troubled and disturbed. The letter I had written to Aurelius meant that I was effectively condemning two people to death.

The situation was one that was new to me. I was very accustomed to delivering bad news and dealing with its consequences, but usually I was imparting information to those who already suspected the words I would say. Usually I would have been able to prepare the ground in anticipation. Usually I would have had the assurance of knowing that I had done all in my power to delay the last journey that each of us must make.

This time I had concealed my intentions. Lies and half-truths had flown from my lips with ease. I had gone out of my way to deceive. But then, these people had done the same to someone else. They had murdered Corolius, and would have had others killed to protect themselves.

I do not doubt that my life, and that of Gallius, would have been in danger if Germanicus or Julia had suspected that I considered them guilty. A man who has killed once, may not hesitate to do so again to protect his freedom. A woman who would see four innocent slaves executed, would not give up easily.

No, uneasy as my sleep was, I was sure I had done the right thing. I knew the four slaves who, hopefully were resting peacefully in the infirmary, were innocent. What kept me awake was why Germanicus and Julia killed Corolius. Despite my own protestations that there was no connection with the deaths of Lucius and Victor, I was not totally convinced. The obvious link, in who had committed the crime, was not there, but something tied these killings together. Something intangible, out of reach, yet I could sense it. Corolius had been absent from his farm several times, with no indication of where he was or why. Was Corolius himself involved in the earlier murders? If he was, then the obvious supposition was that Corolius was linked with the druids. If so, then surely the cult would seek revenge for his murder. Germanicus and Julia may have made a mistake when they killed Corolius, and might have put their own lives in danger.

What was Memno's part in all this? Corolius had been at the garrison recently. Germanicus had assumed it was to consult with me, but it was Memno who received the visitor. If Corolius was associated with these druids, then that could mean Memno was as well. But no. I could not see Memno forsaking the religion of his childhood so easily. However, I could not forget that he had wished to tell me something, so long ago. What was his secret? Was someone I considered my friend mixed up in all this? I could not believe him to be part of this local cult, but what other explanation was there? I found it difficult to accept that he might have killed Lucius or Victor, or had any part in their deaths? He and Lucius were great friends and he had seemed very moved by his demise, so much that his very heart seemed as if was literally being wrung. But that could be an indication of how much he felt the loss, or it could mean a guilty conscience. And so my thoughts revolved round and round, as the stars do likewise in the firmaments, till dawn.

Day Nineteen

The request I received, on rising the next morning, meant that some of my questions might be answered. Along with my breakfast was a message from Memno, asking to see me urgently. I was eager to meet with him, and as soon as I had partaken of some sustenance, I hurried across the courtyard. I could see a road-building party heading out of the main gate, surveyors and soldiers all well wrapped up against the inclement weather. The wind tugged at my cloak, and ran cold fingers through my hair. Glancing inside the surveyors' office and finding it empty, I continued on. Reaching Memno's quarters, I stepped inside, glad to be in the shelter of the building. The door was slammed behind me, as if the air currents were frustrated at the loss of a playmate.

'Tiberius, it's good to see you. How are you?' The words that emerged from Memno's mouth were not the ones written on his drawn and pale face.

'I'm fine,' I replied, 'but you look as if you haven't slept for at least a couple of nights.'

Memno put a smile onto his face, and indicated a chair, which I took, as he did likewise. 'I had hoped that … is it true?' He seemed to struggle to articulate the words. Perching on the edge of his seat, he reached his hand out towards me, as if to take and understand my reply better.

'Is what true?' I asked.

'The news about Corolius. Is it true he's dead?'

As I nodded I contemplated how he had gained this knowledge so quickly, but then I must accept that rumours travel fast in the garrison. The messenger from Corolius' farm would have known that his master was dead, despite the cryptic message he had delivered. Memno dropped his head, his mouth forming words that only he could hear, his chin resting on his clasped hands.

'You seem very concerned about him. I didn't realise you knew him that well.' As I spoke, Memno raised his head, and looked at me with bright eyes.

'We … knew each other. How did he die? Was it an accident?'

I hesitated before speaking. Should I keep the manner of his death a secret? There was probably no need, as rumour and gossip were likely to have spread the story wide.

The messenger who had originally summoned me must have talked to others. At the very least, he would have required a few drinks to steady his nerves. 'His body was found. Like Lucius and Victor, he had also been beheaded.'

Memno let out a long, low gasp. He stood up and moved to look out of the window, his cloak wrapped tightly around him. 'Do you know who did it? Was it the same person, the same cult?'

'I really can't say at the moment.' I didn't want to add to the gossip by publicly denouncing Germanicus and Julia. The authorities would act soon enough. 'I'm surprised that you knew Corolius, although he did come here to see you a few times, didn't he?' My words were directed at Memno's rigid back.

'Yes.' There was a pause, before Memno continued, 'He was consulting me on something.'

'Oh, what was that?'

'A water mill … yes … he had ideas for a water mill on the stream. Thought he'd be able to harness the power to grind his corn. We talked over a few ideas.'

'A mill? On the stream that runs by the villa?'

Memno turned back towards me, resting his hands on the window ledge behind him. 'Yes, that's the one.'

'I would've thought it too slow to use for a mill.'

Memno smiled and nodded vigorously. 'That's the same conclusion I reached. That's what I told him. Now, I must thank you for coming over so promptly, but I have rather a lot of things to get done today, so if you'll excuse me.'

Almost without realising it, I found myself standing looking at the outside of Memno's door. Why was he lying to me? Corolius had been visiting him, but it was most certainly not to consult about the design and construction of a water mill. The stream that ran down by the side of the villa was too small for the idea even to be considered. Additionally, I could not envisage Julia or Corolius wanting to spoil the view down the valley from their reception room window. No, whatever Corolius and Memno had been discussing, it had not been how to grind corn. I felt sure that Memno had wanted me out of his quarters, so that he could go somewhere else, meet someone else. I would have to follow him. The idea sickened me, but I knew I needed to keep an eye on my old friend, if only to prove his innocence. I hoped that I would not be proving his guilt.

Having decided that I would stalk my friend, I weighed the relative merits of telling Gallius.

On the one hand, it would be beneficial for someone else to know what I was doing. A shudder went down my spine as I recalled the previous solitary excursion I had made, resulting in injuries to more than my pride. On the other hand, finding Gallius would take time, during which Memno might evade my observations. The haste with which Memno had effected my exit from his quarters, pointed to an early departure. It seemed that all Memno had wanted from me was the confirmation of how Corolius had died. While I was thus cogitating, my feet appeared to have made their own decision, and I found myself at the stables. My mind agreed with my body that a longer, rather than shorter, journey seemed likely, and I asked for my horse to be made ready.

As the stable hand did as he was ordered, I heard the approach of another person. Sinking my body back into the shadows afforded by the dimly lit building, I turned my head away, for I had caught a glimpse of Memno. He, too, was requesting his horse, and I thanked the gods that I had spoken to the slower of the two grooms.

The journey we made was moderate in length, but felt long; the sun was warm, but I was chilled; the road was easy, but seemed arduous.

Making sure I kept Memno in view while staying far enough behind to ensure that he was unaware of me, meant I could not maintain a steady speed. At times I had to be close, to check he didn't turn off, or get lost in other traffic. As we traversed long, open sections, I fell back or took advantage of what sparse cover there was along the route. On one straight, undulating stretch, I could see a small figure approach, disappearing into the dips, and re-emerging, larger and in more detail. When he was midway between Memno and myself, I could recognise a messenger from the urgency with which he pushed his mount. Was he bearing a reply to my letter of last night? If so, I could only hope it was not one that required an immediate answer.

A hunting party cut across the road, heading into the thick woods I could see to my left, the small, squat dogs pulling on the leash, towing their handlers behind, who were running to keep up. Tonight, someone would be planning the cooking of boar, hare or deer. A group of riders, some seven or eight, joined the road from a side turn, siting themselves between myself and my quarry.

I had a few moments of anxiety when they stopped on the road to converse, before the party split at a fork, some continuing on the main highway, others turning off down a track through woodland.

Once I had overtaken them, I could see Memno ahead of me, and I relaxed again. Soon afterwards we passed through a herd of goats, being driven erratically along, the two herders using wooden swatches to maintain some order in their haphazard group.

And so we continued, Memno in front, riding at a steady pace, always onwards, never looking back. A column of soldiers marched up, the noise of their iron shod sandals announcing their approach, and wordlessly ordering all on the road to vacate it. I shaded my eyes against the reflection of the sun on their armour, as I steered my horse onto the soft grass that bordered the carriageway. Further on we passed a slow moving cart, groaning under its load of sacks, the mules plodding on at their own pace, regardless of the encouragement of the driver.

After some miles, we came to the town of Lindinis. Was this our destination or would Memno ride on through? I closed the gap between us, fearing to lose him in the bustle and confusion of the settlement. Memno made his intentions clear, as he turned off the main thoroughfare, and stopped at the public stables.

He quickly surrendered his horse to the stable hand, then purposefully strode off. Emerging from the gateway I had sheltered in, I had just time to dismount, and hand the reins to the startled boy, together with a few coins, before hurrying after Memno.

In many ways, it was easier to keep him in view, now that we were on foot. I could be closer, there was more cover to hide me if necessary, the shops and taverns proving to be my allies. However, there were also more people to obscure my vision: more people wearing the same type of olive green cloak, more people of a similar height, more people to block my path. At one point I was sure I had lost my quarry, after a compact crowd had prevented my passage. I could see the hood of the cloak I was following, disappear into a side alley, and I hurried after it. Yet when I reached the spot, I found a stranger. I was close to panic as I whirled back to scan the main street. Where was he? Had my shadowing been in vain? Was I to lose my objective now? Should I continue further down the road, or turn back?

While I vacillated, a man in an olive green garment walked purposefully along on the other side of the street. The hood of the cloak was pushed back, so that I could identify the visage as that of my friend.

My feet led me across the road, while my mind wondered how long he would continue to be my friend. Surely this surreptitious escorting meant that I would forfeit any right to comradeship, and for that, I was sad. Pushing such thoughts aside, to a time when I could consider them more clearly, I trailed behind Memno.

The door that he stopped at, down a side turning, was set back from the surrounding wall, creating an alcove. I found a recess with a good view on the other side of the street, into which I could retreat. The sun slanted down to strike the building opposite me, highlighting slight imperfections and rough areas in the render. My hiding place was shadowed and my concealment was aided by my dark, grey cloak, helping to merge me into the weathered wood.

The door opened in response to Memno's knock and a tall gentleman, dressed in a finely worked maroon tunic stood there. I had expected a slave or servant to act as door sentry, but the ease and familiarity with which he and Memno greeted and embraced, indicated otherwise.

A few words spoken in a low tone were exchanged between them, before Memno entered the house. The unknown man glanced briefly up and down the street, then he, too, withdrew, closing the door behind him.

I stood, looking at the sealed building opposite as if I could force it to reveal its secrets by will power and the strength of my gaze. It remained stubbornly silent. I pondered my options. I could stay where I was, until Memno reappeared. I could make enquiries as to the owner of the house. I could imagine some innocent reason for Memno's visit and return to the garrison. I could storm the building and demand an explanation.

Silently laughing to myself at the notion of the last idea, and while weighing the relative merits of the first three, I found I could delay the decision a little longer. Three people approached from the main street, apparently heading for the same house that Memno had entered. At the same time, four smaller figures appeared at the further end of the alley. The group of three halted outside the door of the building I had under observation, but turned, after one had knocked, to watch the antics of the four children who had started playing.

Two small boys towed a third, who was sitting in a home made cart. One wheel wobbled, threatening to upset the whole contraption. After making it safely to one end of the street, they swapped places and attempted a return journey.

The trio of adults at the door entered the house before disaster struck. The precarious wheel detached itself from the rest of the framework, tipping the occupant out. A bloodied knee and elbow seemed to be regarded as trophies as the boys collected together the broken pieces of their home made chariot. Throughout this, a small girl of about four, stood watching, clutching a doll to her chest.

'Hello.' A voice drifted up to me, accompanied by a tugging on my cloak.

'Hello', I responded, bending down to address the girl who now stood in front of me.

'What are you doing?'

'I'm waiting for someone. Do you know who lives in that house?'

She shook her head, her tousled hair flying about. 'He's a nice man. He gave me my dolly.' She held out the toy at arm's length, and I duly admired it.

'Are you very old?' was her next question, leaving me at a loss as to how to answer. She didn't seem to require a response, as she continued, 'My name's Ally. What's yours?'

'My name's Tiberius.'

Our conversation was cut short by the re-emergence of one of the former steeds of the broken chariot, calling out, 'Ally, Ally, come on.'

'I've got to go. Goodbye.' And with that she turned and ran down the street. As she did so, she nearly collided with a stout man, making his way heavily along, again heading for, and then entering, the mysterious doorway opposite. I stood still, waiting to see what would transpire. My best course of action seemed to be observation of the house.

Leaning against the support of the buildings at my back, I recapped all the events that had happened, trying to put them into some sort of order. As the shadows lengthened, so did my list. The deaths of Lucius, Victor, the unknown Roman, and latterly of Corolius, how were they all connected? They had all been beheaded, but I knew that Corolius' death had been different. Secret meetings. There had been too many secret meetings, by too many people. Memno, in the house opposite. Corolius, with his unexplained absences from his farm. Gallius, when he was trading cures with the local women. Agricola, with his knowledge of at least one local girl, and being able to converse with her in her own language.

So many people carrying on so many different activities. Some innocent, some sinister and to be prevented, others with reasons that were personal and private. But which was which?

I rubbed my hands together and blew some meagre warmth back into them, as I shifted my weight from one foot to the other. What was I doing here? Was this the right location for me to be?

What could I learn from standing in this spot? Only that Memno had entered a house, and that others had also gone into the same building. That a 'nice man', who gave toys to children, owned the dwelling. A man who greeted his guests at the doorway, rather than having them shown in by a servant or slave. I wondered if this was from choice or necessity. The house appeared too grand for there to be no assistance for the owners. The wind snatched one edge of my cloak from my hand, billowing it out, until I could recapture it.

What had I gained from any of the locations I had been to? Just deductions and suppositions. Only in the case of Corolius had I gleaned enough evidence to implicate Germanicus and Julia, or rather prove Germanicus' guilt and, by extension, that of Julia.

What had I learnt from my trips to the riverbanks where the first two bodies had been found? I hugged both arms round my torso, a twinge of remembered pain running round my ribs.

I was sure of what I had seen in that grove of trees, or was I? I had been certain at the time, but when the soldiers investigated they had found nothing. I still could not reconcile this with the fragment of cloth I had found, which indicated by its whiteness, that someone had passed that way recently.

While I pondered, the sky above me had been gradually clouding over, obscuring the sun, but a few shafts of light suddenly illuminated the street, to disappear as quickly as they had appeared. My feet were growing colder the longer I stood, but I feared to move. I felt on the verge of a discovery. If I walked about, I would displace the thoughts that were slowly drifting together, and they would be lost in more turbulent waters. I closed my eyes to block out all extraneous distractions.

The soldiers had found nothing where they had looked, but could I be certain they had looked in the same place I had been? How had they known where to go? I had been in no fit state to guide them. I opened my eyes again, as the realisation hit me.

I was in the wrong place. I might wait all night and all tomorrow here, and still not get the answers I sought. No, I must actively seek out the truth I was looking for, and I would not find it here.

I must get back to the garrison, and quickly, for it was there that I must conduct, and complete, my enquiries.

My ride back seemed both longer and shorter than the outward journey. I had no need for caution, as I was not following anyone, and so I could push my horse to a steady canter. But I knew my time was limited, before others would return. Each obstacle that I encountered - the hill that my mount slowed to climb, the broken down cart on a bridge, the column of soldiers that had right of way - made the distance seem longer.

My thoughts had bifurcated, each line proceeding along its own independent track. What if I were too late, and that which I would be searching for, was already destroyed or disposed of? How long would Memno be at the house in Lindinis? My plans would be in tatters if he returned too soon.

What if? How long? What if? How long? The two phrases echoed in my ears to the beat of the horse's hooves. I scarcely noticed the passing countryside, or the traffic on the road, except mentally to curse the slow moving carts that held me up.

The shadows were growing long as I rode back through the gates. Heading for the stables, I abandoned my mount and hurried off to my nephew's rooms. I wasn't sure how much time I would have. Although it was some hours since I had last eaten, my head over-ruled my stomach. Food could wait. It was with this thought that I burst into Valerian's quarters.

'You've got to come with me. I need you and some soldiers. They may be needed, but we must go now.'

Valerian's bemused look penetrated my gabbled words and I ground to a halt. He was sitting at his desk, an open wax tablet in front of him. He carefully laid his stylus down, before speaking.

'Tiberius, you're not making any sense. Are you ill?'

I shook my head, and tried again, as calmly as I could. 'Valerian, I need you to come with me, and I also need you to bring some soldiers.'

'I think you need to tell me just what it is you want, and why.' He motioned to a chair. 'Sit down and explain, please.'

I walked up and down his room. I was too agitated to sit. If I used some of the energy I had, I would be able to articulate better.

'Valerian, I know who killed Lucius and Victor, and I'm sure I can prove it, but first I need you to help me find the last piece of evidence. We need to go now, before they return.'

'Who did it? Before who returns?'

I paused and took a deep breath, stopping my walking to stand in front of him. 'Please trust me. I don't … we don't have much time. I can't go into all the details now. I need to search the surveyors' office and quarters, but we must do it now, while they're empty.'

Valerian sat for a few seconds, seconds that stretched into an eternity. His anticipated movement sent a shock wave through my taut nerves. He stood up, putting one hand on my shoulder. His voice was soft, as he said, 'Don't let me down.'

Our eyes met, and I tried, with mine, to match the trust I could see in his. Our contact broke and we headed for the door.

'You said I might need some soldiers. How many, and for what?' Valerian's voice was business-like, touched with the edge of steel that had made him a successful soldier.

'A contuburnium, I think. That should be sufficient.'

Eight would be plenty to keep watch and prevent my quarry from fleeing. 'I need them well hidden, but so they can watch the buildings, while we are inside, and also to stop anyone who might try to leave.'

A few short and succinct orders were given, and I could hear men running to obey. Valerian turned to me again. 'Why do you want to stop people leaving? You said the offices and quarters were empty.'

'I don't want anyone getting away when they do return. If they see the soldiers at the door, they might just slip away into the night. No, I would like the guards hidden, but so that they can see the doors.' If I was right, the evidence I was going to find would mean that the case was proven, and I did not want my prey arriving back to find his quarters being overtly watched. If the soldiers were too visible, he might disappear. In which case Lucius and Victor might never be avenged.

Valerian nodded, as if in approval of my strategy, as we arrived at our destination.

I stepped across the threshold into the empty office. Valerian was close behind, and for a few moments we both stood still.

His voice was hushed as he asked, 'What are we looking for?'

My answer was as softly spoken, 'I'm not sure. I'll know when I see it.'

A lopsided smile and a shake of his head appeared before he turned to the soldier who gently tapped at the door. I glanced round the room. The desk stood to one end, with its cubby-holes and drawers for wax tablets, scrolls and ink. In one corner were a few gromas, their pendulums hanging from the cross bars like toy gibbets. I contemplated closing the shutters over the open window to conceal our presence, then decided not to. I needed the light from the late afternoon sun and a sealed room would arouse suspicion far more than one with glimpses of movement inside.

Valerian returned to my side as he whispered, 'The men are in position.'

Next to him a soldier stood nervously to attention, trying hard to correct his unevenly belted tunic. I looked back round the room, my gaze resting on the large table, squatting in the centre.

Moving forward, I could see the map spread out on the flat surface. Garrisons, towns, farms and roads, all miniaturised and carefully positioned. Rivers were shrunk down to a thread of blue, woodland reduced to a splash of green.

'What now?' asked Valerian.

I scratched my head, and frowned. 'I'm looking for something odd, out of the ordinary, unexpected. Something that seems out of place.'

Valerian glanced round the room. 'Shouldn't be too difficult to find. Not many places to hide things here. Where shall we start?'

I shook my head. 'No, I don't think it's in here.' What I was looking for was unlikely to be in the office. This room was too public, too open, too transparent. I walked out and towards the surveyors' quarters, stopping outside my selected door.

Pushing it open, I entered the room. Here I would find my evidence. Here, where there was privacy, secrecy, and hiding places that could be exposed. I slowly stepped forward, Valerian at my back. In fact there were few areas to search, a wooden chest, a cabinet and a tall cupboard. These, along with the bed, a table and two chairs, constituted the sum of furniture.

The iron bound chest, standing at the foot of the bed, drew me like a magnet. With my concentration fixed on that, I momentarily forgot my companions. It was only when my ears registered sound, that I realised the soldier was doing his best to help by rummaging through the cupboard.

Spinning round, I shouted in a hoarse whisper, 'No. Stop!' Although some feet from him, I stretched my arm out, striving to prevent him from disturbing or destroying the clues I needed.

The soldier froze in mid-movement, one hand on the handle of the cupboard door, the other reaching in to rifle through the contents. He looked over at me with wide eyes, the breath in his body arrested at the moment of expiration.

'Please, don't touch or move anything.' My voice was softer as I continued, 'You might … the evidence may be lost if you do.'

The soldier let the air escape from his lungs as I added, 'You might do it inadvertently.'

'Yes, sir. Sorry, sir.' He took two paces backwards, and positioned himself next to the door, his eyes firmly fixed on a point just beyond the walls.

Valerian flopped into one of the chairs, leaning back until he was supported on the two rear legs. 'So what exactly do you want us to do?' he asked.

I didn't answer. I was concentrating on the contents of the cupboard, which included a thick burgundy cloak, with a green stripe. The day, although sunny, was cool, as would be expected for the lateness of the year.

No-one would venture far without protection, and indeed, I knew for certain that the normal occupant of the room had gone out that morning wearing his cloak. I lifted it out and fingered the fine woollen cloth, luxuriating in the thickness and warmth. It was an expensive garment, costing the equivalent of several months' wages. The quality indicated it was from Gaul and would be excellent in keeping out even the most persistent wind and rain.

Surely this would have been the first choice to insulate against whatever the heavens might produce. It seemed very strange that someone would leave this cloak in the cupboard, and go out in a thinner garment this late in the year. It was feasible that the owner might have been able to afford two cloaks of this quality, but the cost would have been well beyond the means of most.

Valerian let the front legs of his chair down with a thud, then came over, enquiring, 'What have you found?' He, too, felt the fabric, seeming reluctant to relinquish it. 'Nice cloak. Wish it were mine,' he continued.

'But it isn't. What're you doing here? What in Hades is going on?'

The angry and unexpected voice caused us both to jump. My fingers tightened on the cloak I was holding, so as not to drop it. My mouth was dry, and I could not work my tongue to form the words I wanted. The very event that I had been hoping to avoid, had now happened. Memno had returned earlier than I had anticipated, and was now standing in the doorway.

He took a pace forward, and again demanded, 'What do you think you are doing here?' His eyes scanned the room before again resting on me, waiting for, and demanding, an answer.

'Memno, I didn't expect you back so soon.'

'Obviously.' Memno was standing, arms folded and eyebrows arched.

'I'm doing what I need to do.' I could see the soldier silently position himself behind Memno. Valerian also moved, almost nonchalantly, to his side.

'What gives you the right to search this room?' Memno's face was hard and his chin thrust towards me.

I nodded to the soldier, who laid a hand on Memno's shoulder. He turned, striking the limb away from him and made for the door. The soldier, solid and immovable, blocked his exit, wrapping his fingers about the wooden hilt of his sword.

Valerian gripped Memno tightly about his upper arm, saying, 'You can try and run, but you'll have to fight off both me and him. Then there's seven more out there.'

Memno's body sagged as he swung his gaze back to me, repeating his question. 'How dare you? What right do you have?' He struggled ineffectively, saying, 'Let go of me.'

'Memno, just sit down, so that I can finish here.' My words emerged colder and harsher than I had intended.

Memno was silent, but his face told me much. I looked down at the cloak I was holding, more so that I could not see the misery and betrayal in his eyes, and I moved across to the window to examine it in greater detail. Valerian followed me, as Memno was firmly pushed down in a chair by the soldier, who then shifted his guard position to stand behind Memno, pinning him in his seat by a hovering hand and a directed steadfast gaze.

My attention returned to the cloak. Opening it out revealed a number of hairs on the inside, some clearly visible against the dark fabric, others more concealed. As I laid it on the table, letting the light from the window illuminate its contours, Memno leaned forward.

He lifted the material nearest to him, gazing into its rich depths before asking, in a voice lined with broken glass, 'Where did you get this?'

'Do you recognise it?' I countered.

He half nodded, a bundle of the fabric clutched in his hand. Suddenly I, too, knew to whom the cloak belonged. Before I had only suspected, now I was almost certain the confirmation that would issue from Memno's mouth would echo my own thoughts. As I paused, hesitant to have my last lingering doubts dissolved in truth, Valerian spoke.

'Who does it belong to?'

Memno looked up at us, the pain in his eyes hiding behind an onslaught of fear. 'I'm not sure. I don't really know. I've not seen it before.' As he dropped the cloth, he leaned back in his chair and looked away, out of the window.

Valerian leant forward, seemingly ready to pursue the answer, but I didn't feel the need. I already knew.

'Maybe you could explain how this cloak ... Lucius' cloak, came to be found in that cupboard.' My words caused Memno's posture to stiffen, as he rigidly turned back to face me. His lips were clamped together forming a straight line, balanced by his round eyes.

'How did you know?' escaped his barely moving mouth.

I waved the words away with a flick of my hand. My interest was in answers, not questions. Glancing around the room, I returned to my original destination, the wooden chest.

'Valerian, could you look in the cabinet over there? You know what to look for, anything unusual, but be careful.' Valerian reached it with two or three strides, and commenced his search, holding onto the door, as if unwilling to let more than his eyes inside.

Kneeling down in front of the chest, I ran my hand over the flat surface, which was interspersed with bands of iron. The box was strong, and solidly made, complete with an inset lock on the front. This was one receptacle that its owner intended to keep private. I grimaced to myself, but then Valerian's voice cut across the air.

'Would a key … no, two keys be considered unusual? I think one of them may belong to that chest.'

At last I felt that the waters were beginning to run my way. Maybe this marked the turning point, when I was no longer having to fight against the current, but could use it to speed me on. I held out my hand, as Valerian tossed over to me one of the heavy, iron keys attached to a broken length of leather. I missed the catch and there was a clunk as it hit the floor, sliding a short distance. Retrieving the key, I held my breath as I inserted it into the lock. It fitted. I turned it slowly. It operated the mechanism, and I let my lungs empty with a rush of air. Prising open the heavy lid, I looked inside.

The usual personal effects looked back at me. A leather pouch, full of coins, gave a muffled jingle as I moved it aside. A ludus latrunculorum board was there, complete with its gaming counters and dice in a small wooden box, the glass discs catching the evening sun, as I opened the container.

A freshly fullered toga lay, neatly folded, ready for wearing. At the bottom was a package, which I unwrapped to reveal two lares and a genius. I sat back on my heels, holding the small statues in my hands, feeling the heavy weight of bronze and religion. Why would the spirits of the ancestors and the protector of the owner be wrapped up in the chest? In my own room, in most rooms in the garrison, the lares and genius were sat out on a small altar, ready to provide their protection over the area and occupier. It didn't make sense to keep them wrapped and hidden as if they had no further use. I glanced over at Memno, sitting silent and still.

'Why would these be in here? Why not out, so that they can protect the room?' I was not aware I had spoken aloud, until I received an answer from Memno.

'Some people would think otherwise and not put their trust in a bronze statue to provide protection.'

He seemed about to say more, but then sealed his mouth and looked away again. I resumed my search of the chest, finding some personal letters from family in Rome, and dated some months previously. Underneath these was a small leather bag. Lifting it out, I untied the mouth, and emptied the contents out onto my hand. Attached to a leather cord was a small bronze phallus. There must have been several dozen in the garrison alone, as it was a common choice, but as it sat heavy on my palm, I knew that this was one amulet that had signally failed to protect its owner. Replacing the other items back as closely as I had found them, I re-locked the chest, and stood up.

Limping slightly, as one foot had become numb from the pressure while I was kneeling, I sat down at the table. Valerian brought over the other key he had found, and I took it in my hand. I turned it over, feeling the balance and contours. The shape and weight were as familiar to me as my own keys. Not surprising, as when I reached down for the small bundle tied to my belt, I could find its twin. The key that Valerian had found, and that I now held in my hand, was identical to that which would open the dispensary. Up till now, I had assumed that only Gallius and I had access to that room. It appears I had been wrong.

'That's all the room searched, Tiberius. Now what?' Valerian's decisive voice cut through the air.

I remained looking at the two keys I held, one in each hand. What now? I felt justified in keeping the duplicate key, the amulet and the cloak, for they would be needed as evidence.

'I'll take the cloak, and these.' Holding the two keys and leather bag in one hand, I picked up the cloak in the other. I glanced across the table at Memno, before turning to Valerian, as I said, 'Could you arrange for the guard to continue on this door and outside. Arrest anyone who tries to enter, and let me know immediately.'

'And him?' as he tilted his head towards Memno.

Feeling pain behind my eyes, that threatened to make them water, I said, 'Keep him under guard, until we have a few more answers. Valerian, could you then meet me in my quarters.'

Standing up I strode out of the room, forcing myself not to look back. Out here, in the fresh air, the sun was showing off her finery in the evening display, but I had no eye tonight for such magnificence. It was with a heavy heart that I walked away.

Valerian was not long in joining me, as I sat at the table. A lamp created a pool of light on the wooden surface between us. He pulled up a chair, positioning himself opposite me.

'So, it was Memno after all. I'm surprised, and I can't see why he would have done it.'

I shook my head, 'I'm not sure yet.' I looked at the objects I had brought away with me. A key to the dispensary, a phallus amulet and a thick burgundy cloak. Valerian picked up the key, tossing it up in the air before catching it again.

'Didn't you say that some of your stocks were low?' he commented.

I nodded, smiling ruefully at my accusal of Gallius, but that was when I thought there were only two keys in existence. Now it appeared that someone else had been able to come and go in the dispensary as they pleased.

'Memno must have been helping himself to whatever he liked,' Valerian continued. 'I wonder how long he's had that key, and what other keys he might have.'

'We didn't find any others,' I reminded my nephew, before he got too carried away with proof of guilt.

I turned my attention to the cloak, wondering what secrets it might hold. I cast my mind back, remembering a sight of Lucius showing off his new cloak, sent over from his family as a present.

And if I could remember, having been prompted, it was no wonder that the cloak had been left in the cupboard. It would be some months before it was safe to wear it openly, or even to sell it.

Opening the folds of material around the hood, I saw once again the hairs caught in the fabric. Carefully removing one, I held it up to the light, then compared it with a second. One was fair, the other dark.

'What have you found?' enquired Valerian.

'It looks as if the cloak has been worn by different people, at least two,' I replied.

'If the cloak did belong to Lucius, then he might have left some hair.'

'I know it was Lucius', but he had fair hair, so we can assume these,' as I collected together seven or eight strands that all appeared to match, 'are his. But who else has worn that cloak?'

'Why do you think that the cloak has been used by others?' Valerian asked. 'Might it not be that someone jostled Lucius, when he was in a crowd?'

I shook my head emphatically. 'No. It's obvious from where they were that only the people wearing this cloak could have left these hairs.'

I lifted up my own cloak, showing him. 'See, the hairs were only on the inside, around the hood. If Lucius, or anyone else, had had someone knock against him, or even embrace him, the hair would have been on the outside. The only way these were left here,' as I pulled a filament of my own from the fabric of my cloak to demonstrate, 'were by someone wearing this.'

I sorted out the two types. The fair ones I could mark down as belonging to Lucius, which left some that were short and dark.

'So Memno must have worn that cloak after he killed Lucius.' Valerian declared.

'If these hairs match his, then, yes, but ...'

A soft, but firm knock interrupted me. Valerian was on his feet and at the door before I had even thought about moving. A few words were exchanged, and Valerian turned to me, saying, 'The soldiers have just detained Agricola, as he tried to enter his room. He's being locked in one of the storerooms, next to Memno.'

'Let's go and talk to them.' I pushed my chair back and stood up, collecting a sample of the darker hairs from the small pile on the table. 'Then I can compare their hair to these.'

'Why Agricola? Where does he come into this, when we know the cloak was found in Memno's room?'

I paused at the doorway, and looked back at Valerian. 'But it wasn't.'

'Of course it was.' Valerian briefly lifted his hands and eyebrows, before continuing, 'We just found it there.'

'Yes, yes, I know, except that we weren't in Memno's room.'

Creases appeared between Valerian's eyes and he pulled his head back, as if searching for the right words.

I continued, to answer his unspoken query, 'The room we searched was Agricola's.'

'Then what was Memno doing there?'

I shrugged my shoulders, 'That's one question only he can answer.'

We stepped out into the chill of the open air. I glanced up at the sky, dark and heavy above us, with glimmers of stars, preparing for their night-time journey. With Valerian at my side and the soldier in front, we headed for the storerooms.

'I didn't get them taken to the main guard room, as I didn't think you'd want it public knowledge, just yet,' Valerian explained, in answer to my puzzled look.

I could just hear him mutter, 'Especially since it seems we've locked up two people, when one of them's innocent.' In a louder voice he asked, 'So if it was Agricola's room, why don't we just arrest him and let Memno go? The cloak, amulet and key were found in his quarters.'

'But how do we know who put them there?' I stopped as we reached the door leading to the many storerooms from which the garrison would be fed through the coming winter. 'Anyone could have just walked in. We did. So could Memno, and left the items there, so that suspicion would fall on Agricola.'

'So you do think it's Memno.'

I shook my head, and smiled at his desire to reach a definite decision. I, too, wanted the final outcome known, but I would wait to gather my proof. 'I need to check which of them has worn the cloak, and to do that, I need some hairs that I can compare.'

We entered the complex, to find two soldiers sitting on boxes pulled from a store, to act as stools and a table, on which stood a lamp. They sprang to attention at our approach.

'Sir, first prisoner's in here, sir,' as one indicated a door, 'and second prisoner's in there,' pointing out the next door along. 'One guard in each room as well, sir.'

'Who'd you want to see first?' asked Valerian.

I had been intending to enter the makeshift cells and remove four or five hairs from each person myself, but found myself baulking at the thought. I decided it would be easier, and leave less room for error, if the soldiers asked for and collected the sample. That way, I would have witnesses to say which head the hairs had come from, and I would not be able to influence the outcome. Accordingly I gave my orders, which were relayed to the interior guards.

I went to stand at the doorway, looking out into nothing, while behind me I could hear my instructions being carried out. An angry cry from one room, indicated that one guard was less gentle than the other. Turning round I found the soldiers each with a clenched hand, from which protruded a few strands. I sat down at the temporary table, which now held a second, brighter lamp, and laid out my originals. Valerian claimed the other seat opposite to me.

'Give me one set,' I ordered, holding my hand out. I was given six or seven short, dark hairs. Holding them up to the light, I carefully compared them to the ones I had taken from the cloak, running my fingers down to analyse the texture, and peering closely to check the colouring.

'Take these back, and then give me the others.' I held out the first sample, which was taken and replaced with the second. Again, I looked for parallels and similarities.

'Well,' asked Valerian, 'what have you found?'

In answer, I handed him one hair, 'This is one from the cloak.' I picked up a strand from the second sample, handing it over, 'And this is from one of our prisoners. What do you see?'

He held them both up, examining them closely. 'Looks the same to me,' he finally pronounced.

'What about this one?' I took a filament from the first soldier and gave it to Valerian.

This time he compared all three, singly and in pairs, before slowly saying, 'The last one you gave me feels much coarser than the first two, and I don't think it's the same colour. It seems to be lighter. I think the first two match, in both texture and shade.'

I smiled at him, only then aware how tense my shoulders were, as I consciously relaxed them. 'That's exactly what I thought.' Turning to the soldiers standing around us, who were all concentrating on our actions, I asked, 'Which room did the second sample come from?'

'Sir, that was mine, sir, from that door, sir.' The soldier's eyes gleamed in the lamplight as he pointed out where he had collected his bounty.

I stood up, knowing who had worn that cloak after Lucius had died. I now knew for certain which of my two friends was a murderer.

'I need to speak to him,' I said as I nodded towards one of the doors. 'There are still a lot of questions I need answers to.' Although guilt was proven for one, the other's innocence was still very much in doubt.

'I'll come with you,' was Valerian's response, as he moved to my side. He opened the door I had selected, and we both stepped into the room. I put my lamp down on a cask, to match the one already burning in the opposite corner. Next to the door, a soldier stood, alert and ready for action. His gaze was directed at a figure sitting on the hard floor, by the wall, with his elbows resting on his knees, and his head in his hands. He barely even glanced up at our entry. I sat down on a box, across the room. If I were too close to him, I might not be able to question him adequately, as the bonds of friendship would intervene. I was now grateful for Valerian's presence in the room.

I steeled myself to speak, 'We need some answers.'

He looked up at me, the flickering light from the lamps creating moving shadows across his features.

'Memno, what is going on?' I asked.

He didn't answer immediately, as he leant back, and turned his face to the ceiling, closing his eyes for a few moments. I waited, putting one hand on Valerian's arm, who appeared more anxious than I that the proceedings be hurried.

'Memno?' I said again, and this time he replied, first taking a deep breath, as if drawing courage from the lamplight.

'Could I speak with you two privately?' he said, 'Then I'll tell you.'

I nodded, and sensed, rather than heard, Valerian ordering the soldier to wait outside the door. Only once it had closed again, leaving the three of us in the room, did he continue, 'Tiberius, I give you my word that I have had nothing to do with Lucius' death or Victor's.'

'But what have you been doing? I ... we need to know.' I put as much pleading into my voice as I could.

'Do I have your word that ...' he paused, before continuing in a stronger voice, 'that what I say will remain within these four walls, and that it won't be made public knowledge?'

I was ready to nod in agreement, but Valerian's smooth voice cut in, 'I think we'll be the judge of what happens once you've told us.'

Something in Memno's eyes drilled into mine, and he must have seen reassurance there as he started to speak, 'You must have heard stories about the Jews, about the man they called King of the Jews. The one who was executed, crucified in Hierosolyma. The one they said was seen again, after he had died.'

'But that was thirty years, or more, ago. He was just a common criminal.' Valerian threw up his hands. 'What has that got to do with now?'

'Hush,' I wanted Memno to continue, without any further interruptions. My curiosity was aroused. I had heard several stories from people who claimed to have seen this person when I was stationed in Judea, some twenty years ago, but obviously there had been no truth in any of them. How could there be? 'Carry on,' I said.

Memno looked down at the floor, before resuming his narration, 'There have been lots of stories, about how he was seen again, walking about and talking to people, after he had been buried. Many people claim to have seen him, this Jesus.'

'But Memno, surely that was just lies, put about by the people who called themselves his followers, trying to justify their belief. It's all a pure fabrication, a pack of lies.' I threw both hands up, before resting them flat on my knees.

Memno's eyes were closed, and his jaw was tense. 'Not everyone believes they were lies. Some people believe it was true, and that by following his teachings, we, too, may live forever.'

'Going to get a bit crowded then.'

'We?'

Valerian and I found we had both spoken together, and I repeated my question. 'We? You said we.'

'Yes, I know.' Memno scrambled to his feet and came across to me, taking both my hands in his. His attention was focussed on me, and he appeared to be ignoring Valerian. 'I believe it, too. I believe in my heart,' and relinquishing my hands, he put both of his over his chest, 'that now I have been baptised in water, if I follow the teachings of Jesus, that I, too, will gain eternal salvation. Not on this earth, but in Heaven.'

I sat, lost for words. Here was one of my closest friends telling me that he truly believed in some minor cult, as short-lived as it was ridiculous, that had sprung up from the execution of a criminal, many miles away. I shook my head in amazement.

'Now you understand why I don't want you to tell anyone else.' Memno seemed to be gaining courage from my bewilderment. 'There's a small group of us, we meet when we can, to discuss the teachings.'

'At a house in Lindinis.' My voice was dry.

'How did you know?'

Now it was my turn for confessions. 'I followed you this morning. I saw you go into the house.'

A small frown appeared on Memno's face. 'I thought I saw you in the town, but convinced myself it couldn't be. As you said, we usually meet in a house in Lindinis.'

I felt the need to absolve myself of any crime. 'I had to follow you. I had to know what you were doing. You've been acting strangely of late, and your rapid departure this morning, after our chat, was suspicious.'

'Yes,' said Valerian, 'Why did you go there today? It appears to have been a sudden decision.'

Tears rapidly filmed Memno's eyes, and he wiped them roughly with his sleeve. 'It was the news of Corolius, the confirmation of his death. I needed to tell the others, so we could pray for his soul.'

I seemed to be fording uncertain waters. One moment I had a solid footing, the next the ground threatened to send me flying.

'Corolius? Why would you pray specifically for Corolius?'

Memno looked up at the ceiling, before gazing back at me. 'Because he also was one of us. He, too, believed in Jesus' teachings.'

I spent a few moments mentally shifting my perceptions. That would explain Corolius' many unexplained absences from his farm, and why he preferred not to discuss his reasons. Association with a cult, like these Christians, could have seriously impaired his social standing and his business dealings. It could result in Memno needing to give up his post as chief surveyor, or worse, if it became public knowledge.

I shuddered as I thought about the stories I had heard from Rome. The Emperor made no secret of his dislike for this particular cult, and was employing some brutal methods to wipe it out.

'I knew Corolius wasn't really consulting you about a water mill?' I muttered.

The unexpected sound of a laugh spread round the room, helping to lighten the corners from their accumulated gloom. 'No,' Memno admitted, 'but I was so shocked that it was all I could think of at the time.'

I turned to face Valerian. 'I don't think this is relevant to the investigation into the murders, do you?'

'What he does in his spare time, even if it is a load of nonsense, is his own affair, but I want to know what he was doing in Agricola's room this evening.' Valerian's voice was hard and firm, reminding me of my duty to Lucius, Victor and our unknown victim.

Memno turned away to pace up and down the room, as if wrestling internally. When he spoke, his voice was hesitant and broken. 'I went to warn him. I had heard rumours, gossip, about a cult of druids, and ...' His words ran out, as if he had no will left to utter them.

'There've been lots of rumours about the druids. Why did you need to warn Agricola?' I prompted him.

Memno made no effort to control the flow of tears as he continued, 'Fabius, the leader of our group, said he'd heard about a Roman at the garrison who was involved with the druids, and who had betrayed his compatriots in order to gain favour with them.' He stopped his movement to stand in front of me. 'What could I do? I knew that it had to be Agricola.'

'Why did you know it was him?' I asked.

'I had some time to think on the journey back from Lindinis. Agricola was the only other person who knew where Lucius was going. No-one else was in earshot when I gave him his instructions, only Agricola. In fact Agricola encouraged me to send Lucius, and then advised him on the route to take.' Memno perched on the edge of a cask, as he said, almost to himself, 'I knew Agricola was jealous of Lucius' position, and he certainly enjoyed his temporary rise when I was ill. He definitely didn't want me to recover and return to my post.' Looking back up at me, Memno continued, 'Then, when I added that to the fact that Agricola had rescued you … had known where you were … when you had your fall, I felt certain.' He looked at me, with wet eyes. 'Tell me I'm wrong, please?'

I couldn't. The knowledge I had of who had worn Lucius' cloak lay heavy on my mind. I shook my head sadly, before asking, 'Why were you going to warn him? Didn't you want the deaths avenged?'

Memno closed his eyes, saying, 'I thought I would be able to reason with him, to get him to admit how wrong he'd been. I thought I'd be able to get him to give himself up, and maybe reveal who else was involved. When I saw you with Lucius' cloak in your hands, I wasn't too sure what I was saying.'

'It looks like we've both come to the same conclusions, but from different angles.' I stood up and moved over to Memno, putting my hand on my friend's shoulder. 'But I now have definite proof of Agricola's guilt, although I can't say the same about his accomplices.'

'How can you prove Agricola was involved with these murders? Surely a cloak, an amulet and a stolen key are not enough.' Memno waved his hand about in the air. 'I can't see how you can be so definite.'

I smiled at him, feeling more than a little smug inside. 'Whoever had Lucius' cloak, must have been involved in his death. Agricola wore that cloak, which both you, and I, know belonged to Lucius. There were two sets of hairs on the inside of the hood. One set, which was blond and curly, belonged to Lucius. The others, which were dark, are identical to those pulled from Agricola's head.' Valerian nodded in agreement at my words.

Memno reached up his hand to run it through his greying mop, as he muttered, 'So that's what the soldier was after. I did wonder.'

I considered many of the things Agricola had spoken of, as I said, 'I feel sure it was that girl, Etain, who got him involved with the druids, the one who looked after me after my fall, and she won't pay for her crimes at all.'

'Unless Agricola tells us,' Valerian put in.

I very much doubted that Agricola would betray his former conspirators. I thought back over some of the events of the last weeks. The pieces all fitted into place, except one, and I voiced my annoyance aloud, 'I wish the soldiers had been able to find the druids grove. That would strengthen our case.'

'Are you sure you took them to the right place?' Memno asked. 'You might have been mistaken in the location.'

'But I didn't take them. I was too unwell after the fall.' I turned to Valerian. 'Do you know who commanded the soldiers that went?'

He shook his head, 'Wasn't me, but I did hear that the head surveyor showed them the spot.'

Memno and I looked at each other, as he almost whispered, 'I, too, was ill at the time.'

'No wonder they didn't find anything. It must have been Agricola.' Of course Agricola wouldn't have taken them to the grove I had seen, the grove that was in use, but to one that had been abandoned many months ago. The last piece slotted into place, and my puzzle was complete.

'What will happen now?' asked Memno.

I looked at Valerian, saying, 'I don't think what he's said about being a Christian needs to go any further, do you? I think this could just stay between ourselves.'

Valerian slowly nodded, adding, 'I can't see that there has been any crime committed by Memno, provided all this can be verified, of course. I'll need some names and addresses, but as long as your beliefs are kept strictly to yourselves, I don't think it needs to go any further.'

Memno visibly relaxed.

After Valerian had left us, to check on Agricola's incarceration, Memno and I sat for a few moments in silence. The relief I felt at the innocence of one friend was tempered by the guilt of the other. I had no desire to confront Agricola. I had completed my task, which was to provide evidence for Aurelius. Now that he would not only have the proof, but a prisoner as well, he would act, as he had promised during our conversation two weeks previously.

I looked at Memno. We had both passed through stormy waters, and our relationship would never be the same again.

But then, maybe it was for the best. Maybe friendships need to weather a few squalls in order to be strengthened. Only time would tell. Right now, what was needed was some food and wine. I indicated the door with my open arm, and followed Memno as he walked over the threshold. Together we crossed the courtyard to my quarters.

Two Months Later

And so I complete my story. Agricola was tried, condemned and executed, for his part in the murder of Lucius. In my mind, I know that Agricola was also directly involved in Victor's death, but I could offer no proof, and therefore Aurelius was unable to include it in the charges. The unknown Roman who also died was never able to be named or avenged, but I know that just as the spirit of Lucius will rest in peace, so shall his and Victor's. Despite the best efforts of Aurelius' men to coax a confession from him, Agricola remained silent about these deaths, and the names of his co-conspirators to the end. They have escaped the justice that was meted out to him, as they evaded all efforts to find them. Their attempt to aid Boudicca's efforts resulted in failure, as she herself fell under the might of the Roman army, although I suspect that Agricola's motives came more from personal greed and desire.

Germanicus was also executed for murdering his master, Corolius. At his trial, he attempted to implicate Julia, by saying she had been slowly poisoning Corolius over several months, gradually increasing the dose, so that it appeared to be an illness. Julia escaped justice, more by dint of money than lack of guilt. She, and her son, Petronus, returned to her family, back in Pompeii.

Gallius will soon have his freedom, now that I am seriously considering my retirement. I believe he will do well, as he will be able to develop his practice amongst the local people. He has an extensive knowledge of herbs and cures that are native to this island. Lydia, as well as Alena, Zera and Thalia now belong to me. Julia's need for money during her trial meant that I was able to purchase them at a very reasonable price.

Lachlan stayed at the tavern for several days and nights, initially drinking in a private world of his own. It transpired that Victor did indeed have extensive assets, which, in the absence of any will, passed to his cousin, leaving Lachlan destitute, fulfilling Victor's mock prophecy, when I declined to buy a blue glass bowl. Barris, the landlord, then encouraged Lachlan to pay off his escalating bill, by working there.

It is notable how fewer fights and disturbances there are, now that he helps to maintain order. He does not appear to be hampered by his lack of hearing, and he needs to speak no words to encourage peace.

I encourage Gallius and Lydia together as much as possible, and have told him how much I would like to see them marry. I'm old, compared to Gallius, and it would not be fair to expect Lydia to spend her days with me. But I shall take pleasure in their enjoyment together, and anticipate many children. I shall devote my time to study and relaxation, and maybe soon I'll manage to read the books that arrived from Alexandria, so many weeks ago. The copies are now finished, and the originals have been returned, but I haven't had the opportunity to peruse the contents until now. They will provide a welcome distraction as the long winter evenings lighten into spring.

'Master, your meal is ready, and Memno is also here.' Gallius entered with a dish of olives, two cups and a jug of wine.

'Thank you, Gallius.' I turned to face my guest, 'Please, be seated.'

As Memno sat down, I could see the enthusiasm in his face. 'Tiberius, I've just heard. There's going to be a circus built, between here and Durnovaria. It'll be great to see some racing again, won't it? I know one of the builders, so I think I can get us to the opening ceremony. What do you think?'

I smiled. Memno had a passion about chariots, and had been known to bet much more than he could afford. He could not resist the excitement of the circus, and I was not averse to a gamble. At least it would be quieter than the previous few months. I could not imagine anything more dramatic happening than a wheel coming off, a favourite losing, or a bet being won. Certainly no murders.

'Of course we'll go.' I declared.